THE KILLER ORGANISM

Lockton was mesmerized by the rhythmic contractions of the virus, followed by long chain-spurts of RNA. Ejaculations of death, he thought. They hunt. They breed. They kill. Not just the host cell, but the whole—the complex community of cells that make up a rodent, a mammal or a human being.

A few years ago, what he was viewing could only have existed in the imagination of a good science-fiction writer. Now it was a reality. There on the screen in living color. A mutant virus created in the lab. Sponsored by the Central Intelligence Agency. Made in the U.S.A.

QUARANTINE

"No reader
will be able to escape...
It haunts you into the small hours!"
said JOHN SAUL of Josh Webster's *Ceremonies*.

JOSH WEBSTER

QUARANTINE

WORLDWIDE.

TORONTO · NEW YORK · LONDON · PARIS
AMSTERDAM · STOCKHOLM · HAMBURG
ATHENS · MILAN · TOKYO · SYDNEY

QUARANTINE

A Worldwide Library Book/March 1988

ISBN 0-373-97063-3

Printed in U.S.A.

Dedicated to my parents,
Glorianne L. Webster and Kenneth L. Webster,
with love, respect and gratitude.

Thank you for always being there when I needed you.

THE MAINLAND

Chapter 1

12:51 a.m., November 1, 1976

THE BIRTH WAS PROCEEDING without complications. Elizabeth Lockton had been in labor for just over three hours. It was her first child and the doctor did not expect it to go quickly.

For the past two months, the young couple had been preparing themselves for this monumental moment by taking weekly Lamaze classes. The course included a trip to the hospital and delivery room to familiarize them with the medical procedures. It was supposed to help them relax.

It didn't.

Liz tried to remember what she had been taught about deep muscle relaxation and proper breathing. When the next contraction struck, she muffled a scream and forgot everything but the pain. Her husband, James Lockton, checked the time of the latest contraction, coaching her to breathe through it and relax.

"Easy for you to say," she grunted, wet with perspiration. During the classes, she had felt as if they were a team, husband and wife, preparing to give birth together. But now, in the reality of labor, after hours of pain, she felt alone. It seemed she was doing all the work.

"Want to switch roles?" She tried to smile. "I'll watch. You finish up here."

At 9:38 p.m., James Lockton had been rereading *The Tao of Physics* in their den, hoping no more trick-or-treaters would ring the doorbell; there were only three Hershey bars left in the Halloween basket on the table.

"The water broke," Liz had calmly announced from upstairs.

James Lockton bolted out of his chair, swept up the hospital bag that had been sitting by the front door for the past two weeks, and dashed to their bedroom.

"I'll carry you." He started to lift her under the legs, but she stopped him.

"It's easier if I waddle." She slowly descended, bent over her ripe belly like a question mark.

"Nine months and two weeks," Lockton commented, helping her into their Subaru. He gently patted her swollen stomach. "Just like Mom. Always late to the party."

University Hospital was three miles due south, in the university district, north of Seattle. James Lockton was a full professor at the University of Washington. The youngest in the biology department. He had met Elizabeth Thurber two years ago in one of his postgraduate classes. She was working on her master's in molecular biology—his specific field, although he preferred calling himself a genetic engineer. He liked the strength and the practicality of it: *genetic engi-*

neer. Builder and bridge maker, spanning the turbulent waters of existence with the spiraling, double helix of DNA, the blueprint of life.

They were married six months later.

Even the grandeur of modern molecular biology had not prepared James Lockton for this, the greatest miracle of all—creating life the old-fashioned way. Nothing in the laboratory could hold a candle to it. All his other genetic research and experimentation was anticlimactic in comparison.

The Four *L* Experiment he had titled it, when they decided it was the proper time to have a baby. Start with the main ingredient, Liz, add a lot of love, a little luck, and a large portion of undiluted lust, and see what happens.

Worked like a charm, he thought, grinning proudly as he backed out of the short driveway.

The streets in the U. district were overrun with college students masquerading in Halloween disguises, from Dracula and Darth Vader to Boy George and four-color spiked hairdos. Lockton was amazed that Nixon masks were still popular.

A crowd of macabre costumes stopped in the middle of the avenue to pass around a pint of peppermint schnapps. Lockton honked impatiently. His no-more-than-eight-minute ride to the hospital had turned into a quarter of an hour and they were still five blocks away.

Liz winced in pain as she watched the raucous festivities.

"I hope the baby still wants out—" she laughed "—after seeing this."

"THE HEAD'S BEGINNING TO BREACH," Dr. Shapiro announced. Liz already had a pretty good idea what was coming. "Push now. Push. That's it."

James Lockton swallowed his coaching techniques and silently stared in awe.

It had all started with one lonely egg and an adventuresome hard-swimming sperm. Together they had combined the evolved genetic code of a hundred thousand generations to produce...

A miracle.

Arching up against the bed, Liz dug her fingernails into James's hand and screamed. A trickle of blood oozed down between his fingers.

The nurse placed the wet, pink-and-red dappled baby onto Liz's belly. It stopped crying immediately. James wiped the sweat under his mask.

Nothing in the world could be as beautiful as this, he thought, nervously counting its fingers, its toes, its...

He smiled behind his mask.

It was a boy.

And it was perfect.

JAMES LOCKTON pulled the stiff metal chair up next to the hospital bed. Liz had fallen asleep after the nurse had cleaned the baby and taken it to the nursery. Twenty minutes ago, Lockton had checked on the child. He was sleeping peacefully, just like Mom.

Lockton still couldn't get over just how minuscule, yet perfectly proportioned, his hands and feet were.

Liz opened her eyes. "James?"

Lockton brushed her hair back off her forehead. "You did well, Mrs. Lockton."

"You, too, Mr. Lockton," she assured him weakly. He kissed her cheek. "James?"

"What, honey?"

"What do we call him?"

They had discussed names often in the past three months, but had never reached a final decision.

"We can talk about it later. When you're stronger," he advised.

"He needs a name now, James." When she took his hand, she felt the bandage. "Did I do that?"

"Don't worry about it. It's the least I could do."

"I'd still like Nick," she said.

"I know." He really didn't want to argue about it now.

"Uncle Nick was . . . special."

"Anyone who could convince your father that a girl was capable of competing on his beloved baseball team had to be. Speedball Liz, the only little-league pitcher in pigtails."

"It's better than Homer," she argued.

"I always liked Homer. I had a professor that . . ."

Suddenly Liz catapulted up off the pillows as if she'd been slammed in the back by a battering ram. Her face contorted and she clutched her chest.

"Liz?" Lockton grabbed her shoulders. Her body was beginning to convulse. "What is it?"

"I don't know," she gasped. "Pain. My chest. Can't...breathe."

"Doctor!" Lockton screamed. Too terrified to leave his wife's side, he buzzed the nurse's button.

A nurse opened the door. One look at Mrs. Lockton and she was running to the bed.

"Chest pains," Lockton reported. "She's having trouble breathing."

The nurse pressed the intercom. "Code Blue, room 355. Code Blue."

Seconds later a doctor, intern and two nurses burst into the room with a crash cart. The older, heavyset physician darted to the bed and shoved Lockton aside.

"Get him out of here," he ordered.

"That's my wife, goddamn it," Lockton protested. A second intern and a big-shouldered orderly dragged him toward the door.

"She's thrown an embolus," the doctor stated above the organized chaos. The first intern pushed the cart beside the bed. "Get the defibrillator ready."

Holding the doorframe, Lockton kneed the big orderly in the groin. "I'm not leaving, you bastards. Let me go!"

"Let him stay," the doctor lamented. "Just keep out of the way."

Lockton stood against the far wall, facing the foot of the bed. The intern handed the doctor two saucer-shaped disks connected to the defibrillator by heavily insulated wires.

"She's gone into shallow respiration," the doctor announced. "Stand back. I'm going to shock."

During birth, a small portion of amniotic fluid had backed up into Elizabeth Lockton's circulatory system through a vein in the uterus. The fluid blocked the pulmonary artery between the heart and lungs, causing an amniotic embolus.

Fifteen minutes later, the emergency team silently backed away from the bed.

Elizabeth Lockton was dead.

DR. SHAPIRO took Lockton to a small interns' lounge on the fourth floor. Neither spoke. James Lockton looked as if all the blood had been drained from his body. He sat down and stared at the floor.

Shapiro put an uncomfortable hand on his back. "I'm sorry."

Suddenly Lockton stood up. His eyes riveted on the doctor's. "I want his name on the crib. I don't want him lying in the nursery without a name. It's Nick. His name is Nick. Nick Lockton."

Chapter 2

JAMES LOCKTON ambled across the nursery he and his wife had spent the past six months preparing. It had been the most joyous room in the house. Just peeking in the door usually evoked an expectant chuckle.

It was no one's fault. That was what Dr. Shapiro had said. It just happened. Embolism was the most common cause of death during childbirth. Twenty thousand a year in the U.S. alone. Lockton did not care about statistics. Liz was not a number. She was his wife.

The angry sky looked like a huge gray-brown camouflage net. He stared out the window at an obese mother in curlers and bright pink stretch pants pushing her child in a carriage.

Why? he asked himself.

Why Liz?

And not her?

He had just returned from the funeral.

The phone in the master bedroom rang. He trudged down the hall. It was Dr. Shapiro.

"Mr. Lockton, could you come to the hospital?"

It was all a mistake, his imagination screamed. A terrible mistake. It wasn't her they had just lowered into the black, uncaring earth. It was someone else! A stranger! Liz was alive!

"It's your baby, Mr. Lockton," Shapiro continued, not having received an answer. "He has an obstruction in the small intestine. We need to operate. Immediately."

"How scrious is it?"

"Very."

James Lockton arrived at the hospital eight minutes later.

"We took X rays," Shapiro informed him, as they hurried across the lobby. "From the appearance of the loops in the intestine, we suspect a large portion of the small bowel is impacted. Probably by meconium. The bowel will have to be opened and cleared, then irrigated with a proteolytic enzyme solution."

They took the stairs instead of the elevator. Lockton needed to keep moving.

"What caused it?" he asked.

"We don't know. After the operation we'll need to do a number of tests. For diagnostic purposes."

"What are his—" Lockton stopped the doctor by the fifth floor door "   chances?"

"Mr. Lockton, it's hard to . . ."

"Doctor?" Lockton pleaded. "Please. Give me something."

Shapiro waited to catch his breath. "It's too early to tell. I'm sorry."

FOR THE NEXT FOUR HOURS, James Lockton felt as if he were battling fierce canyon rapids on a partially deflated air mattress. Whatever resentment he had felt toward the baby during the past two days dissolved while he paced the hall outside the operating room.

The baby couldn't die. He wouldn't allow it. His entire being remained focused on that single self-willed proposition. Liz's death would be reduced to a meaningless statistic if the baby died. Another absurdity in an absurd and godless world. He would not let that happen.

At 8:46 p.m., Dr. Henry Furgeson, the head surgeon, walked out of the operating room. James Lockton ran up the hall.

"Mr. Lockton?" the doctor inquired.

He nodded, opening his mouth to ask the fatal question. The words remained anchored in his throat.

Like a lost key, Dr. Furgeson's exhausted smile finally unlocked the steel box that had encased Lockton's heart.

"I think he'll be all right," he said.

The last ounce of James Lockton's strength was used to utter "Thank you."

Dr. Furgeson gently nudged him to a vacant office and helped him into a chair.

"No one will bother you in here. Stay as long as you like." The doctor closed the door.

When the tears finally came, they poured from his soul like an early-spring rain, melting the frozen soil that had entombed his battered dreams.

Chapter 3

JAMES LOCKTON SAT before Dr. Shapiro's desk, his hands vised between his thighs.

"It's a relatively simple test, really," Shapiro explained. "We stimulated the sweat glands in a small area of the baby's forearm with pilocarpine and iontophoresis. The results indicate a high sodium-chloride content in his perspiration."

Lockton had been listening to medical jargon for over a month. He wanted his baby. Nick had survived the operation, but they had kept him in the hospital for continued testing. James did not want to hear any more about pancreatic-enzyme deficiency, or how mucus in the bronchi caused respiratory obstruction. He wanted his baby. In his nursery. With his daddy. At home.

Lockton had been granted a full year's maternity leave—a first in the university's history for a single male parent. Only a few uninformed colleagues were so callous as to joke about it.

The family health-insurance policy had covered the cost of Nick's birth, as well as the unexpected expenses of Liz's death, but not the funeral. With Nick's operation and prolonged hospital stay, the policy's fifty-thousand dollar limit for a newborn child had almost been reached.

As long as Nick was released soon, Lockton's financial situation would remain tolerable. All their savings had been drained to buy and remodel their new house, but if he could combine Liz's school loans, the home-improvement loan, the furniture loan, and the five thousand dollars he owed the funeral parlor into one four-year loan, he could meet the monthly installments, with enough left over for mortgage payments and living expenses. Further medical complications could force him to sell the house.

That would be like burying Liz a second time.

James Lockton despised being haunted by financial worries at a time like this. He leaned toward the desk, struggling to retain his optimism. His son had had a problem. And now he was cured.

"You said the tests have been completed." He straightened against the chair. "What's the verdict?"

Dr. Shapiro had been dreading this all morning. Lockton had been through enough already.

"Mr. Lockton, your son has cystic fibrosis."

Lockton slumped down in the leather chair, looking everywhere but at the doctor. Shapiro couldn't help comparing James Lockton's last six weeks with the biblical story of Job. He just hoped Lockton had half the faith Job had. He would need it.

Lockton crossed his arms and stared blankly across the desk. "Is it curable?" He was hugging his chest as if struggling to keep his guts from spilling out.

"It's treatable. We've made a number of advancements in the area. Medication, therapy, et cetera."

"Is it curable?" Lockton repeated.

"No."

"Then it's..." His arms tightened around his ribs. "Fatal?"

Shapiro hated this. "Eventually everything is fatal, Mr. Lockton. Life is fatal. Being born is..."

"I don't need undergraduate philosophy, Doctor. I need an answer."

Shapiro wished he hadn't quit cigarettes. He could use a smoke screen right now. "Yes. It's fatal."

"How long does he have?"

"Children are now living an average of fifteen years or more. With future developments, who knows?" Shapiro could not read Lockton's reaction. The man didn't even appear to be breathing. "Mr. Lockton, the life span of a child with C.F. depends largely on the course of the pulmonary disease and the degree of damage to the tracheal-bronchial tree in the lungs at the time of the diagnosis. Because of the operation, we were able to diagnose Nick extremely early. That should mean his life expectancy will more than exceed the average."

"How will he die?"

"Eventually he could die of heart failure, but..." Shapiro turned away. He did not want to go on.

"But what, Doctor?" Lockton had to know.

"But more probably, he will drown in a buildup of mucus in the lungs."

When James Lockton stood up, Shapiro flinched. He was half expecting the leather chair to come flying across the desk. Lockton walked to the window and shoved his hands deep into his trouser pockets. The muscles in his neck and shoulders continually flexed and unflexed.

"Can I take him home?" He knew it wasn't the doctor's fault but he hated even looking at him then. Lockton peered down at the parking lot. "Now?"

"I believe so. Yes." Dr. Shapiro swiveled his chair sideways and took a card from the Rolodex file on the corner of his desk. "Here's the name of one of our hospital social workers who specializes in this field. There's a lot you need to learn. The treatments are lifelong and complex. Give her a call as soon as possible."

Lockton took the card without reading it, walked to the door and turned. "Thank you, Doctor."

Shapiro tapped a pen against his chin. "For what?"

Lockton stared at the rug. "I don't know."

Chapter 4

IT TOOK A LONG TIME for James Lockton to come to terms with the guilt of having been half of the hereditary cause of his son's horrifying fate. At times his sense of regret and helplessness was almost immobilizing.

But, although caring for Nick Lockton during his first year of life was a difficult and exasperating job, James Lockton wouldn't have traded it for anything less than a sudden and miraculous cure. He became an amateur pharmacist, physical therapist, nurse and diagnostician.

There were the prescriptions of animal-pancreas extracts, vitamin supplements and antibiotics to be administered daily. To help keep the lungs clear, there was the ever-present mist tent and intermittent positive-pressure breathing machine.

The child also had to be bathed frequently to prevent skin irritation and to eliminate the stench of his partially undigested stools. Diapers had to be changed constantly, the character of the stools accurately noted and charted. Because of his vigorous appetite, Nick had to be fed promptly, never without the recommended daily dietary modifications and medications.

To drain the lungs, physical therapies had to be performed, including as many as twelve different postural drainage techniques, twice daily.

It was the mist tent that Lockton hated the most. He despised putting his baby to bed and zipping it over the crib. He hated the way the moist, cool air fogged the clear plastic. He abhorred how it separated them into two different worlds. He hated how it muffled the sound of his baby sleeping. The tent was a constant, agonizing reminder of his son's inevitable fate, and zipping him in at night was like closing the glass lid of his coffin.

For the first six months, Lockton battled himself and his psychologist twice a week. Guilt, anger, fear and resentment were the four horsemen of his bitter apocalypse. Like an alcoholic struggling to stay sober, he taught himself to face life one day at a time. One hour at a time, if necessary.

But always, there was the baby.

Lockton's entire existence focused on Nick. The complications of modern civilized life had been broken down into the simplest components of survival. Like all babies, healthy or otherwise, Nick needed his parent, without conditions or reservations.

James Lockton needed that, too.

Late at night, when he would scream himself awake on the mattress he had moved to the floor of the nursery, he would stand naked beside the crib, unzip the tent and whisper, "Just you and me, kid. All the way."

Invariably the child would open his eyes, look up at his father and smile, as if he understood exactly what he meant.

That, more than anything else, more than the bi-weekly therapies or the C.F. clinic, got him through the first year.

A WEEK AFTER Nick Lockton's first birthday, his cold developed into pneumonia and he had to be hospitalized.

The fifty-thousand-dollar cap on the insurance policy had long since been spent.

In the middle of December, Lockton was forced to put the house on the market.

In January, his maternity leave was up and he had to hire a full-time R.N. to take care of Nick.

He sold the house in late February. His asking price had been $137,000. He settled for $129,999.

He rented a small but charming three-bedroom town house in West Seattle. It was cheaper than the university area, Queen Anne or Capitol Hill. The commute to the university took twenty minutes, unless traffic on Interstate-5 was bad. It usually was.

During the next two years, he went through four full-time R.N.s. One left to be married in San Francisco. One became pregnant. And two quit because the job wasn't as fulfilling or challenging as their previous careers in city hospitals.

Nick was not the easiest child to care for. Almost as soon as he learned the word *Daddy*, he also learned to say "No!" The child grew to despise the twice-daily postural drainage therapies almost as much as he abhorred the mist tent. Screaming temper tantrums continually echoed through the house.

James Lockton had as difficult a time controlling his son as the nurses did. He understood and commiserated with Nick's resentment of his limited, regimented life-style. It was no way for a boy to grow up. Disciplining the child was almost more than he could stand.

It's for your own good, Nick. To keep you healthy, to keep you breathing, to keep you active and strong and . . .

No! No tent! No! No!

It has to be, Nick. I'm sorry.

Why? Other kids don't sleep in tents. Why me? Why? Does God hate me, Daddy? Do you hate me? I won't sleep. I'll scream. I will.

Between the tantrums, the forced therapies, the tent and the unanswerable questions, James Lockton's heart often felt like an open sore, festering and painful to the touch.

In the spring of 1980, the money from the house was gone and he could no longer afford a full-time nurse. The C.F. counselor at the hospital suggested the possibility of a live-in R.N. With free room and board, he could cut the previous salary expenditure in half. With luck, skipping lunches, selling the car and the furniture, he figured his professorial wages could cover the added four hundred to six hundred dollars a month.

The discomfort of mismatched garage-sale furniture and a rusty '64 Ford station wagon that sucked exhaust fumes through any number of holes in the floor meant nothing, compared with Nick's health.

ONE ADVANTAGE of having a live-in nurse—he would finally be able to resume his research. He missed his viruses and transposons, the antiseptic smell of the security lab and the camaraderie of his fellow scientists struggling against nature's genetically stacked deck in the hopes of one day combating certain cancers and hereditary diseases on their own microscopic battleground—the very nucleus of cells themselves.

For three years, he had been living in exile, confined to theoretical research at home. He yearned to return to his scientific homeland. The constant challenges, the excitement, the sudden electrifying discoveries had always been his soul's spiritual sustenance. It was there, in the laboratory, that his genius blossomed. Teaching was moderately satisfying, but he was a scientist, explorer and engineer first, a professor second.

He thrived in the laboratory. It was his narcotic. His incurable addiction.

Only his unyielding love for Nick could have kept him away so long.

THE FIRST NURSE he interviewed for the live-in position was Anna Marie Lehrer, a short, robust, gray-haired bulldozer of a woman in her early sixties. She shook his hand vigorously. Lockton doubted he could beat her arm-wrestling.

He told her about himself and his work, Nick's medical history, the child's emotional problems with the disease and his wife's death. He was also honest about his financial predicament. She listened with an intensity that allowed him to elaborate without feeling uncomfortable or self-conscious.

When he had finished, he realized she had turned the interview around with only a few strategic questions. He would have resented it if she hadn't immediately begun to tell him about herself with equal candor.

Her husband, Hartmude Lehrer, had died of cirrhosis of the liver a year ago. Now she was alone. He had been a doctor in Germany during the war. They had met in a hospital in Hamburg. He was tall and handsome and had beautiful hands. As the war grew old and bitter, so did her husband. He had seen the results of Gestapo interrogation, having had to repair the mangled victims, only to have them sent back for further questioning. When he refused to continue, the Gestapo had taken him away. She knew of a man in the German resistance who said he would help. His people attacked the small caravan of trucks that were taking prisoners to a work camp outside Heidelberg. Although her husband was one of the few survivors of the rescue, his leg was severely wounded. That night she had had to amputate it herself, without anesthetic.

After the war, they had come to America. Although her husband remained a gentle, loving man, something deep inside him had broken. He tried to get it back with drink and sometimes, in the early years, it worked, but he never practiced medicine again.

She had moved to Seattle a month ago to start a new life, but she did not enjoy living alone. A live-in nursery job would suit her needs perfectly.

She also had very good credentials and letters of recommendation, as well as an impressive résumé. The majority of her nursing career had been spent working with terminally ill children in Portland.

Lockton hired her that afternoon. He had the instinctive feeling she could give Nick the kind of structure and discipline he had not been able to provide.

In less than a year, the Lockton household was transformed.

Nick fought Mrs. L. every inch of the way, but eventually gave in to her uncompromising authority. Frequent tantrums were not to be tolerated, and that was that. Therapies were necessary and beneficial and kept children with C.F. out of hospitals, and that was that.

Did Nick like hospitals? Did he like having pneumonia? Did he like being bedridden for long periods and not being able to play outside with his friends? Then it would be best to do as Mrs. L. said, and that was that.

What startled Lockton the most was Mrs. L.'s ability to use Nick's burgeoning imagination to her own benefit. The mist tent was transformed into an exotic planet on a solar system far, far away. The intermittent positive-pressure breathing machine contained a special atmospheric mixture that kept children, whose ancestors had arrived from planets far, far away, alive. Didn't Nick know that children with C.F. were very rare and special, and that they could trace their bloodlines back to extraterrestrials that had crashed on Earth eons ago? The physical therapies were necessary because the heavier atmosphere of Earth clogged their lungs. Remember how sick E.T. became when he was out all night and caught a cold? Just like children with C.F.

By the time Nick was four, he was able to read aloud to Mrs. L. His vocabulary soon equaled that of a fifth grader. Instead of letting him dwell on his limitations, Mrs. L. constantly reinforced his strengths. They read and wrote together incessantly.

Every night, Mrs. L. would interrupt their dinner. "You think you're so smart, Mr. Genius? Listen to this." Nick would then recite what he had learned that day.

After the applause, Nick would tap his forehead and grin. "Aliens, Daddy. Just you and me. All the way."

No matter how often he said it, it always evoked the memory of their first year together and the long dark nights on the floor of the nursery.

Mrs. L. quickly took over all the household chores, including shopping and cooking. When Lockton told her it wasn't necessary, she scoffed. When he offered her a raise, she was insulted.

"The boy needs a clean house and good food," she said.

"I did okay for three years," he argued.

She countered with "Okay isn't good enough for our Nick."

She got no argument from him.

The Locktons, James realized on the first anniversary of Mrs. L.'s employment, had been adopted.

Chapter 5

November 24, 1980

THE BURLY, HARD-JAWED MAN scrutinized James Lockton's campus office like a wary real-estate agent assessing an overpriced new listing. When they shook hands, his thick arm stretched the seam of his gray suit coat. He was in superb shape for a balding man in his late forties. He introduced himself as Richard Stone. He had told the secretary he worked for the government and was looking for the right man to head a new research-and-development program. He assured her it would be more than worth a few minutes of Dr. Lockton's time.

"I'll be brief, Doctor." Stone sat on the leather couch below the bookshelves. "What I have to say is confidential. I would rather it didn't leave this room. If you have a problem with that, we'll . . ."

He knows how to get your attention, Lockton thought.

"It won't," he agreed.

"We've spent a good deal of time checking the credentials of a number of professed leaders in the field of recombinant DNA research. Your name has been mentioned often by your colleagues. Your work with viruses as possible vectors for gene therapy, using transposons, so-called jumping genes, to alter the genetic structure of specific organisms, is considered by most as bordering on pure genius."

"Do you work in the field?" Lockton asked.

"No, no," Stone protested. "I'm in the—well, management end of it. For the last year, we've been following your work with great interest."

"And who exactly is—we?" Lockton had the feeling he wouldn't get a straight answer.

"I'm not at liberty to disclose that information . . . yet."

"Are you offering the university some type of federally funded research grant? My department could use it."

"In a way, yes." Stone took a pack of Camels from his shirt pocket. "Do you mind?"

Lockton shook his head. There was an ashtray on the corner of the desk. Stone put it on the arm of the sofa.

"I don't mean to be evasive, Dr. Lockton, but—" Stone lit his cigarette "—what we are offering is not exactly a university grant. We're looking for the right individual for a rather unusual position. You'd probably have to take an extended leave of absence."

"How long a leave?"

"Three to six years. It would all depend on the research's success. But there would be considerable compensation. I've been authorized to offer you your own lab outfitted with all the latest state-of-the-art equipment. And a house adjoining it. Both to be built in the area of your choice. Within certain limitations, of course. The salary is excellent. Suffice it to say, it would far exceed your present income." Stone blew a thick smoke-ring. It floated down onto Lockton's desk, spreading like a pond ripple before breaking. "We understand you have a growing financial problem, Dr. Lockton. We'd like to help if we could. As part of the benefits, we would underwrite an insurance policy for your son that would cover one hundred percent of his medical expenses—hospitalization, prescriptions, the salary of your live-in nurse, everything. We would also pay off all your outstanding debts as a bonus for signing the contract with us."

James Lockton wiped his palms on his trousers. "That's quite an offer." Stone had painted a picture that only existed in the consequential plots of a Dickens novel. He hated to put a match to it, but he had to ask. "What type of research are we talking about?"

Stone stamped out his cigarette and put the ashtray back on the desk. "Biological weapons."

"Can you be more specific?" Lockton watched the corner of that beautiful picture catch fire.

"Not about the research." Stone noticed the subtle change in Lockton's body language. He had tightened up, stiffened. "I'd like to explain what I can, however."

"Please." Lockton tipped his chair back against the window frame. During his college years in the late sixties and early seventies, he had participated in a few antiwar demonstrations. Like his male contemporaries, he had received a 2-S deferment from the draft. By the time he graduated, the lottery system had been introduced and his number, 263, had kept him out of the military. Although James Lockton's antiwar sentiments had waned as the passing years fogged the televised memories of Vietnam, he still had an instinctive distrust for anything that resembled a covert military operation.

But it wouldn't hurt to listen, especially when the argument came wrapped in such a beautifully tempting package.

"Let me give you some facts," Stone suggested. "Soviet-made chemical and biological agents have been used in very recent times. Where and what type is confidential. Our intelligence has discovered at least six major C.B. research-and-production installations in the Soviet Union. They have even tailored one of their strategic rockets to deliver multiple C.B. warheads. The United States, however, quit making C.B. weapons well over a decade ago. One of Nixon's legacies."

"And now the government thinks we should resume production?"

Lockton reached around to open the window after Stone lit another cigarette.

"It's the only way to persuade the Soviets to seriously negotiate a C.B. weapons ban. Eventually we're going to bring them to the negotiating table to consider a comprehensive nuclear weapons treaty because we stood firm and began deployment of our cruise missiles in Europe. Mark my words, Dr. Lockton. The same goes for C.B. weapons. You don't sit down at the table and try to bluff the Russians. You need a strong hand or they'll scoop up the pot every time."

"The theory has a certain nebulous validity, but..."

"No buts. That's the way it is, I assure you." Stone realized he was pushing too hard. He decided to take another tack. "Doctor, I'm sure you're familiar with the fact that the United States hasn't used any C.B. weapons since World War I. Although both the Allied and Axis powers had C.B. capabilities in World War II, neither side committed them. That's what parity is all about."

"I think your facts are a little faulty." Lockton rose and opened the other two windows. "The Japanese used chemical weapons in World War II and we used them in Vietnam. Take Agent Orange, for instance."

"Agent Orange was a defoliant. It was not considered a lethal or severely injurious chemical agent. Our country has a prohibitory policy against first use of all lethal C.B. weapons."

"There are a number of Vietnam vets who would disagree with that assessment."

"Mistakes are made in any war, Dr. Lockton."

"That's exactly what worries me."

"Don't make any hasty decisions." Stone paused to give his next statement weight. "Think of your son."

Lockton realized his decision could affect both the length and quality of Nick's life. And Stone had made some pertinent points. Since World War I, the U.S. had been in three major military conflicts and had never resorted to the kind of C.B. warfare used in the trenches. Even in World War I, Lockton remembered, it was the kaiser who first introduced C.B. weapons. In 1915, during the second battle of Ypres, six thousand cylinders of chlorine were wafted over the Allied lines by the wind, and modern chemical warfare had officially begun.

Lockton walked to the door. One way or another, he would take care of Nick without resorting to that.

"I appreciate your generous offer, Mr. Stone, but I'm afraid I'll have to decline."

"We'll be in touch." Stone offered his hand. "In case circumstances dictate a change of mind."

Lockton smiled politely. "I assure you they won't."

IN THE SPRING of 1982, Nick Lockton developed cirrhosis of the liver, trapping enough blood elements to also produce anemia. In the year and a half following Lockton's meeting with Stone, Nick had been hospitalized three times. James's debts now exceeded seventy thousand dollars. The hospital had filed a suit against him the same day Nick was to be readmitted. He also owed Mrs. L. six months' back salary and Radke Drug Store twelve hundred dollars.

He discovered that abstract sociopolitical philosophies meant little when you were financially pinned against the ropes, trying desperately to protect your son while getting pummeled about the head and body with lawsuits and bankruptcy.

Stone arrived at his West Seattle apartment the day after Nick went into the hospital.

"You said the offer still stands?" Lockton handed him a cup of coffee, black.

"We've been working on the project for almost two years. We haven't accomplished a single major goal." Stone lit a cigarette. This time he didn't ask permission. "We need your genius, Dr. Lockton."

"My debts have increased substantially since our last meeting." Lockton put his coffee on the plastic table beside one of Nick's toy crates.

"That's $74,855," Stone said. "Not including lawyers' fees and your son's latest hospitalization, which should run you upward of thirty grand. I'm sorry about Nick."

"The doctor said we caught it in time."

"I'm glad." Stone sank deep into the sofa. "I've brought the contracts and the insurance policy. Officially you'll be working for BIOGENTEX, a private biotech corporation in Texas."

"And unofficially?"

"The CIA."

Lockton hadn't expected that. "Then this isn't going to be a large-scale military weapons system? Something to be used at the bargaining table? Deterrence through parity? Weapons negotiation and all that crap?"

Stone ignored his sarcastic paraphrasing of his earlier conversation. "The project is highly classified, Dr. Lockton. Top top secret. One of the contracts is a special loyalty oath similar to the one signed by our people. You'll be working on the project alone. Everything you need will be made available through me. Are you still willing to sign?"

"Yes."

"Good." Stone opened the briefcase on his lap.
"Now where would you like your new house and lab
to be built?"

"Back home."

"And where's that?"

"You don't know?" Lockton wasn't being face-
tious. "You seem to know everything else."

Stone looked up impatiently.

"Vashon." Lockton pointed out the window.
"Where that ferry's docking. Vashon Island."

July 22, 1983

"IT LOOKS LIKE ONE of the big dinosaur skeletons we
saw at the museum," Nick said as he continued kicking a crinkled Pepsi can up the rutted dirt driveway of
their new house. Three weeks after the basement
foundation had been completed, the carpenters had
already framed the entire house. One crew was on the
roof, nail-gunning plywood sheets to the rafters. The
other was putting up the siding on the garage.

Lockton put a hand on his son's shoulder. "You're
going to like it out here, Nick. The island's a great
place to grow up."

"Are we going to get a boat?"

"Maybe."

"And a puppy?"

"As soon as we move in."

"Awesome!" As Nick gleefully skipped into the
garage, a white van pulled into the driveway.

"Moving right along, huh, Doc?" Richard Stone
said as he got out. The driver hurried past them with-

out a greeting. Lockton watched him circle past the house and disappear into the basement.

"Who's that?" he asked.

"One of our people." Stone shaded his eyes to examine the progress. "He wanted to see the house and the lab before planning the alarm systems."

"I ran into an old high-school friend in town. He's an electrician. He wanted to know..."

"I told you before, Doc. We do all the contracting. No exceptions."

"Hey Dad! Look at me!" Nick was standing on top of a ladder between two open rafters on the roof.

"What, are you nuts, Charlie?" Stone screamed up at the carpenter below him on the ladder. "Get the boy down from there. Now!"

"I just wanted to see what it looked like from up here," Nick confessed.

"That's all right, Nick," Lockton interceded. "You look around. But stay on the ladder."

"Charlie shouldn't have let him up there," Stone protested angrily. "He doesn't know about the kid's..." He looked awkwardly down at the mud. "Sickness."

"I try not to overcompensate," Lockton explained, startled by Stone's concern. "I don't want him to feel like he has to live his life shut up like an invalid. It wouldn't be fair." They walked down the hill to the basement. "And besides, he's not. Not really."

"Boys," Stone said, shaking his head philosophically. "They're always getting into trouble."

"You have children?" Lockton suddenly realized just how little he knew about him. In the past few months, he had gained a sort of depersonalized respect, but this was the first time he had thought of Stone as a family man, a person with a life outside of the "business."

"Boy and a girl." Stone smiled to himself. "My wife threatened to divorce me if I let George follow in..." Stone caught himself and shrugged.

Lockton followed him into the dark, cool basement. "In his father's footsteps?"

The slightest hint of pride creased Stone's face.

"Now let me show you just how secure this P-3 lab will be," Stone announced, stepping farther into the darkness.

Chapter 6

7:45 p.m., December 19, 1984

THE FERRY FROM STRALSUND arrived at Putbus, on Rügen Island, twenty-five minutes behind schedule. George Stone, dapperly dressed in a Czechoslovakian business suit containing papers stating he was a marine engineer named Klaus Furstenfeld, drank a cup of sweet hot chocolate with cream at a table by the window of the Fulder Café, two blocks from the Rügen ferry terminal. His winter coat was hung on the back of his chair. Under the bright white lights, he could see the big, double-decker ferry pitch up against the log pilings as it docked. The sea was choppy with whitecaps. The winter wind was bitter.

This was to be George Stone's last assignment in East Germany. In three days, he would be home in Fairfax, Virginia. It was hard to keep from thinking about his kid sister and his mother as he watched the terminal. It would be even harder not to tell them that he and Dad had finally worked together on an assignment.

SIX WEEKS EARLIER, Dick Schraeder, a fifteen-year veteran in the Operations Division of the CIA, had been assigned as the case officer to a "covert defection" of a renowned East German physicist. He had immediately called Richard Stone at the Intelligence Division, where he had been transferred five years earlier.

Stone had been Schraeder's first case officer. He had taught him how to survive in the dangerous world of espionage and had saved his rookie ass more than once in those first few years. Because George Stone was one of Schraeder's available operatives in East Germany, he knew his father should be in on this one.

He owed him that.

They met for lunch at Lapolla's, an Italian restaurant in the ritzy Georgetown section of Washington, D.C.

"I've checked it through Williams," Schraeder told him, finishing his fettuccini Alfredo. "It's been okayed. You can take over as case officer on this one if you want."

Stone was beaming as he reached across the table to shake his friend's hand. "I don't know how you scammed this through, but thanks." He had barely touched his meatball sandwich.

"This is big, Richard." Schraeder lit his old case officer's cigarette, then his own. "This physicist is important. His name is Dr. Heimlich Koplenz. He's at the forefront of particle-beam technology. For the last ten years he's been working on a top-secret, space-based particle-beam weapons system. The Pentagon is creaming in their pants to get him."

"With two Stones on it, how can we fail?" He grinned. Schraeder must have called in a lot of favors, he thought. If it wouldn't have embarrassed both men, he would have reached across the table and kissed him.

During the following weeks, Richard Stone checked every detail of the operation dozens of times. The pressure and the regimen made him feel ten years younger. He was going back in the field. One more mission. And he would finally be directing his son. His dream had come true. Good old Schraeder. If there was a way he could pay him back for this, he would find it.

Richard Stone had been working for the Agency almost thirty years. He was one of the best spies Operations had ever employed. The transfer to Intelligence was supposed to have been a promotion. But Stone had felt he had been sent out to pasture. To him, analyzing data collected by his colleagues in Operations was the same as growing too old to play football and becoming a coach. He missed the action on the field. Heading security for the CIA's top-secret biological weapon project was also supposed to have been a special honor. Stone thought of it as classified babysitting.

Now he had one more chance to quarterback in a play-off game. Hell, he thought, this one's the goddamn Super Bowl and the kid's my star receiver.

Richard Stone's proudest moment was when George had been accepted by the Agency, which received a quarter of a million applications yearly. George had made his dad promise not to pull any strings. He wanted to make it on his own and had. His linguistic skills—he spoke fluent German, Russian and Spanish—with a master's in postrevolutionary Russian history—and his athletic abilities—he was the starting quarterback at North Carolina State—had sacked it for him. In the past three years, George Stone had also proven himself extremely capable in the field of Cold War combat.

The Stone legacy would continue after the old man retired, Richard Stone decided.

What father could ask for more?

WHEN GEORGE STONE spotted the rotund, balding scientist scuffling up the terminal with his old leather suitcase, head bent against the wind, he quickly slipped on his jacket and finished his chocolate. As Koplenz entered the café, two clean-shaven men in fur hats ran across the street. Two other men hurried past them and slid into a 1972 Volkswagen. Stone caught the slight nod of recognition as they passed. The two on the sidewalk, backs to the wind, pretended to window-shop as Koplenz skittered through the restaurant foyer.

Stone left his table and went to the bathroom. Koplenz drew a chair up to the table where he had just drunk his chocolate. The scientist stared out the steamy window at the men across the street. When they saw him watching, they started down toward Putbus town square. Koplenz lifted the empty cup and saucer and wiped the wet napkin into his lap as if cleaning off cake crumbs. There was one word on it: *toilette*. Leaning back in his chair, he spotted the two men again. They had crossed the street and were starting back toward the café.

Resigned to his fate, either way, Koplenz entered the men's room. A well-dressed, handsome young man was combing his hair in front of the rusty mirror above the sink. The young man quickly walked around him, shoved open the window and climbed out into the alley. Koplenz heard a car idling. Exhaust fumes billowed in through the window.

The young man poked his head back into the bathroom.

"Are you coming?" he asked in American English.

IN THE BACK OF THE VOLVO, George Stone and Dr. Heimlich Koplenz changed into fishermen's clothes and knee-high boots. The driver sped along the windy coast road toward a small fishing village six kilometers north of Putbus.

"It stinks," Koplenz complained in German as he twisted into the oily wool sweater.

"Like fish," Stone agreed.

The driver handed them two Danish passports.

"How did you get my photo?" Koplenz asked, examining his.

Stone grinned and tapped the driver's shoulder. "There's Weidenberg. Turn here."

The dirt road descended through the village of Weidenberg to the sea. Only a few houses had lights on. Early to bed, early to rise—a fisherman's life, Stone thought. Nets were hung on long poles behind the high seawall. Three piers jutted out into the water. Thirty- to forty-five-foot fishing boats twisted and moaned against their lines, tied to individual slips on the piers.

The driver got out of the car and ran up the center pier. Two fishermen climbed down the sixty-foot vessel secured at the end of the dock.

Koplenz followed the driver.

George Stone leaned on the roof of the Volvo, his back to the sea, and scanned the coast road with binoculars.

Two pairs of headlights flashed into view, coming north on the coast road. Bumper to bumper and doing at least ninety, Stone calculated. They turned onto the dirt road to Weidenberg.

Stone spun around and yelled into the hard sea wind. His driver glanced back at the approaching lights, turned and spoke to the two fishermen.

One climbed aboard and helped Koplenz up onto the deck. The other cast off the bowline. The vessel's powerful engine rumbled and the second fisherman jumped up onto the bow. Stone's driver ran back to the car and took the binoculars.

"How did they know?" he muttered.

Stone saw the boat leave the pier and turn out to sea. "What the hell are they doing?"

He started toward the dock, but was pulled back.

"Get in," the driver ordered.

They sped around the block of small, dilapidated warehouses and parked behind what appeared to be the town hall. They had not turned on their headlights.

"Why did they leave us?" Stone demanded.

"I told them to."

When the two cars passed, the Volvo turned onto the street leading back to the coast road and flicked on its headlights.

"What are you doing?" Stone looked out the back window. The two cars squealed to a halt, kicking up a wall of dust. The driver floored it.

"Had to give them time to get out to sea." They bumped up onto the coast road and turned south, back toward Stralsund. "Our orders were simple. Ensure Koplenz gets safely to Bornholm. Hopefully, they still think we have him."

"What about us?"

As they veered down the steep hill, their headlights suddenly illuminated two military trucks blocking the road.

The driver didn't have an answer.

RICHARD STONE REMAINED on Bornholm after Koplenz had been delivered to Denmark, making the eighty-mile ocean voyage to the town of Wiek on Rügen Island every four days. If something had gone wrong, his two operatives were to meet his boat in a small harbor two miles north of Wiek by the abandoned lighthouse.

After eight trips, he was ordered to return to the States. The coded message revealed that a member of his surveillance team on the top-secret biological weapons project was being replaced. Stone was told to fly to Seattle to personally oversee the transition. No one else could do it. Only he and one other man, Jack Lieberman, divisional head of Intelligence, knew the exact details of the project. The other agents involved were kept on a need-to-know basis. Even the surveillance personnel had only a limited knowledge of the project's true nature. Stone refused to leave until he had elicited promises from his two operatives on Bornholm Island to continue the sea voyages to the lighthouse until they heard directly from him.

Eight days later, on their second cold, storm-tossed journey, the two agents spotted George Stone and his driver.

Their bullet-scarred bodies were hanging upside down, their feet nailed to the lighthouse door.

RICHARD STONE had been able to forgive the company a myriad of ethical discrepancies over the years. Leaving his son to die on a godforsaken island in the Baltic Sea was not one of them. He understood the military and strategical importance of Dr. Heimlich Koplenz, but they still could have taken the chance and all left on the boat together. He would have. It was a big ocean out there. To Stone, the driver had been too protective of his prize defector and had sacrificed himself and his son without just cause.

Jack Lieberman told Stone he wasn't being objective about the incident. Agents had been sacrificed before and would be again. It happened. His son had known the risks. He was a brave man. The Company honored him. Now let it go.

Stone took three months off. For the first month, he locked himself in the house and drank. By the time he sobered up, he had decided he couldn't tell the good guys from the bad guys anymore. What the hell was the difference between a capitalist military industrial society run by a minority of corporate bigwigs and a totalitarian military industrial complex run by a minority of Communist elite? Either way, the rich got fat on the bodies of our sons.

Honor? What the hell was that anymore? Just a word for people still living in the previous century. Like *loyalty* and *duty*. They were all words developed by the elite, the corporate aristocracy, to get other men's sons to die for their causes. Just like Vietnam, he thought. The rich got deferments. The poor got their skinny asses blown away.

Two weeks before he was to return to work, Richard Stone received a phone call from Dick Schraeder.

"Did you hear about our prize defector?" he inquired.

"No. And I don't give a..."

"He's refused to work on our S.D.I. program. No Star Wars for Dr. Koplenz. He's decided it's immoral. After they got everything they could out of him about the Soviets' space-based weapons technology and he was officially granted political asylum, he confessed. The main reason he defected was because of his acute abhorrence of military weapons. He wants to work with particle accelerators to find out what the universe was like a millionth of a second after the big bang. In other words, our East German firecracker was a dud. I'm sorry. I thought you should know."

Richard Stone ripped the phone from the wall and threw it through the kitchen window.

In his way of thinking, Dr. Koplenz had just spit on his son's grave. A grave that had been dug for him.

Thirty years of his life. And his son's life. Wasted.

It had all been for nothing. Duty, patriotism, honor. All one big fucking joke.

Richard Stone poured a double shot of brandy into his coffee and stared through the broken glass at the upper-class suburban landscape. His divorced wife had moved in with a twenty-eight-year-old dentist; his daughter had married an alcoholic drug counselor; his son was dead and his job was bullshit.

In four years he would retire with a pension, stocks and social security worth about twenty-eight grand a year after taxes.

It wasn't enough.

Not for thirty wasted years.

Not for his son's life.

They owed him. Blood money. And he knew just how to bleed them.

Richard Stone decided his pound of flesh was alive and breeding in a laboratory on Vashon Island in the Puget Sound of Washington State.

THE ISLAND

Chapter 7

5:15 p.m., March 14, 1986

THE TWO BIG MALE RATS remained in opposite corners of cage three, snarling and twitching, spittle spilling down through their bared teeth. The lone female bunched her three surviving babies under the water tube. She originally had had a litter of seven. The other four's mutilated bodies were strewn across the metal floor of the cage, dead. One's decapitated carcass lay propped over the edge of the plastic food dish like a dead French aristocrat left under the guillotine.

Suddenly the gray male caught one of the young by the front leg and began dragging it across the cage. The other male charged, gnawing and ripping at the baby's haunches. Like a pack of hyenas, they began tearing their screeching prey apart.

James Lockton had witnessed many similar assaults over the past three months, but had never become immune to their horror. It took all his self-discipline to retain enough scientific detachment to chronicle the event on the cage's chart. His mouth tasted of cement dust. To most people, the only good rat was a dead rat.

It was different with Lockton.

All forms of life on earth, from *E. coli* bacteria to the great sperm whale, were miracles that reaffirmed the planet's natural symbiotic relationship, both to its billions of species and to the nature of the Earth itself, its climate and atmosphere. James Lockton believed in the GAIA hypothesis: the planet and its life were one, but to sustain itself, the battle of opposite forces was continually needed to balance the rhythm of life—yin and yang, good and evil, life and death. One could not exist without the other.

In terms of evolution, the rise and fall of numerous species over millions of years, Lockton could understand and respect the interrelating balance of life and death on the planet Earth.

But when viewing the brief flicker of a single Homo sapien's life span, specifically his dead wife's, he could not. Human beings were not viruses; they were not supposed to die in order to propagate.

Death, however, had become a daily occurrence in James Lockton's life. He stepped back from the four cages in the enclave, sickened.

For four years, he had been able to retain a scientific detachment from the project and keep it a difficult but exciting theoretical challenge. In the past three months, however, all that had changed. His research was no longer confined to the microscopic world of viruses. Now the fruition of his genius was the systematic murdering of a living species....

Rats.

To test his genetically altered virus's capability to infect a much larger host...

Man.

Lockton slowly surveyed the carnage in the four cages. All the rats in the first two were dead. Their mauled corpses littered their cages like the dead bodies of a retreating army, abandoned on the battlefield.

The lone female in cage three stared up through the wire meshing at the huge figure in surgical garb. Her black-caviar eyes helplessly pleaded for clemency from her godlike tormentor. Lockton knew it was already too late. If the infected males didn't kill her, the disease eating away at her brain soon would.

In the fourth cage, five or six rats appeared healthy. The biggest male, however, seemed agitated. Standing guard at the water tube, his left hind leg kept trembling in sudden bursts, like a plucked string on a fiddle.

His nervous disorder was one of the first signs of the disease.

Taking a Kleenex from the center table, Lockton dabbed the sweat around the perimeter of his surgical cap and mask, then tossed it into the plastic-lined aluminum trash can. After unwrapping a disposable hypodermic syringe, he pinned the big male against the side of the cage with a pair of plastic tongs and drew a sample of blood.

When he closed the enclave's transparent hood, the rats' tortured squeals were muted by the heavy drone of the P-3 security lab's overhead ventilation system. He was grateful for the noise as he prepared the sample for the scanning electron microscope. When the sample was ready, he removed his surgical gloves and entered the back room.

The scanning electron microscope was more like a television system than an optical microscope. The finely focused electron beam swept across the specimen, stimulating the emission of secondary electrons from the minute area struck. As the probe's signal was collected in the cathode-ray tube, another beam scanned the tube's face, and an almost three-dimensional image appeared on Lockton's computer terminal.

He began to direct the microscope's beam across the specimen as if it were a video camera. A row of bowl-shaped red blood cells stood in a line like a bent deck of cards. Zooming in, he spotted one of the syringe-shaped virus mutations frozen in the process of injecting its pearl-necklace strands of RNA into the ectoplasm of a blood cell. Roaming farther, he found a cell caught in the process of bursting—unleashing the mutant virus that had been bred within it.

Normally, the Formido Inexorbisilis virus had to come into contact with nerve tissue in order to successfully infect its host. From there, it would slowly spread to the peripheral nerves and the dorsal-root ganglia, and finally, the brain. Once it reached the brain, the virus was irreversible. The mutant virus, however, had been bred to travel and reproduce in fresh water as well as the bloodstream.

Lockton estimated that it could reach the brain of its host within two hours.

The mutant virus's natural cousin was more commonly referred to as rabies.

After filing the test data in his 9000 series H.P. 320 computer, Lockton removed the blood sample from the S.E.M. and replaced it with a sample of water from the first cage's trough which had been infected five days earlier.

This was the experiment that concerned him the most. He had perfected the virus's ability to rapidly infect one-celled organisms in fresh water well over a year ago.

The problem was . . .

How to stop it.

Like some of the scientists at Los Alamos during World War II, who had feared that the first nuclear explosion might cause a chain reaction that would destroy the world, Lockton had feared the consequences of his virus if it was ever unleashed into a large body of fresh water. So, as soon as the virus's ability to propagate in water was successfully coded into its genetic structure, he had begun working on what he called its "half-life factor." The virus had to have a genetic fail-safe "clause" that would ensure its breakdown after a specific infective period. Without that, a body of fresh water, underground or above, would remain contagious and continue spreading—through flooding, underground streams or small tributaries—for centuries.

In the sample he was viewing, over eighty-five percent of the viruses had broken apart and died. Twenty-four hours earlier, more than fifty percent of the viruses had been still functioning. Lockton was pleased by the results. Within six hours, the infected water would be completely harmless again. Five and a half days for infectiousness to break down.

He filed the new data into the computer and reentered the main lab. Slipping on another pair of surgical gloves, he collected the day's pipettes, flasks and syringes and dropped them into the steel autoclave. The super-hot steam oven quickly sterilized the disposable utensils. He discarded his mask, hat, gown and gloves in the trash.

The scrub brush stung his skin as he washed his arms and hands in the large aluminum sink. He rinsed down from the elbows and looked into the mirror. He hadn't shaved in three days. His gray-green eyes were dark-rimmed, as shadowed as his stubbled chin. His short, disheveled blond hair looked like a storm-battered cornfield. The longer he stared, the less he recognized the image staring back at him.

The haunted face in the mirror drew him closer. His breath fogged his reflection.

It was as if he was trying to rediscover who he was.

Or what he had become.

NUMBED BY THAT strange feeling of self-disparity, Lockton opened the laboratory door. Cool air blew in across his face. The suction breeze was a basic component of a P-3 security lab. The air pressure inside the lab maintained a constant inhalation.

Nothing could escape.

Lockton closed the airtight door and switched on the alarm system with two uniquely designed keys. After bolt-locking the door, the green overhead safety light flashed on.

He circled the full-size antique mahogany pool table in the basement den. A stained-glass lamp hung over it like an inverted tulip. The balls were exactly as he and Nick had left them four nights ago. He held back the urge to roll the five ball into a dead three-ball combination in the corner pocket.

Four nights ago, he thought, startled. They were supposed to finish the game the next day.

As he started up the stairs, he could hear Mrs. L. talking to herself in the kitchen. He smiled gratefully. Her coarse voice helped to push aside the hollowness that had engulfed him. It reminded him of real life, of Nick and the island and the deep waters of Puget Sound…and Alex. He let it wash over him like a cool alcohol sponge-bath, until he felt rejuvenated, ready to return to the world of sunlight and natural breezes.

He made a mental note to finish the pool game tonight.

No more excuses.

"SO THE MOLES finally came up for air." Mrs. L. clanked the big iron pot onto another burner.

Lockton opened the refrigerator, popped a can of Rainier, took a long, pleasant swallow and burped abruptly.

"The manners of a German peasant." Mrs. L. slapped the lid on her pot of turkey soup. The kitchen was thick with the gusty aroma.

Lockton inched closer to the stove. "Were you having a good conversation?"

"There's no one here but me." She began to cut carrots on a well-worn oak board. "As usual."

Lockton swiped one of the carrots, narrowly escaping the knife. "I heard you," he teased. Mrs. L. always talked to herself, but would never admit it. "Sounded like a hell of an argument. Where's Nick?"

The knife cracked through a half-dozen carrots. "Nick's over at—" the next two words fell from her lips like lead sinkers "—your neighbor's."

She was referring to Alex McGuire, the most beautiful woman Lockton had ever met. The sight of her doing aerobics on her deck, her leotard cut high above the double arch of her muscled buttocks, rated as one of the seven wonders of the modern world. They had been dating for over a year, exclusively for the past six months. It was the first time in eight years James Lockton had had a relationship that lasted more than a couple of months. Alex McGuire had been the only woman able to compare with the ghost of Elizabeth. It was not easy to compete with a memory, but Alex McGuire had never asked him to forget, only to make room.

Mrs. L. viewed Alex McGuire as an intruder and never referred to her by name. It was always "your neighbor," as if she wasn't her neighbor as well. No wonder Alex always seemed reluctant to visit.

"Is your neighbor going to be here for breakfast, too?" did not make for comfortable dinner conversation, especially when followed by: "This time, remember to close your windows. I can't sleep during all that racket."

James Lockton snuck a kiss on Mrs. L.'s cheek before she could shoo him away. When she heard the front door open, her head snapped up.

"Dinner's promptly at six, you hear?" she called. "Six-O-five, it goes to the dog. At least he's never late." The door closed and she shook her head. "And I wasn't talking to myself. Only crazy people do that. I was . . . praying."

Mrs. L. had been praying because of the old black-and-white horror movie she had had the displeasure of viewing late last night. It starred Bela Lugosi, a brunette that never made it beyond B movies and Tor Johnson, a barely human creature the size of a cement truck. In the final scene, when the mad scientist and his laboratory exploded in a mushroom cloud, the hero muttered ominously, "He tampered with God's domain."

Mrs. L. couldn't sleep after that.

Chapter 8

March 14, 1986

VASHON ISLAND was fourteen miles long and from two to five miles wide. The only way on or off was by boat. The Lockton residence sat perched on a wooded hill above the beach on the northwest coast. Ten miles northeast, across Puget Sound, lay the Emerald City, Seattle. To the south, Tacoma, a brawny industrial town with a deep-sea port. Giant Fort Lewis bordered Tacoma on the southwest. Vashon Island, like most of the Pacific Northwest, was a mystical blend of semitropical foliage, thick blackberry vines, bright green moss, fir trees, alders and evergreens. Spring came early to the Northwest. The island was already beginning to bloom.

Alex McGuire's beach house was a hundred yards north of Lockton's. The rich, shimmering green forest rose a half mile up between the two homes to the long flat summit of the island. Lockton kept a path open between the houses. Twice a year he macheted the blackberry vines. A rain-washed gully zigzagged through the center of the path down to the Sound.

As he crossed the makeshift bridge spanning the gully, James Lockton spotted a bald eagle perched high on the jagged top of a splintered fir tree. It soared out into the wind currents and down below the tree line. Seagulls cawed raucously.

The path widened at the edge of Alex's property. Fixed to the steep ridge with four-by-four beams, her tall deck jutted out like the bow of a clipper ship. The glass west wall reflected the bright orange-pink glow of the setting sun.

Lockton stopped by the stairs to listen to the harmony of piano and flute. The heavy thump of paws broke the rhythm. Thor, Nick's ninety-five pound golden retriever, bounded down the stairs, his tail gyrating like a helicopter blade. Lockton scratched him under the ears and Thor nudged his bent head up against the man's leg.

Deciding not to interrupt the piece, Lockton watched through the glass door. Nick looked frail and angelic, playing his flute behind the sun-tinted glass. His long blond lashes fluttered with concentration. When he was six, Mrs. L. had bought him a cheap German Meinl flute from a pawnshop in Tacoma. She thought it would be good therapy. Help build his wind. In two years, Nick had graduated to an expensive Dundy and was able to accompany his favorite songs on the stereo, note by note, as if the sheet music were there in front of him. If it wasn't for his lungs, Nick might have been considered a child prodigy.

A year ago, Nick had asked Alex, who played piano, guitar and flute, if she would give him lessons. After six months, she had decided there wasn't much she could teach him, and had started accompanying him on the piano instead.

Alex shook back her thick red mane, her fingers dancing on the keyboard like two graceful water spiders. Her wide, full mouth parted slightly as the piece reached its climax. Her lower lip reminded Lockton of the perfect wave, breaking across the soft white sands of her chin.

Suddenly Thor darted down the stairs and started barking. Lockton glanced around the corner of the house. Something was flashing in the woods up the hill, past the roof of the Hobbit House, so named for its ramshackle construction and hard-angled, wood-shingled roof. No one had lived there in years.

"That's enough," Lockton commanded, angered by the interruption.

The flashing stopped.

So had the music.

Thor leaped up the stairs, unashamed. He had been doing his job.

"Hi, Daddy." Nick limped outside into his father's arms. "Sounded pretty good, huh?"

"Good?" Lockton hugged him. "It was great. What was it?"

Nick glanced inside at Alex. "Deb-bus-sey?" he fumbled questioningly.

"Debussy." Alex corrected.

"I'll never get that right." Nick sighed.

Lockton patted the boy's shoulder on their way to the piano.

Alex leaned up to kiss him.

Thor anxiously paced outside the door.

Nick slapped his thigh. "You can come in now. The song's over."

Nick leaned against Thor's shoulder and the dog adjusted his stance to accommodate the weight.

"Hey, Dad!" Nick rolled his shoulders back like a professional wrestler. "Gettin' stronger. Feel." He flexed his biceps.

"Better use two hands, huh?" Lockton circled his son's arm. The tiny muscle coiled against his palms. It was barely the size of an egg. "Hulk Hogan, look out. Nick 'The Claw' Lockton is gunning for the title."

Nick sneered fiercely as he put Thor in a headlock. The arm he had flexed cramped and he jerked it straight, hoping no one had noticed.

Lockton glanced at Alex. She'd seen it, too. An uncomfortable silence followed.

"Come on, Thor," Nick said. "Let's blow this joint before they start swapping spit again."

"Nick!" Lockton reprimanded.

"Don't forget your flute." Alex held out the case.

"Dad, watch this." Nick pointed at Alex. "Fetch the flute."

Thor crept toward Alex in slow motion, every step calculated by centuries of instinct. When his jaw was a few inches from the case, he snapped the handle out of her hand.

"Good boy," Nick praised.

Together, they departed the world of adults and music and showing-off and journeyed toward the beach and the truer world of scents and imagination.

Alex opened the shuttered mahogany doors of the liquor cabinet under the limited-edition Mark Toby print of The Market in downtown Seattle. Although she had lived in Washington only a year and a half, she was already a loyal patron of Northwest artists, both world-famous ánd unrecognized. Her most prized possession was a small painting by Jake Hollard, a relatively unknown Vashon Island artist.

"Dewar's and water?" she asked, already pouring the Scotch.

"He hates it when anyone catches him in pain." Lockton watched Nick disappear down the beach.

"Especially his father." Alex slid onto the bench beside him.

"He doesn't need to hide it from me."

"He thinks so." Alex handed him his glass. "He's worried you're mad at him."

"Why?"

"Because you've been living down in that lab of yours for the past few months. He said you even forgot about your pool tournament."

"Shit!" Lockton downed half his drink.

Alex led him to the sofa. "We're all worried, James. You emerge from that lab like it was a damn morgue. You're not eating. Not jogging. You don't sleep well. At least when I'm there."

He finished his drink. "It's not because of you."

She refilled his glass and returned. "For God's sake, James, you've already perfected your lab tan. It's enough to make any vampire jealous."

Lockton was relieved to smile. "I haven't exactly been a barrel of laughs lately, have I?"

He looked across the room at Hollard's darkly mystical, surrealistic painting of an evergreen forest populated by half-human, half-animal creatures. His smile slowly drifted away like an unmoored boat. When he looked back at Alex, she felt an intense, physical tugging, as if a cord in her groin was being drawn taut.

"I want it finished. I want to be rid of it." His quiet cadence reminded her of how she had spoken to the priest as a child, when she still believed in the confessional.

Lockton slowly walked to the glass wall and rapped his knuckles against it. "I wish I'd failed."

"No, you don't." Alex hugged him from behind. "It's not your way."

Lockton turned and embraced her. "Come over for dinner. And bring one of those Frederick's of Hollywood items."

Alex pushed up tight against him. "I've got a piano lesson at five-thirty."

"So come at six-thirty."

"There're some things I've got to do. Grocery shop. Some paperwork my lawyer's been . . ."

Lockton pulled away. "Why is it always so hard for us to be together?" He was getting loud. "It's been nearly a year and I still feel like I'm being pushy."

Alex flicked her hair back. "I just thought I'd let you and Nick have some time together. You've got a game of pool to finish, right?"

It took a moment for Lockton's jaw to unclench. "Sorry." His eyes softened. "I've been apologizing a lot lately, haven't I?" He opened the sliding-glass door. "Please, come over. Please?"

"I'll be there at eight. Tell Mrs. L. I'll already have eaten and that, yes—" she smiled "—I will be there for breakfast."

She walked out onto the deck as he headed for the beach. "And tell her to try closing her own damn windows."

JAMES LOCKTON'S five-foot-ten-inch frame galloped down the beach in a comfortable rhythm. The running loosened him. The beach extended twenty yards to the water. During high tide, it disappeared, leaving only seawalls, small concave cliffs and uprooted trees. Lockton hopped over a driftwood log the size of a telephone pole and slowed to a walk. He was already winded and chastised himself for getting out of shape.

When Thor spotted him, he charged. Lockton snapped a dead branch off the driftwood log and Thor eagerly leaped at it. When he heaved it back up the beach, the dog flew past Nick like an orange tracer round fired from a high-caliber weapon.

With a thin stick, Nick stabbed a jellyfish and held it up. "Look, Dad. A coelenterate."

Thor saw his master holding the stick, dropped the one he had fetched and ran back toward him. The boy quickly heaved the jellyfish and the stick out into the water.

"Thor, stay!" he screamed. The dog broke into the waves. "Thor. No!" The dog halted and looked back confused. "Come, Thor, come!" Thor reluctantly obeyed and Nick petted him roughly. The large jellyfish would have stung his mouth, and his tongue would have been swollen again. Some dogs just don't learn, Nick decided.

Lockton joined his son by the water's edge. The sun was gone. Only a thin turquoise hue, low behind the mountains, hinted at its departure. A few stars already poked through the purple sky. From the southwest, a scattered cloud front was approaching. A tugboat slowly passed, towing a drilling barge. The wind was soft and steady, colder now in the dark twilight.

As they started home, Lockton put his hand on the boy's bony shoulder. Thor ran out ahead of them, scouting the trail for his human pack.

"I'm sorry I've been so preoccupied lately, Nick. I don't want you to think I'm avoiding you on purpose. I love you." He squeezed the boy's shoulder. "And I miss hanging out with you."

"Me, too." Nick kicked a rock across the hard mud and Thor retrieved it.

"How 'bout we finish our pool game tonight. And tomorrow we'll spend the whole day together. Do anything you want, okay?"

"Anything?" Nick queried mischievously. "Like go buy a go-cart?"

"Well, almost anything."

Nick giggled. It had been worth a try. He had learned, years ago, that when his dad was feeling guilty, it was the best time to ask for stuff he wanted. And if he asked for something he knew he wouldn't get, then asking for other stuff was a cinch.

"Can we go to Seattle early and buy two Siamese fighting fish for my aquarium?"

"Sure."

"And can we take the boat out and go fishing in the afternoon?"

"Yup."

Works every time, Nick thought.

THE BIG MAN with the black-bearded, pockmarked face had parked the gray 1985 Chevy Impala on an old dirt road off Hillcrest Drive. Hillcrest snaked down from the main highway to a fork that led to three beachfront areas. The dirt road dead-ended high above Cove Road near the locked gate to the Hobbit House.

He was wearing army-surplus boots, sweater and rain gear, although the sky had been relatively clear all day. From the secluded bluff above the abandoned house, he had a good view of the beachfront homes on Cove Road. It had taken a week to find just the right spot.

Twilight had receded into darkness. He put down the Steiner 7×50 mm binoculars and retrieved an infrared night scope. Army surplus from Vietnam.

Just like himself.

Through its reddish lens, he watched the orange figure of a man with a boy on his shoulders cross a driveway. The quick shadow of a dog darted past. The man put the boy down and opened the front door. The lights went on in the house and the drapes were open.

"You've put us off long enough, Doc," the man said, switching back to his binoculars.

Chapter 9

6:42 p.m., March 14, 1986

A PEARL-WHITE LEAR JET, wing lights blinking, a corporate logo in bold green letters reading BIO-GENTEX on its tail, touched down at the Dallas–Fort Worth airport. The night sky was clear. Because of the distant cities, the smog and the well-lit air terminal, only the brightest stars were visible. The jet taxied past the commercial landing bays to a private hangar well beyond the runways.

The engine wound down as it rolled to a halt. The door was opened by the only passenger aboard. Even the company stewardesses hadn't been informed of this flight.

Richard Stone, wearing a gray Hart Schaffner & Marx three-piece, pin-striped suit, opened the passenger door and the stairs automatically dropped to the runway. His tan accentuated the scar that curved like a scimitar from his right eyebrow into his hair. Brushing back his short gray hair, he surveyed the area as he cautiously descended the stairs. His face showed his age—fifty-three—but his boarlike stride and clear gray eyes rejected it as inconsequential.

A white Cadillac stretch limousine was waiting. Stone walked directly to it. The chauffeur opened the back door and nodded. Stone ignored him and ducked inside.

AN HOUR LATER, the sky was black and crystalline with stars. Stone pressed down the automatic window. The desert air was dry and clean. He counted fifteen shooting stars on the western horizon before he reached his destination.

The entire twelve-acre complex was surrounded by a ten-foot brick fence. The interconnected buildings were typical of the Southwest, Spanish modern, with red-tile roofs, arched windows and numerous open-court patios. The nearest town, San Marcos, was thirty miles away. The front gate was made of barred steel. The BIOGENTEX logo was sculpted into the bars. The gate opened electronically.

Stone waved up at the closed-circuit camera perched like a vulture on the white brick arch bridging the gate. The limo stopped in front of the main, three-story building. Steel bars amply secured all windows. The chauffeur didn't get out.

Two guards in white uniforms opened the door.

"Mr. Courser is waiting, sir."

"Good."

The guards ran to catch up and open the security door to the main lobby.

Stone marched down the long sterile-white corridor, past numerous locked security labs. The two guards followed him to the door at the end of the hall. The taller slid his security card into the computerized identification lock. The white door swung open by itself. Stone entered alone.

The office was massive, the decor a gaudy blend of expensive antiques and cowboy paraphernalia. Above the fireplace made for gas-burning iron logs, hung two crossed, pearl-handled Colt .45s, said to have been stolen from Cole Younger, a member of the Jesse James gang, while he was passed out in a whorehouse. Or so swore Jack Courser, president of BIO-GENTEX, chairman of the board of a dozen Texas companies, and a second-generation oil baron.

Courser's attire was the same confused blend of styles. His twelve-hundred-dollar Brioni suit was richly offset by a pair of alligator-skin cowboy boots. His bolo tie was held with a gold nugget the size of a hummingbird.

Courser slammed his desk phone down. "Those slimy bastards. A generation ago they thought the height of sophistication was simmering goat meat over a hot bed of camel shit." Courser's loose cheeks and bulbous nose were mapped with varicose veins. His neck swelled like a puffer fish when he breathed. "Now those lice-ridden camel jockeys think they own the entire goddamn world."

"Don't they?" Stone couldn't help egging on his tantrum.

Irritated, Courser arose from his big leather chair and pressed one of eight buttons on the wall panel directly behind his desk. Two original Edward Curtis photographs, one a profile of the Cheyenne chief, Porcupine, wearing a sunshade of cottonwood leaves,

the other a full-length portrait of Iron Breast, a Pie-
gan chief in headdress and chaps, slipped behind the
wall to reveal a completely stocked bar.

"What would you do if there was a power failure?" Stone lit a Camel. "You couldn't even get out
of your office."

"We have two auxiliary generators." Courser held
a bottle of 101-proof Wild Turkey in one hand and a
bottle of Jack Daniel's in the other. Stone pointed to
the Wild Turkey.

Courser poured two double shots on ice and went
back to his chair. Like the ten-foot wall around the
complex, his huge desk gave him a sense of security
and power. It was the same with owning huge stretches
of land. Stone remained standing by the bar, smoking. He had never needed props to bolster his ego.

"They're growing impatient." Courser scratched
the neck rash he had aggravated by shaving. "The war
is becoming far too expensive. Their enemy continually stocks its front lines with Muslim fanatics, child
martyrs who throw themselves at their bayonets for a
free ticket to the best seats in Allah's warrior heaven.
With the price of gas at a new low, their financial re-
serves are quickly depleting. They want the extract.
It's been over two years since we promised them the
weapon. They don't want to wait any longer."

Stone sipped the sharp, oak-sweet bourbon whis-
key. "Doc says he still has a few—" he couldn't resist
it "—bugs to work out."

"That half-life thing."

"Right."

"Seems to me that's rather a minor problem. Ever think he's just milking you for more bucks?" Courser exhumed a Cuban cigar from a gold humidor and snipped the end. "What do your people think of the delay?"

"The CIA is a relatively patient institution. Our original estimate, before we were even sure it could actually be done, was four to six years."

"Which averages out to just over a half million a year, the vast majority tax-free, if you include the initial 1.5-million investment for the lab and house. I'd say our good Dr. Lockton is doing quite well for himself."

"It all goes into the lab, the latest gene machine, the newest computer, the best electron microscope. The rest goes for the kid's medical expenses. The doc's got exactly $37,952.86 in stocks, bonds and money-market funds. Another six grand in IRA retirement funds. Not exactly enough to skip town." Stone finished his drink, dropped his cigarette in the glass and leaned over the desk. "Since we contracted the doc's services, BIOGENTEX has made over a quarter million off him in contrived expenses. So why bitch?"

Courser stuck the Havana on the edge of his desk and looked up at Stone apprehensively. "If they don't get the extract within three weeks, they'll withdraw the money from our account in Zurich."

"Then they have deposited it?"

"Five million, as of yesterday. Five more when the extract crosses their border."

Stone rapped his callused knuckles on the desk and headed back to the bar. He poured two more doubles, delivered one to Courser and held up his glass.

It was the first time Courser had seen the man grin since his son died. His teeth were nicotine stained.

"To the Formido Inexorbisilis mutation," Stone toasted.

Courser stood up. "And the desert rats."

RICHARD STONE CALLED a north-end number on Vashon Island from a pay phone in San Marcos, Texas. It was six-fifteen, Central Time.

It rang in a small $150-a-month, one-bedroom cabin hidden deep in the forest. The rental's septic system had backed up two days earlier. The cabin stunk. The woods stunk. Daryl Haskell stunk.

The owner had said someone was coming out to pump the tank tomorrow. For the past two days, someone was coming out "tomorrow." *Tomorrow* was a buzzword when you were dealing with services that ran on island time.

Haskell picked up the rust-orange wall phone in the kitchen. Outside, beyond the unfinished porch, the lights from the houses on the peninsula shimmered across the water like sound-wave graphs.

He didn't say hello. He didn't say anything.

Stone said. "Mama San."

Haskell stiffened, instantly forgetting the septic tank. He had never liked code names, identification codes, codes of any kind, including codes of behavior or conduct. He had served two tours in Vietnam, from

1968 to 1970. Special Forces. Worked closely with the CIA in Cambodia and the mountain villages of the central highlands. That was where he had met Stone. Haskell held no respect for authority of any kind. Rules, regulations, codes—they all reminded him of the septic tank; they were forever backing up and they smelled like shit.

Since Vietnam, Haskell had periodically worked for Stone. Sometimes Stone had need of a man outside of the System who would kill cleanly and without remorse, and whose idea of loyalty was reserved for the man who paid him.

"It's a go," Stone informed him. "Tonight."

8:30 p.m.
NICK PLAYFULLY TUGGED the loose skin under Thor's neck. Thor curled around the boy like a scarf and barked.

Nick exploded with laughter. "No, you!"

Thor slapped Nick's face with his front paw and barked again.

Nick shoved the dog back.

"No way, José." He poked Thor's black nose. "You will."

Mrs. L. carried a tray of hot chocolate and Oreo cookies into the dining room. Alex and Mr. Lockton had gone for a walk on the beach. Putting the tray down on the coffee table, she carefully sank her large frame into the sofa, as if testing the temperature of a hot bath.

"What are you two arguing about now?" she asked.

"A bet." Thor nuzzled Nick's ear. "No, you," he giggled. Thor rolled over on his back, legs up, begging for a good stomach rub. Nick happily obliged.

"A bet. On what?" Mrs. L. put six cookies on her plate and sat back with a mug of chocolate.

Nick unscrewed an Oreo, licked off the white cream and gave the rest to the dog.

"On who's gonna live longer," he answered matter-of-factly. "Thor or me."

Mrs. L. put her mug down on the end table.

"Come, here." She patted her soft, full lap. Nick slipped into her embrace. Heat radiated from her ample body like an electric blanket. "That wasn't funny, you know."

"Thor thought so," he argued. His leg kept kicking the arm of the sofa. She stroked his head. Nick tucked himself in against her. She watched him gaze out at places only he knew, places he had invented to hide from the fear.

"Don't you count on winning that bet, young man." She wrapped her big arms around his fragile shoulders. "No offense to Thor, but our money's on you. And don't you ever say that in front of your father. You hear?"

"I hear." Thor laid his head on Nick's knees. Nick leaned over to pet him. "Sometimes I think it's harder on Daddy. My being sick."

"In some ways, I guess it is. He loves you so much. And he worries."

"I haven't been really sick for a long time," he defended. He pushed out of her arms. "I won the pool game. We're tied, six to six, in the tournament."

"My little pool shark." She lifted him off her lap. "Don't you want your cookies?"

"I'm not really hungry."

"That's a first." She looked at him with concerned curiosity. "What's wrong, Nick?"

His face contorted. "Do you think Daddy's in love?"

"Could be."

"Do you like her?" He could tell she didn't want to discuss it. "I do. I'm glad for Daddy."

She glanced over at the wall clock. "It's time for therapy and then bed. Got to get some of Earth's heavy atmosphere out of your lungs."

Nick leaned against her knee, curling his leg around her calf. "I don't really believe that stuff anymore. I'm not from outer space. I just have a bad disease."

Mrs. L. saw it then. She called his sudden depressions simply "the sadness." He almost never threw temper tantrums anymore. The sadness had taken their place. It was not an unhealthy behavior to be corrected, like tantrums. It was completely understandable. What amazed her was how infrequently the sadness came. She drew him back into her arms.

"I don't want you banging on my back anymore." He started to cry. "I just want to be like other kids."

"But look what you can do. You're special. You read so well. You can play the flute like a bird. And pool. Oh, you're good at pool."

Nick quietly sobbed on her shoulder. "I don't care about the flute. I don't care about pool. I don't want to be special. I just want to be normal."

9:00 p.m.
FROM THE SOUTHWEST CORNER of the cabin's tiny backyard, Daryl Haskell could see the second story of Lockton's house. The upstairs-hall light flicked on. Drizzle matted his long hair down over his eyes. He put the infrared scope into its waterproof case and took out the binoculars.

Doc's putting the kid to bed, he thought.

At ten-thirty, the light in the master bedroom clicked on. Because there were no neighbors across the street, Lockton rarely closed the drapes. From his bed, he had a view of the woods to the east, the water and mountains to the west.

It began raining hard and Haskell hiked back up to the cabin. From his kitchen, he could still see Lockton's bedroom and adjoining bathroom. He dialed room ten, in the Best Western Hotel on the outskirts of San Marcos, Texas. As it rang, he focused his Steiner binoculars.

Lockton finished brushing his teeth, walked to the bed, stripped and crawled under the blue quilt. Alex turned off the bright overhead light, leaving only the reading lamp on, on the bedside table. Picking up her overnight bag, she went to the bathroom. She was wearing her blouse and panties.

Haskell was refocusing the zoom lens when Richard Stone answered the call. As usual, Haskell skipped the coded introductions.

"Got a problem," Haskell said.

Alex brushed back her hair and began unbuttoning her blouse. After slipping it off, she opened her bag and took out a red lace teddy.

Haskell held his breath to keep the binoculars steady.

Her upturned breasts reminded him of two large pigeons arched in that sudden moment before flight. Playmate of the Year material, he judged, with legs that could hold you captive for days.

"Is she with him?" Stone asked.

She rolled off her panties and slipped on the teddy.

"She's getting ready for bed." It wasn't the first time she had fogged up his binoculars.

"Lingerie heaven, again?"

"Yup."

"Knocking off a quickie or is she spending the night?"

The bathroom light went off. The binoculars shot to the bedroom window.

"Hard to tell," Haskell answered. "Yet."

Alex pulled back the thick quilt and knelt beside Lockton's hips. As she bent over, her back blocked Haskell's view, but he knew exactly what she was doing.

"Should I go in?" Haskell asked.

Lockton sat up and reached for her, but she gently pushed him back down. He swept her hair over her shoulders.

Haskell was having difficulty keeping the binoculars steady.

"If she stays, don't go in." Stone ordered.

"Looks like she will. She's in no hurry, anyway."

"Then call it a night."

Haskell held his breath again.

"Did you hear me?" Stone asked.

"I'll stick it out a little longer." He slowly exhaled. "Just to make sure."

Chapter 10

THE LATE-AFTERNOON SUN wasn't visible. The wind was from the northwest and the low clouds hid the mainland mountain ranges. Two fog banks, drifting down through the dark tree-shadowed peninsula, reached out across the Sound. Lockton switched on the inboard engine of his thirty-three-foot Egg Harbor cabin cruiser and pushed the throttle forward. They had been drifting with the tide and had lost the cod hole. Fifty yards south, the ferry, *Tillicum*, engines reversed, rocked against the piling leading into the Southworth dock.

Nick waved at the captain, John Holloway, a life-long Vashon resident, who, on special occasions, let Nick come up on the bridge to "help steer." Holloway let out one short blast of the ship's horn and Nick laughed.

Lockton cut his engine and returned to his starboard chair. Five large, rust-backed rock cod splashed in the bucket beside it. Opening his reel, he let the herring sink to the bottom and slowly began rocking the bait. Nick copied the up-down rhythm.

Three seals bobbed out of the water, then disappeared.

"Dad, look." Nick pointed to their ripples. "They're heading north." They scanned the water until the seals popped up again.

Midafternoon was not the best time to bottom-fish, but Nick had decided they should go out early and cruise the coast of the Olympic Peninsula. Nick loved to steer the boat and Lockton enjoyed leisurely sipping Rainier and looking at the waterfront homes. After returning from Seattle with two Siamese fighting fish and an aquarium castle, they had stocked the boat's refrigerator and headed out.

Being on the water was an integral part of island life. Each day, Nick checked the tide chart with the same enthusiasm a Wall Street executive reviewed the stock market. Two months ago, on a Sunday morning in early January, Nick and his father had rowed their ten-foot fiberglass dinghy to the cod hole just northwest of the old pier. Suddenly a six-foot fin sliced the water, barely thirty feet from their bow. It was the first time Nick had seen a killer whale in the wild.

"Hope it doesn't think our boat's a seal," Nick had said as he watched it dive under the dinghy. To Nick, the Puget Sound was a never-ending adventure and he read about it voraciously. He had decided he would be a marine biologist when he grew up.

"You study the little things," he had told his father, "and I'll study the big things."

Although somewhat muted by age and repetition, days like that one in January revitalized the child in James Lockton as well, with all its wonder and inspiration.

Nick's Fenwick rod jerked twice. He yanked it back and felt the weight of the fish tugging against him.

"It's a big one," he announced, pulling and reeling. His father quickly got his own line up to keep it from entangling with his son's.

Suddenly the fish ran. Nick stopped reeling and let it fight.

Lockton bent over the back of his son's chair. "Want some help?"

"I can do it." Nick grimaced. Pushing against the stern with his feet, Nick used his body to raise the rod back up.

"Keep reeling," his father coached. "Slow and firm."

Nick got his rhythm back and became the aggressor again.

"I'll get the net." His father leaned out over the side. Nick held the pole against his chest as it bent to a U. "I see it." James glanced back at his son, disappointed. "It's a shark." The gray dorsal fin cut the water in a quick, angry circle.

"Don't let it wreck our net," Nick warned. Lockton grabbed the Swedish knife on the cutting board and cut the line. Nick slumped forward, exhausted.

"That was something," the boy said. Shaking, he pushed out of his chair and rested against his father's chest. Lockton felt Nick's skin. It wasn't good for him to sweat too much. If he lost too much salt, he could become acutely ill. It had to do with the high sodium-chloride level of his sweat. He was not perspiring excessively.

"Feel all right?" he asked.

"I'm okay," he emphasized, trying to shake off his light-headedness. He could see his father was not convinced. "A little tired, I guess."

"Let's head in." Lockton turned on the ignition. "Want to steer?"

"Sure."

Lockton lifted him up into the pilot's chair. Nick opened the throttle to ten knots and turned the bow southeast toward Vashon.

"Boy, Mrs. L. sure was grumpy this morning," Nick said, opening the throttle to fifteen knots. Lockton almost tumbled aft, but caught the top of the wheel. Nick giggled quietly.

"She's always grumpy," Lockton said. "It's her way."

Nick turned sharply to starboard to avoid a dead-head hidden in the swells and Lockton lurched against the cabin door.

"Especially when Alex stays overnight," Nick said, hiding his playful grin.

When Nick turned nine, they had had a man-to-man discussion about sex. Having thumbed through numerous biology books in his father's library, Nick was way ahead of his father's first lecture. The how of the matter, Nick understood. It was the why that confused him. His father had explained about men's and women's needs, about love and sharing and the beauty of the sexual union, but Nick still thought fishing was a much better way for a man to occupy his time.

"I know what would cure her grumpiness." Nick kept the bow targeted on their buoy.

"So tell me already, smart guy."

Nick cut back on the throttle. "Marry Alex."

Lockton hadn't been prepared for that at all. He elbowed his son in the ribs. "Oh, yeah?"

"Yeah."

"What about you?" Lockton hunched over the chair. His voice was gentle, but serious. "Think that's a good idea?"

"You love Alex, don't you?"

"Yes. I do."

"Me, too."

Lockton smiled. "Where's this leading to, counselor?"

Nick straightened up the chair. "Mrs. L. isn't going to be around forever, Dad."

"So?"

"Well, you're just not that good at taking care of yourself. If it wasn't for Mrs. L. and me, you'd be living down in your lab, eating potato chips and hot dogs, drinking too much beer."

A bubble of amusement formed in Lockton's throat. "So you don't think your old man could make it on his own, huh?"

Nick laughed. "Nope."

Lockton chuckled and put his son in a bear hug.

"She's everything I'd want, Dad. If I had to choose a mom, I mean." Nick took one hand off the wheel and held his father's thumb. They both stared out at the approaching island in silence. Laughter was inappropriate now. They felt a bonding, deep and warm, flow between them.

Suddenly it hit him—what Nick had really meant. He wanted to make sure his father would still be loved when he, not Mrs. L., was gone. The role of caring protector had been reversed. Lockton rested his chin on Nick's head.

9:55 p.m.
AFTER PUTTING NICK TO BED, Lockton had called Alex to tell her he was coming over at ten with a surprise, and hung up.

It was all very mysterious.

He decided to take Cove Road to Alex's house. The path was shorter, but he didn't want to muddy the dress shoes he had just spent fifteen minutes polishing. He was wearing the suit he had bought on sale seven years ago at the Bon in Seattle. He had even ironed his tie.

As he walked, he thought about the first day they had met. He had just finished jogging three miles and was walking down the hill to the beach in his old gray sweats, nursing a recurring case of shin splints. A red Trans Am with Maryland plates pulled up beside him.

When the driver rolled down the window, the sun caught her dark red hair. It was like looking at a full moon through a glass of Burgundy. Lockton remembered wishing he had washed his sweats after his last workout instead of hanging them over a chair to dry.

Her car was stuffed with suitcases and boxes. She asked him where the Hollingworths' house was and he gave her directions. When she offered to give him a lift, he refused because of the rankness of his sweats.

That night, he had brought her a bottle of Washington State chardonnay to welcome her to the island.

It surprised Lockton to realize how little he really knew about Alex McGuire. Her father had worked for the Department of the Interior and was retired. Her mother, an accomplished cellist, had played with the National Symphony until she was fifty-two. Alex had lived in private boarding schools since the sixth grade. She received her B.A. in political science, with a minor in music, from Georgetown University. Her grandfather, Kevin McGuire, had built a small construction empire in Baltimore. When he died, he left separate trust funds for his children and grandchildren. Alex supplemented that income by teaching jazz aerobics at the old grade-school gymnasium on the island and giving piano lessons.

Before he could ring the bell, Alex opened the door.

"Must be a hell of a surprise," she said. "To get you to dress up."

Like a teenager on his first date, Lockton stood outside in the light awkwardly combing his hair with his fingers. He was holding his gym bag and a single long-stemmed red rose behind his back.

"You look..." He stepped back, fumbling through a mental list of superlatives. "Ravishing."

"So do you. And your tie isn't even wrinkled."

His shyness gave the moment a certain innocence that touched Alex. Here was a man, considered a genius by his peers, stumbling over words like a junior-high student with a crush on his music teacher.

A year ago, she had witnessed an entire auditorium full of scientists, professors and graduate students instantly hush when he was introduced as the guest lecturer.

"Everyone has gifts," he had told her on the ferry ride home after the lecture. "You're a talented musician, for example, and I'm tone-deaf."

He actually seemed embarrassed by it all. He had even pleaded with her not to attend. He thought she would find it boring and pedantic. It was that night, on the ferry, six months after they had met, that she realized she was falling in love with a man she had only begun to understand.

"Aren't you going to come in?" she asked.

He sidestepped around her to keep his gifts hidden. After she closed the door, she was met by a proffered rose and a boyish grin.

Alex held the rose like a newborn child. "I'll get a vase."

James Lockton followed her into the kitchen. He had planned to be debonair, or at least gracefully romantic, but he felt more like a rugby player in a ballet class.

After putting the rose in a tall cut-crystal vase, Alex centered it on the dining-room table.

"It's beautiful," she said, kissing him. He was still holding his gym bag behind his back. "So what's the big surprise?"

Lockton swung the bag around. It thumped heavily on the table.

Alex's eyebrows curled in confused amusement. "We're going to run a marathon?"

Ignoring her, he retrieved two champagne glasses from her china cabinet. Alex looked over his shoulders as he unzipped the bag. It contained a bottle of Dom Perignon embedded in ice.

"For the winner?" she asked.

He rolled the bottle around in the ice as if he were trying to unscrew it.

"Now that you have me absolutely bubbling with curiosity..." Her jokes were getting no response at all.

He popped the cork, but when she reached for a glass, he stopped her.

"Champagne doesn't need to breathe, James. What's the..."

"With this expensive stuff, you have to give it time—" he finally smiled "—to let it burp."

She laughed. "Didn't know that."

"You're talking to a biologist. We know about things like that."

"How much time—" using his tie, she pulled him up against her "—do we have to give it?"

"I had a talk with Nick today," he said. Her breath was warm and sweet. Her lips feathered against his cheek. "Let me finish."

She slipped back and waited.

"I'm not doing well at all." Frustration wrinkled the corners of his mouth.

"What is it? What are you..."

He interrupted her with his hand.

"That night in the hospital, when Liz died, I wanted to kill someone. To get even, somehow, for her leaving me. So I did. I killed someone. Me. I killed my ability to love. Nick soon gave me back my heart, but...something was still missing. I didn't completely understand it, until I met you. I love you, Alex. And I need you. You've made me whole again and I never want to lose that."

"James, I..."

"Alex." He moved nearer. Neither touched. "Will you marry me?"

She closed her eyes and turned away. Suddenly, he felt as if he'd fallen into a huge empty bottle. The glass was growing dark and blurred. He watched her slump in the pass-through between the kitchen and dining room.

This was supposed to have been one of those few perfect moments in life, a moment of oneness that bridged the physical gap between two human beings. Instead, ice-brown liquid was slowly filling the bottle.

Why now, James? her mind cried. Just a few more weeks, and...

"I thought..." He watched her head slowly sink below her shoulders. "It was supposed to be..." She finally looked back. A thick lock of hair hid one eye. "A happy occasion."

He hadn't felt this claustrophobic, this trapped, since that night in Liz's hospital room when she bolted up from the bed clutching her chest. The look on

Alex's face reminded him of the doctor's as he wheeled out the crash cart.

"I love you, James." Her words were soft, but distant, as if spoken through a black veil of regret.

"So marry me. That's what people do when they love each other."

"I can't."

"Why?" The bottle was almost full now. He was holding his breath to keep from drowning. "Nick said you were the only one. For both of us. And you know how perceptive he is."

"Give me time, James. Please? We've never really talked about this and . . ."

"It's been a year." He crossed his arms. His hands were too conspicuous to leave in view. "Is it Nick?"

She stared at him, stunned. "I love him, too. You know that."

"I'm not sure I know anything right now," he murmured angrily.

"James, please, it's not what . . ."

"Tell me why. Just tell me why?"

Hugging herself, she turned back toward the pass-through. "I can't."

When the sliding-glass door slammed closed, she hunched over as if someone had cracked her in the ribs with a tire iron.

THE RAIN STRUCK LOCKTON like hailstones. He was running. Hard. He felt as if he was in a silent movie with the film-speed up. His lungs burned. He ran until his foot slid on the mud-packed gravel, sending him somersaulting into the narrow ditch by his driveway.

Rising, he punched in the side of the mailbox. The metal door flopped open.

"She ain't worth it, Doc," Daryl Haskell said, watching his rain-blurred outline march into the garage. Daryl Haskell tossed his unlit cigar into the bushes across the street and sneered like a jackal sniffing a rival male's scent mark.

Lockton's black Mazda RX-7 squealed out of the garage in reverse and bounced over the gravel onto Cove Road. Kicking gravel and mud, the low, sleek car fishtailed into the night.

"That's right, Doc." Haskell scooped up his backpack. "Make it easy for me."

10:52 p.m.

A BLACK HOODED FIGURE slipped across Cove Road. The rain was hard and steady. Only Lockton's outside front light interrupted the darkness. The apparition moved with pantherlike stealth, darting from tree to bush along the edge of the lawn. Once past the southeast corner of the house, he was safely beyond the yellow perimeter of the front light.

Crouching, Daryl Haskell slipped across the open lawn to the kitchen door. Pressed against the wall between the windows and the door, he was protected from the rain by the overhanging gutter. A thin flower garden, only beginning to bud, ran along the entire south wall of the house. The toes of his boots sank into the mud as he peered into the window. The first floor was uninhabited. No lights were on.

He removed his parka and hooked its hood and his backpack on the screen-door latch. With a two-inch key-chain flashlight, he checked his boots. They were mud clogged. He untied them and set them on the dry inside corner of the cement step. He unpocketed a set of seven keys, put the flashlight in his teeth and chose the proper two in the small circle of light. He turned off the outside alarm above the door first, then unlocked the door.

His rubber surgical gloves were wet and slippery. Once inside the house, he dried them on his shirt.

He had twenty seconds to find and disconnect the inside alarm system.

The two-inch flashlight severely limited his vision, but it wasn't important. He had already memorized the floor plans. He sneaked quietly across the long kitchen in stocking feet. He paused in the foyer, by the second-floor stairs. Only the rain broke the silence.

He had ten seconds left.

The alarm was built in the wall of the foyer. He had a duplicate key and turned it off with four seconds left.

The basement door was around the corner under the stairs. It squeaked open and he froze, one foot halfway down to the first step.

NICK WAS SLEEPING ON HIS SIDE, one arm around Thor's shoulders. The dog's head snapped up from the mattress. Nick's sleep-heavy eyes opened slightly. Thor growled deep from his belly.

"Shh." Half conscious, he stroked Thor's neck. "Just a squirrel on the roof."

The dog's ears remained erect as he nuzzled Nick's cheek. Nick grumbled incoherently and rolled away from his cold nose.

Thor hopped off the bed and stood guard by his door. He knew it wasn't a squirrel. Whatever it was, it was in the house.

But it would not get to Nick.

AS HASKELL PASSED the pool table in the basement den, the small light swept across the laboratory door to the alarm system. If the three keys weren't used in proper sequence, the alarm would trip and the reinforced steel door would be impossible to unlock.

First the long key, then the short square one.

The green overhead light switched off.

Last, the bolt-lock key to the door.

There were no windows in the foot-thick cement-walled bunker that housed the lab's three rooms. The ventilation system droned like an old electric motor. A temperature-controlled water bath clicked on. The echoes in the lab disoriented Haskell. It took him a few moments to reacquaint himself with his mental diagrams and find the light switch. The far door led to the electron microscope and the darkroom. The gene machine was in the southeast corner. He scanned the shelves, the enclaves, the counters, the center table.

It didn't look as impressive as he had thought it would. More like a high-school chemistry room than a state-of-the-art genetic engineering P-3 security lab. He had expected it to resemble the helm of the star ship *Enterprise* at least.

As he walked around the center table, he stopped to inspect the rat cages. All except three in the last cage were dead. Good riddance, he thought, pleased. He hated rats. They were the only species that really prospered in wartime. A constant horror in Nam. He had seen what they could do to a body during the night. Removing his government Colt .45, he pointed it at each of the live rats and grinned.

Although the lab maintained a constant temperature of seventy-four degrees, he was suddenly sweating. It took all his discipline to put the pistol back into its holster without wasting the rats.

He tied on a surgical mask from the drawer and headed for the hooded enclave across the room. The small seventh key on the ring fit the round steel lock on the hood's bottom frame. When he slid it up, he felt a slight pulling breeze. He removed the second of six test tubes in the plastic holding case. It contained a murky brown solution. His fingers were hot and wet inside the rubber gloves.

He did not know what was in the test tube, but had been warned to use extreme caution. It was the uncertainty that made him stare at the liquid as if it were bile from the stomach of a leper.

ALEX McGUIRE WAS SITTING at her dining-room table, staring at the Dom Perignon and twirling the stem of her champagne glass. For the past hour, since James's departure, she hadn't moved from her chair. A puddle had grown around the gym bag and was dripping between the table leaves onto the rug. The dripping slowly grew louder, until it was pounding the walls like a bass drum. Her heart kept beat with the steady dripping, as if it were her blood leaking out onto the rug.

James had caught her completely off guard. She hadn't had time to think, to explain.

Then he was gone.

Love had been mentioned often, but never marriage. They hadn't even discussed living together. It hadn't seemed necessary. As next-door neighbors, they were all but living together already. If it wasn't for Mrs. L., they probably would have been sleeping together every night, instead of once or twice a week.

She should have been prepared. She should have realized when he called, that . . .

She felt as if each of her limbs was tied to the saddle of a horse, all galloping in opposite directions. A line of black mascara ran down across her cheek. She hated to cry. She hated any loss of control.

So many secrets, she thought. So many lies.

But not their love.

That was real. And true. And it hurt. Like nothing that had ever hurt her before.

It wasn't supposed to have happened. But it had. She couldn't stop it. She had tried. She had fought it.

Oh, God, how she fought it. But it had been the one thing in her life she finally couldn't control.

She hadn't even realized just how much she loved him, until she heard the door slam. It had struck her heart like a scythe. Every cell in her body seemed to have cried out.

Nothing had ever consumed her like this before.

How could she explain it to him? The fear. The lies. The waiting. Without losing his trust forever?

She had only needed a few more weeks. Just a few more weeks and she would have been free.

"Damn you, James," she murmured to the champagne bottle, standing cold and silent before her. She peered into the shallow bowl of the glass, smudged with fingerprints. She felt just as empty, just as smudged.

Suddenly she bolted from the table.

"The hell with them!" she cursed, heaving the glass at the big stone fireplace. The shattered echo reverberated in the room.

Sweeping up the bottle, she yanked her raincoat off the hall tree and headed for the door.

HASKELL PUT the empty plastic vial on the counter next to the open enclave. Using one of the lab syringes, he extracted 5 cc of the thick fluid from the test tube and injected it through the vial's sealed rubber top. He placed the test tube back in the enclave and locked it. The syringe, gloves and mask went into the autoclave. Once sterilized, he tossed them into the aluminum trash bin. After rolling on another pair of gloves, he inserted the vial into a cotton-stuffed plastic container, secured its lid and pocketed it.

He looked around to make sure everything was back in place. In the white glare of the lab, he suddenly felt exposed, as if some genetically mutated deity was watching him desecrate its temple.

The memory of Tom Shank began haunting him again. Tom had been his closest friend in the war. For six months they had fought, slept, drank and cried together in the jungles of Nam. One night, as they moved out of base camp on a routine patrol, Tom pulled him aside and said that he didn't think he was coming back. That night, he took three rounds from an AK-47, splattering pieces of his brain across Haskell's chest. As Haskell locked the lab, he couldn't shake the ominous feeling that Shank's ghost was calling him.

Daryl Haskell put on his parka and boots, and reactivated the outside alarm system. It was too damn easy, he thought, too perfectly executed. No matter how well an operation had been planned, the unexpected always happened. The human factor, Stone called it. An incalculable aspect of all operations, military or civilian, legal or illegal.

Not this time, he reassured himself. The hell with Murphy's Law. Or Tom's superstitions.

ALEX SAW THE HOODED FIGURE outlined by Lockton's front light. It was heading across the street to the dirt access road that dead-ended up the hill where the

Lowery Lumber Company had leveled twenty acres of trees a decade ago.

She called out, "James?"

The figure scurried out of the light into the woods across the street. Alex backed up into the shadow between two poplars. Squinting in the rain, she saw him slide down the shallow gully and run up the old lumber road.

It wasn't James. The figure was too quick, too smooth, too attuned to the night. It moved like a nocturnal predator hiding its kill.

A car engine started. She heard the vehicle bump over a deep rut. A puddle splashed close to Cove Road. Whoever it was, they were driving without headlights to hide their identity.

Alex began running back toward her house. The car slammed up the gully onto the road. It was a big old American car, but she couldn't tell the make. Before turning into her driveway, she saw it pass under the streetlight. It was an old Chevy Impala.

Throwing the bottle aside, she sprinted to the carport and jumped into her Trans Am.

Almost perfect, Haskell thought. He knew she had spotted him.

Good, he thought. Takes the jinx off.

He would soon be on the old west-side highway, heading down to the south end. There he would exchange the car, which he had stolen in Olympia a week ago, for the Ford, parked on the unused horse-trail between the property lines of two large estates.

As he passed the gate to the island dump, a pair of headlights caught his rearview mirror. He checked the side mirror. Running the stop sign, he turned left on Lamb Road, then a quick left on 131st Avenue by the Jehovah's Witness church.

The car appeared to be following him.

There's one way to find out. After the curve, he let off on the gas, flicked off his lights, slid into a driveway, backed out and headed back toward the car. Whoever it was hadn't seen him turn around. He passed the Trans Am in the middle of the curve.

Alex slammed on the brakes and twisted the wheel. The car spun sideways on the wet road. Her back wheels caught the gravel and she accelerated in pursuit.

It was her, all right. Haskell decided he would have to lose her before heading back to the stolen car near the south end.

The heavy rain was making visibility extremely difficult. He was forced to turn his lights back on. Should have stolen a newer car, he growled at himself. One with decent radials, the way it rains around here.

James Lockton had driven to the Islander Restaurant and Lounge with the intention of getting extremely drunk. He had forgotten it was Saturday night. Bill Brown and the King Bees, a rock-blues band, was playing in the lounge. The place was packed. He tossed down a Windsor and water and decided to go home. Getting plastered had completely lost its appeal. People were dancing and shouting and having a good time, and he wanted none of it.

He decided to take the back way home, up Bank Road to the old west-side highway. His anger dissipated as he thought about Nick. His son had known about the surprise. It would be hard for him to understand Alex's refusal. Hell, he didn't understand it, either. He just wished he hadn't told Nick his plans. Knowing Nick, he'd probably march over to Alex's tomorrow and demand an explanation. Which is what I should be doing now, he realized, instead of driving around feeling sorry for myself.

He pulled up to the stop sign where Bank Road dead-ended at the old highway. What was it that was wedged between them? It had always been there, since the beginning. A certain reluctance. An unspoken emotional trepidation. Even when they spoke of love, there had always been a trace of sadness in Alex's posture.

He pulled out onto the narrow two-lane highway. Driving to town had been a lousy idea. The windshield wipers rhythmically cleared the glass. His body felt drained, but his mind was charged like an overheated circuit board. Memories and emotions crosswired, making concentration difficult. He slowed where the hill had been cut open, like the pocket of a worn catcher's mitt, by a mud slide.

Rain pounded the car in waves. Lockton kept alert for deep puddles that could catch the wheels like flypaper.

An old Chevy zipped past him on the straightaway, kicking up a back spray that momentarily blinded him. Lockton let off the accelerator just as the red Trans Am sped by his side window.

He recognized it immediately, but checked the license to make sure. It was Alex, all right. Doing over seventy.

He honked his horn and pushed the Mazda into passing gear.

Lockton honked again as he slid into the hard turn at the top of the rise. A half mile after the second sharp S curve, there was another slide area. Although the city had cleared the eight tons of dirt off the road, half of the highway had caved in, sliced completely away like a glacier sheared by a spring thaw.

Haskell's Impala was no match for the Trans Am. And who was in that Mazda coming up behind her? He hadn't stolen the Chevy for speed, only anonymity.

Balls to the walls, his mind cried, pumped up on the fear high he had grown addicted to in Nam. If you can't beat 'em with equipment, beat them with guts. He was pushing the Impala past its limits. The rain burst in front of his headlights like electrical sparks.

Then he saw it.

The half-eaten section of road.

His right tires caught in the puddle caused by the excavation of mud from the upper slide. Swerving, he spun the wheel in the opposite direction. His bald tires slid across the wet road, out of control.

The Chevy catapulted out over the 150-foot cliff and free-fell between the trees. For a moment he was weightless, sailing in the dark like a two-ton metal eagle.

"Tommy!" he screamed, as the gully rose up to meet him.

Alex held her Trans Am in tight to the curve, waiting until she had passed the washout to brake. Lockton pulled up to the precipice and hopped out. Two feet from his left tire, the road was completely gone. Alex backed up next to him.

"He was coming from your house," she explained breathlessly. "I yelled to him and he ran. I thought he was a burglar, so I . . ."

An explosion ripped through the darkness like a fiery tidal wave. Eighty feet below, the mangled Chevy was engulfed in flames.

"Why didn't you call the cops?" Lockton started climbing down the steep embankment.

"I don't know. He took off in a car and I didn't think there was time, so I just . . ."

"Get to the nearest house and call the police. I'll see if . . ." Lockton slid down the mud. He could feel the heat increasing on his back. "If he's still alive."

The front half of the Impala was crushed. The engine had been jammed into the front seat. The smell of burning gas and rubber permeated the gully. Metal and plastic crackled in the flames. Because of the heat, Lockton couldn't get within thirty feet of the vehicle.

Moving around to the driver's side, he saw the charred remnants of a body pinned to the seat by the steering wheel.

By the time he had climbed back up to the road, Alex had returned.

"The police are on their way," she told him. They were both rain-soaked. "They called the fire department."

"I've got to get home," Lockton said. "See if Nick and Mrs. L. are all right."

"I'll wait here." Alex looked down at the burning vehicle. The fire had spread into the bushes, but the rain was holding it back from the trees.

Lockton gently pulled her away from the cliff. "Are you okay?"

"I'll be fine," she lied. "Now, go on. Get going."

Less than five minutes after Lockton left, a squad car arrived, followed by a rescue vehicle, fire engine and water truck.

Chapter 11

12:14 a.m., March 16, 1986

LOCKTON WAS RELIEVED to find his outside alarm system on. Maybe he never got in. He hurried upstairs. Both his son and Mrs. L. were asleep. And unharmed. Lockton seriously doubted the man was just a burglar. Hopefully Alex had scared him away before he could break in.

But she had said he was coming from the house, not to it.

Lockton ran down to the basement and examined the lab's alarm box. It hadn't been tampered with. The green safety light was still on and the door was bolted and locked. He couldn't have gotten in. Both alarm systems were on and functioning. He must have realized it was futile and was leaving when Alex spotted him.

Just to be safe, Lockton decided to check the lab before the police arrived. He walked around the center table, checking the shelves, the rat cages, the enclaves, the back room.

Maybe it was just a burglar hoping to rip off a fancy-looking island home. The project was top secret. No one except himself and a few people in the CIA even knew about the project. You've been watching too many James Bond movies, he told himself. The house and lab were built and secured by the CIA—professionals who knew their jobs. No one could get into this house, let alone the lab, without keys. And they were all specially made. No duplicates. No master-key molds.

Lockton checked the hood lock where the extract was stored. It was secured. Relieved, he dried his rain-soaked face with a couple of Kleenex tissues and stepped on the trash-can pedal to throw them away.

His hand stopped in midtoss.

There was mud on the fingers of the surgical gloves on the top of the pile. He quickly brushed through the first layer of trash. He had used three syringes on Friday. There was a fourth on top of the extra mask and muddy gloves.

Lockton spun back to the hooded enclave and struggled to fit in the key as he visually checked the row of test tubes holding the extract.

A portion of the virus culture in the second test tube was missing. At least 4 or 5 cc.

But how?

The intruder couldn't have gotten in with the alarm system on. It was impossible.

Lockton backed into the rim of the aluminum sink, horrified.

Whoever had burned to death fifteen minutes ago had succeeded in stealing enough of the extract to breed.

And he had known exactly what he was looking for.

And where to find it.

OFFICER RENTON methodically searched outside Lockton's house for signs of an attempted break-in. Next to the kitchen-door steps, his flashlight caught the footprints in the mud under the window. The toe marks were deep, as if someone had been leaning up to look inside. He studied the lock on the kitchen door. It showed no signs of tampering.

"Could you explain why you chose to chase the intruder, Miss McGuire?" Officer Somners asked, flipping to a clean page in his notebook.

"When I saw him, I called out. I thought it was James."

"Mr. Lockton."

"That's right. When he heard me, he ran across the street into the woods. I heard a car start. He drove onto the road with his headlights off. Obviously, he was trying to sneak away. So I went after him."

"Why didn't you call the police first?"

"No time." Alex felt as if the officer were accusing her of some kind of ridiculous complicity. "He took off. I went after him. I didn't weigh all the alternatives. Is that a crime?"

"Not at all, Miss McGuire. But it is unusual, under the circumstances. Most people would have called the police first."

"By the time the police could have arrived, the burglar would have been long gone."

"You used the word burglar. Why?"

"He didn't act like the meter man."

Alex had had it with Officer Somners. He was trying to be clever, but with no purpose. Weaned on *Dragnet* reruns, she thought.

She was relieved when Lockton joined them.

"Miss McGuire told us you came home. I can understand your concern, but what were you doing in the basement?"

"I was checking my laboratory's alarm system. It was still on."

"Your laboratory?"

"I'm a molecular biologist. I subcontract to a firm in Texas called BIOGENTEX."

"Do you have reason to believe someone might have wanted to break into your lab?"

"Not really. But I do have some expensive equipment."

"Was the outside alarm system functioning when you got here, Mr. Lockton?"

"Yes, it was."

Nick leaned against Mrs. L. sleepily. Thor was lying at his feet. Lockton ruffled Nick's hair while Officer Somners finished jotting down his statement.

"Did either of you hear anything? Anything unusual?" The officer asked Nick and Mrs. L.

"Thor did," Nick said.

Somners squatted down in front of the boy. "And you?"

"Nope."

"Well, what did the dog hear?"

"Something. He woke me up. He was growling."

Officer Renton came in the front door. "There were footprints by the kitchen window, but the door was untouched. Same with the front door and the garage. All the windows within reach on the first floor are locked. Looks like she scared him off, all right."

Somners's radio crackled. He took it from his leather belt and walked into the living room, away from the civilians.

"Fire's completely out."

"And the suspect?" Somners turned down the volume. His partner hustled to his side.

"Not much left, I'm afraid."

"Looks like he didn't get in."

"Lucky break. At least for them."

"Should I bring Lockton and McGuire to the station?"

"Tomorrow. They've been through enough tonight. Listen, Somners. The suspect was carrying a standard military-issue .45. He also had a semiautomatic .22 rifle, a sawed-off shotgun and an Israeli Uzi in the trunk. This guy was ready for a war."

"We'll be right out. Over."

The two officers returned to the hall.

"Hopefully there won't be," Somners announced, his thumbs hitched in his broad leather belt, "but if there is a next time," he glanced at Alex, "don't play cop. Call us. We get paid to chase people."

AFTER THE SQUAD CAR DEPARTED, Lockton walked outside with Alex. She looked pale under the front light. Her hair was tangled and matted. Mascara smudged her left eye like a bruise.

"You look terrible," he said.

"You don't look so good yourself." Alex smiled awkwardly. Lockton wanted to draw her to him, but there was a chasm between them now that seemed too wide to cross.

"You going to be all right?"

She shrugged. "I just want to go home."

"I'll drive you."

"No."

There was so much more to say, that needed to be said, but it was not the time. Death, in all its grisly horror, was too close. The stench of gasoline and charred flesh clung to Lockton's clothes and hair like an obscene perfume.

The thought of a professional agent breaking into his house undetected was like hearing that someone in his family had been brutally assaulted or raped. Lockton never thought he would have felt this way about another human being, but he was glad the man was dead.

LOCKTON POURED three fingers of Scotch over two small ice cubes. It would be a relief to slip into the hazy numbness of alcohol.

But he couldn't afford the luxury. Not tonight. He took one long sip and poured the rest into the kitchen sink.

What if the man hadn't been working alone? What if there were others? Here on the island?

Sleep was not on Lockton's agenda, either. He probably couldn't have anyway, not without an ample supply of Scotch.

He went upstairs to check on Nick.

"I'm still awake," Nick said when he saw his father looking around the door.

Lockton sat on the bed. "How you doing?"

"Who was it, Daddy?"

"I don't know. Probably just a prowler. Don't let it worry you. Our alarm system kept him out. Nobody can ever get in this house unless we want them here."

"What happened to him, Daddy? Did the police catch him?"

"It's over. Don't worry about it."

"Thor would have got him good if he'd gotten in." Hearing his name, the dog crawled up against Nick.

"He sure would have." Lockton kissed his son. "Now, go to sleep."

Lockton remained with Nick until he was sound asleep. While he waited, he tried to remember the phone number he had memorized four years ago. Stone had warned him never to use the number unless it was a life-and-death situation. He had said it was merely part of security procedures, and really wasn't something he'd ever have to worry about.

James Lockton went to his room and picked up the phone on the table by the bed. He did not sit down. He did not want the damp, musty smell of fire and death on his blankets. He dialed the long-distance number to Langley, Virginia.

The call was received, but no one spoke. Lockton was told they wouldn't. He repeated the introduction Stone had given him with the number.

"This is the dog. There's been an accident."

A woman's voice said. "One moment."

The call was forwarded to Dick Schraeder. "Doc?"

"Yes?"

"Hang up and wait. Stone will call you in a couple of minutes."

Lockton stripped off his jacket and tie and hung them over the chair by the closet.

The phone rang.

"Doc?"

Lockton recognized Stone's voice. "There's been a break-in."

THE SOUNDPROOF ROOM was the size of a walk-in closet. A desktop counter, running the length of the south wall, was stacked with surveillance receiving equipment. The other three walls and ceiling were barren except for the soundproof padding.

The intelligence officer readjusted the headset and turned up the volume on the phone tap. The conversation was being taped.

"That's right," Lockton said. The agent raised the volume another click. "He's dead."

"You sure he got in?" Stone asked.

"I'm sure."

"Was the body... recognizable?"

"They couldn't get him out. He was pinned to the seat."

"What about the police?"

"What about them?"

"Do they suspect anything?"

"I don't think so."

"Good. Cooperate, but don't volunteer anything."

"Good?" Lockton could barely restrain his fury. "What the hell is good about it? The man got in and out of here as if there was no damn security at all. What if Nick had wandered downstairs, for Christ's sake?"

"Take it easy, Doc. We don't know for sure he..."

"Take it easy—hell!" Lockton marched across the rug until the cord pulled him back. "I want protection. For my family. Now!"

"The man didn't escape." Stone's voice was chillingly calm. "I'll take care of it. I'm taking the next flight to Seattle."

Lockton almost pulled the cord out of the phone. He was incensed by Stone's condescending tone.

"Top secret. Full security," he mimicked scornfully. "What a fucking joke."

"The intruder's dead. The extract's safe. Our status is still intact."

"No thanks to you."

"Maybe. Maybe not."

Lockton wasn't in the mood to play ego-saving guessing games. "One other thing. The virus was probably incinerated in the fire. But if it wasn't. If, let's say, it was thrown out one of the windows as the car flipped, we could have a problem." The other end of the line was finally silent. No quick Band-Aid answer this time. "It was raining hard. It's a long shot, but you should be aware of the possibility." Lockton hadn't really digested it yet, either—the worst case scenario. It began to tear everything that seemed normal and natural in his life out by the roots.

Stone interrupted the long pause. "Talk to me, Doc."

"What if the container broke on impact and the virus was washed down with the rain into a small stream. And the stream feeds one of the underground tributaries that resupplies Vashon's water tables. You can figure the rest out."

"Tomorrow, Doc." Stone hung up.

Lockton turned to the window and looked out across the Sound. The peninsula was barely visible.

It burned up, he reassured himself. It's a million to one it was thrown out in the first place.

A gust of wind blew in across the water through the trees. A cracked branch on the big hemlock near the west side of the house scratched across the aluminum gutters. Lockton froze. Another blast of wind and he recognized the sound. It immediately took his mind off the extract and redirected it toward his more immediate concern . . .

His family's safety.

THE PEARL-WHITE LIMOUSINE hurtled Richard Stone across the desert at a hundred and five miles per hour. He used the car phone to make reservations from Dallas–Fort Worth to Seattle. He would arrive, via Salt Lake City, at 11:46 a.m. From one of the airport's pay phones, he planned to make two calls. Both to CIA employees who owed their true allegiance to the five million dollars in his Swiss bank account.

So Haskell had blown it, he thought. Too bad. But he was going to die anyway. He liked his drugs and booze too much. He couldn't have been counted on to keep his mouth shut.

They would have to move the project now that security had been breached. That wasn't a problem. The Company would be told 10 cc of the extract had been stolen, not five. That would still give him the 5 cc he needed. No one would know, except Lockton. But Lockton reported directly to Stone, so it didn't matter. Stone was the one who would make out the final report.

Everything could still proceed according to plan, with a few minor adjustments. He had already recommended Lockton's termination from the project.

In Stone's estimation, the mutant rabies virus had been perfected. It was able to successfully breed in water and infiltrate a human host's brain directly through the bloodstream. Symptoms would begin hours after ingestion and there was no antidote. Its self-destruct mechanism was sufficient.

A devastating weapon. Stone had imagined one like it for years.

It could easily be slipped, undetected, into an enemy's water-supply system. Because of the five to ten hours' lag time before infection, escape would be relatively simple. It wasn't like planting a bomb. You just traced the water system back to its source.

The possibilities were numerous. It could be used as a broadly defined assassination weapon to eliminate a well-guarded paranoid like Khadaffi, or it could wipe out a military enemy's entire chiefs of staff. It would wreak havoc in the Ayatollah Khomeini's little Muslim palace. The psychological devastation would be immense, as awesome as the clandestine physical destruction.

Imagining Khomeini going totally insane as the virus ate away his brain, barking orders like the mad dog he was, brought a smile to Stone's face.

Hell of a concept, he complimented himself. More than worth ten mil!

JAMES LOCKTON had built a sturdy worktable and tool cabinet in his garage. He wasn't much of a handyman, but having the tools available made it feel more like a home, not just an expensive extension of his laboratory. His father, Paul Lockton, had been a wizard with tools, but he had never felt comfortable with them.

Lockton lifted the big double-edged ax out from between the table and the shelves. It felt natural, and balanced in his hands. He had been chopping and splitting wood since he was ten. It had been their only source of heat in the winter. There was a certain strength, a security, in just holding it. It was as if part of his father radiated through the smooth wood handle. It was a feeling James Lockton needed then.

He carried the ax with him as he checked all the window latches and doors in the house. He only put

it down to carry his favorite overstuffed beige chair out
of the living room and into the foyer.

THE INTELLIGENCE OFFICER switched monitors to
trace the sudden low, squeaking noise. It seemed to
originate somewhere near the front hall. It ended with
a thump.

Next came the sound of a key turning, followed by
the clink of a bolt lock. Then the quick scratching of
metal on wood.

What had he gotten from the garage? the agent
wondered, focusing the monitor on the sound of a
body dropping into cushions.

The gray phone to the left of the first-floor surveillance monitors buzzed. The intelligence officer had
been expecting the call.

"Long night ahead," Stone said. "Did you monitor his call?"

"Yes."

"I think we'd better discuss how the intruder slipped
through your surveillance." The statement was flatly
underplayed. "But it can wait until I get there."

"Who sent him? How could they have gotten
keys?"

"No idea. Keep all your ears on. If the doc even
breathes funny, I want to know."

EVERY SOUND, EVERY CREAK, every time the electric
heat kicked in or the refrigerator hummed on, Lockton popped off his chair with the ax. At five-thirty, he
called the emergency number again. It took ten min-

utes for Stone to call back. He was at the Dallas–Fort Worth air terminal.

Stone's first words were, "The flight to Salt Lake is boarding, Doc. Can't this wait?"

Lockton knew Stone wasn't going to like what he was about to suggest. "I want to notify the authorities. Warn the island residents not to drink their tap water until all the wells can be tested. I realize there's almost no chance of infection, but . . ."

"You said the odds were a million to one, Doc."

"Probably higher."

"We can't risk our security status just to ease your troubled mind. You tell no one, understand? If you do, I'll have you arrested. You break security, the contract's gone, the insurance policy void, and you'll be in prison. How are you going to support Nick in prison? He'll end up being institutionalized. You want that, Doc?"

"Security has already been destroyed. What the hell's the difference now? We're talking about people's lives, Stone. That's not something to gamble with, no matter what the odds."

"This is none of the American public's damn business. Think of the mass hysteria it would cause on your precious Vashon. Just the idea of a mutant virus possibly seeping into the ground would be enough to ruin the island's economy. All for nothing. Except to soothe your overzealous humanitarian instinct. We both know it had to have been destroyed in the fire!"

"We don't know that for sure."

"Who can know anything for sure, Doc? If you want to invest in a million-to-one shot, go buy a lottery ticket. But don't even consider breaking our contract. This is still top secret. And it will remain top secret."

Realizing he had no choice, Lockton hung up.

He knew Stone was not one to make idle threats.

Chapter 12

THE TOW TRUCK from Jim Willano's Shell station lowered its woven steel cable down the steep embankment. The new mechanic, Harvey Poke, led the big gray hook down through the burned-out underbrush and clamped it onto the bent back axle of the Chevy, between the wheel and the drive shaft.

"Okay, Jim," Harvey called up through the mist. "Crank 'er up."

The dark blue Ford tow truck heaved like an old mule against its plow. Harvey followed the vehicle's slow, creaking ascent up the cliff. The hydraulic engine whined like a huge rusty fishing reel.

"Someone tried to break into your house, eh?" Jim queried.

It didn't surprise Lockton that the news had already begun to spread. The island, like most small towns, was famous for that.

"Didn't get past the alarm systems," Lockton shouted over the whine of the hydraulics. The car crept up the hill like a half-squashed beetle.

"Heard your honey scared him off. Chased him right into the next life." Jim had never been known for his tact. He was far more familiar with cars than people.

Lockton ignored him and stepped to the edge of the cliff. A slight southwest breeze sent up hints of oil and burned upholstery. The sky was clearing, but patches of mist still slithered through the trees. The damp air was beginning to dry as the new sun filtered into the woods.

Harvey surveyed the mud slides on both sides of the road. "Clay and sand." He spit down the cliff. "Worthless glacier shit."

The car rose up like a breaching whale and crashed backward onto the road. Harvey studied the crest of the slide above the road. It looked like a giant wave breaking. A two-hundred-foot fir tree had been uprooted at the top of the slide. Its gnarled roots twisted out from the trunk like the snake-haired Medusa.

"Piece by piece, this island's slowly sinking back into the Sound," Harvey prophesied. "Someday, the last tree will fall, the last knoll will break and what's left of the island will slide into the water, gone forever. Probably just before the glaciers return to start the whole damn process all over again."

Lockton nodded, anxiously waiting for them to finish and leave. He hadn't expected the truck this early. If his car had broken down, Jim's tow truck wouldn't have shown up until late afternoon. If he was lucky. But this job was just too juicy for the gossip circuit to let Island Time slow it down.

After an in-depth discussion on the art of towing, they finally left, dragging the car away like conquering heroes.

As soon as they disappeared around the turn, he started down the embankment. The mist was rising quickly. Dust-yellow rays from the early-morning sun tunneled down through the lush green forest like the golden fingers of a multiarmed Hindu god.

It was easy to follow the car's descent. There were deep gashes in the earth after each sideward flip. Lockton checked the fall area thoroughly. There were no signs of a canister. He was praying there wouldn't be.

Halfway up the cliff, Lockton began to lose his footing in the rain-drenched mud. He regained his balance on a rock jetty protruding from the newly formed gash in the earth. Only a small portion of it was aboveground. The stone was cracked cleanly into two pieces. A five-inch crevasse disappeared deep into the hill. Pulling himself up over the stone, he reached for the severed tree root. Using it like a rope, he tugged himself back up to the road.

It was almost impossible for the extract to have been ejected, he reassured himself, walking back to his car. Even if it had been, once it was subjected to the open air, the decomposition factor would have rendered the virus harmless in a matter of hours. Besides, the entire area around the wreck had burned for at least a half hour.

The virus couldn't have survived that.

If it just hadn't been raining all night, he thought.

It was the rain that kept him from completely shrugging off the threat.

9:40 a.m.
AFTER A BIG BREAKFAST of pancakes, soybean sausages, eggs and orange juice, Mrs. L. drove Nick to the Methodist church near the cemetery. She liked it because it looked like a real church—white, with a tall steeple and hard-angled roof—and because it ran the best bingo game on the island.

James Lockton carried his third cup of espresso down to the lab. He hadn't slept all night and Mrs. L.'s sanctimonious chastisement hadn't helped. She was upset because he had not gone with them to church for the past two months. He had never even met the new woman minister, Alice Soddersby. Mrs. L. said her sermons were far more relevant than old Reverend Huckley's. This Sunday's service was titled: "If God Can Forgive, Why Can't We?"

Lockton thought the reevaluation of the time-element data from his last fifteen experiments with the two decomposition factors was far more relevant than forgiveness.

Ten of the experiments concerned the half-life factor, the decomposition capabilities of the virus after activation in fresh water. The other five involved the decomposition time of the virus when subjected to the atmosphere. The data showed a fluctuation between two and twenty-three days in fresh water. The decomposition of the virus once subjected to the atmosphere, however, was constant: six hours.

It had now been over twelve hours since the accident.

AS NICK AND MRS. L. were listening to Reverend Soddersby quote from the Book of John—"Beloved, if our heart condemn us not, then have we confidence toward God"—a shaft of sunlight filtered into the narrow crevasse in the split stone bulging out of the mud slide above the accident site. Shards of clear plastic sparkled like tiny bits of ancient silver coins. Two feet below the surface, deep in the sheared stone, lay the shattered remains of the plastic vial that had once contained the stolen mutant virus.

During the night, the rain had created a small waterfall in the crevasse. Wave after wave washed the extract deeper into the soil. Like an iceberg, the section of rock jutting out of the mud was only the tip of a much larger boulder lodged into the side of the hill. For centuries, the winter rains had eroded the crevasse until it had finally cut completely through the stone into a layer of sand and dirt. From there, it tunneled eastward, through the northern belly of the island.

The virus flowed along the rainwater path until it found a home in an underground pool. There, it began to infect and breed among the microorganisms that lived in the pool. Like submarine wolf packs, the viruses pursued their prey, stalking them with chemical scent-traces as they moved in for the kill.

Their numbers grew geometrically. Nothing could stop them. They soon became the dominant predators in the microscopic world of the pool.

The pool's current drew the ever-expanding virus horde through a number of small arteries, all leading into an underground stream. The stream wound eastward, across the north end of the island until it broke off into three tributaries, one flowing east to the beach, one southeast and one directly south.

The viruses continued their life cycles of hunting and breeding as they journeyed toward their final destinations—two underground water tables high above the deeper aquifers of Vashon.

10:05 a.m.

ON THE NORTHEASTERN SHORE of Vashon, a quarter mile south of the ferry dock, John Walters was working on his greatest achievement, the limited-class hydroplane *Suzy Q*, named after his wife, Susan Qually Walters.

John Walters was a mechanical maestro. His wife was certain his blood was three-fifths gas, one-fifth nitrogen, one-fifth motor oil, and one-fifth Jim Beam. If someone reminded her that that made six-fifths, Susan just said her husband never went anywhere without an extra fifth. For the past eight years, John had been the head mechanic for Tommy Fairwood, world-famous driver of the unlimited-class hydroplane *All's Fair*, sponsored by one of the larger bank chains in the Northwest.

"Three-sixteenth," John ordered.

His son Terry quickly retrieved the wrench socket from the four-foot, red metal toolbox on wheels and slapped it into his father's palm.

"Three-sixteenth," he reiterated, as if assisting a surgical operation.

The *Suzy Q* was up on the lift in the boathouse, built at the pinnacle of a concrete ramp rising from the sea. The boat lift could be lowered onto iron tracks and rolled down the ramp into the Sound, enabling it to be launched no matter what the tide.

Terry liked to watch his father work. The reverence John held for combustion engines was the same as a surgeon's for the human body. Terry was a chubby kid, prone to Twinkies and Doritos, who never went anywhere without his All's Fair baseball cap and a wad of grape bubble gum. His hair was permanently creased. He had just turned ten and was already able to disassemble his go-cart engine and rebuild it himself. His grades were miserable, but he could tell jokes like nobody else in class. His best friend, Nick Lockton, helped him with his homework, but it didn't change anything.

"Screwdriver," John handed the socket head back to his son. "That small, red-handled one."

"Screwdriver." Terry circled the concrete platform that surrounded the hydroplane to get a better view. The bright red fiberglass engine cover was resting on a blanket on the platform. He squatted down and petted it, as if it were a cat, while he studied his father's next adjustment. The dash in the *Suzy Q*'s cockpit was finished, but the seat and its aerodynamic back frame were still being built. Eventually there would be only room for the driver, but now two or three people could still go out with him on test runs.

John Walters got up off his knees. "She's ready."

"Awesome," Terry said.

Neither smiled. This was far too important a moment. John stepped up off the boat onto the platform, ceremoniously held his grease-smeared hands above his head and waited. Terry hopped up onto the wooden bench and slapped his father's palms.

High fives. All systems go.

11:31 a.m.
AFTER CHANGING from Sunday-school clothes into jeans, Nick Lockton began sprinkling pinches of Tetra-min fish food over the surface of his aquarium. He loved his fish almost as much as he loved Thor. He could watch them for hours. Each fish had its own subtle but distinct personality. Last year, he finally got his father's and the doctor's permission to take scuba lessons. When he joined his father, John Walters and Terry on his first dive in Puget Sound, Nick was in heaven. Less bound by gravity, he felt strong and agile, freer than he had ever felt before. It was the one place where his disease didn't matter.

"You've got it made," he told the fish jealously. "No mist tent. No hospitals. No kids teasing you. Just eat and poop and cruise around."

"As long as a larger fish doesn't cruise by with a hungry look in his eyes," his father added. Nick watched the distorted figure approach through the aquarium. "This room needs picking up, bud."

Nick had expected that. He was supposed to do it before Saturday-morning cartoons.

James Lockton bent down on the other side of the aquarium. Nick puffed out his cheeks to make a fish mouth. Lockton chuckled and stood up.

"Dad, when can we go diving again?"

"When the doctor gives us the okay."

Nick sighed dramatically. "When will that be?"

"We have an appointment on Wednesday."

"Then we can go next weekend. We'll take the Walters out on our boat—and go spearfishing off Blake Island."

Lockton winked in agreement and looked back into the tank. His mind wasn't on spearfishing. So much had happened since yesterday. The woman he loved had rejected his proposal. His house had been broken into. The top-secret project had turned out to be anything but secret. A man had died. Part of the deadly extract was still unaccounted for. And Mrs. L. was mad because he hadn't gone to church again.

He looked at his watch. Stone had landed at Sea-Tac and was probably heading for Fauntleroy Dock. He couldn't get his second conversation with Stone out of his mind.

As he watched the fish dart at the falling flakes of food, he decided the odds of the virus reaching either of the aquifers that supplied the vast majority of water to the island were even more remote than he had first thought. It took months for the rain to seep that far down through the earth. The virus would break down well before that.

"Dad?"

Lockton glanced up over the aquarium. "Yeah?"

"Are you all right?" Nick had been watching his father's face stiffen into granite. His son's concern softened his rigid features.

"Just thinking." He reached over the aquarium and ruffled Nick's hair.

Suddenly the spine-straightening blast of an air horn pierced the beach. Nick ran to the window and opened it.

John Walters maneuvered the *Suzy Q* closer to shore. Lying belly down on the bow, his head and shoulders draped over the port side, Terry jabbed the water with a paddle to keep the boat from scraping bottom as they glided in.

Nick leaned out and waved. "Hey Terry!"

Terry beckoned with the paddle. "Come on. We're going for a test run."

Nick looked back at his father. "Can I?"

"You bet."

Nick darted for the door.

"But when you get back," Lockton injected before he got out of the room, "this room is to be picked up."

"It's a deal." Nick was already halfway down the stairs.

James Lockton flopped down on Nick's bed. His body ached for the sleep his burdened mind had no intention of giving him.

1:32 p.m.

THE SPRING BREEZE was blowing in from the south-west. Above the dark green peninsula, the snow-topped Olympic Mountains pierced the clean, blue sky like shark's teeth. It was the kind of sunny Sunday that drew even diehard television addicts outdoors. Sunshine was a commodity not to be taken for granted in the Northwest.

Lockton watched the blood-red hydroplane skim over the water, flapping side to side against the tops of the waves. Nick, in helmet and orange life jacket, waved up at his father as they passed the house.

"John must have finally worked the bugs out of his carburetor," Alex said, coming up the porch stairs.

His chest tightened. He hadn't heard her coming. Without turning, he said, "Looks like it."

To get his attention, she dropped his gym bag on the glass table. It thudded heavily. Lockton glanced back over his shoulder.

Alex McGuire's glistening red hair billowed softly in the breeze. She had spent the past two hours searching for just the right outfit. Years from now she wanted him to remember exactly how she looked at this moment.

Seeing her in his favorite black dress with the wide red stripe that matched her hair, the one that clung to her strong curves like wet silk, only fueled his anguish and frustration.

"I have two questions," she stated matter-of-factly. "First, that wasn't just a prowler last night, was it?" When she realized he had no intention of answering, she continued. "It had something to do with your research, didn't it?"

"No," Lockton said. His throat felt like splintered wood. "Why would you think that?"

She reached into her purse. "You're as rotten a liar as Nick." She made herself smile. He looked away. The smile dropped like a rock slide.

"And you're a good one, I suppose?" He meant it to be barbed.

It was going even worse than she had imagined. She held out a snub-nosed .38 and a box of shells.

"What the hell is that for?"

"I bought it when I was living in D.C. After my neighbor was raped." She slid the pistol across the glass. "I want you to have it."

"You're blowing this whole thing way out of proportion." He picked up the .38 and examined it. He hadn't touched a handgun in years.

Sure beats the old double-edged ax, he thought, fighting off the first twinge of a smile.

Alex moved around the table next to him. His first instinct was to back away, but he didn't. He wanted to appear calm, indifferent, as if last night's denial had just been another conversation.

"James." When her fingers brushed his forearm, he jerked away. "Keep it for my sake. I'm frightened. Please?"

"All right," he agreed, secretly grateful. "What's the second question?"

Alex unzipped the gym bag. "Does your offer still hold?"

Lockton searched her face, hoping. "What?"

She lifted the bottle of Dom Perignon out of the ice. "Your offer? Something about tying the knot? Getting hitched? You do remember?"

Lockton couldn't answer. He didn't want to open the wound again. It had already begun to fester and there wasn't an antibiotic in the world that could cleanse it.

"If so—" she unwrapped two champagne glasses packed in tissue "—the answer is—yes. Why are you looking at me like that? A lady's allowed to change her mind, isn't she?"

"Only once." Lockton drew her to him, still wary. "Change it again and you'll be swimming for the mainland."

"I won't, James." She kissed him deeply to seal her promise. "Not ever."

"Alex, I love you so much." Her body writhed in his embrace. "Don't ever leave me, please. I couldn't take that. Not again."

"I'll never leave you, James." She was attacking him with quick, trembling, desperate kisses. "Oh, God, James. Love me. Now."

Lockton lifted her into the living room, her squirming body wrapped around him like a python.

She tugged at his shirt, ripping the top button. He lowered her to the rug. Hunching her shoulders, he slipped the dress straps down her arms. His lips followed the descent across her chest and she guided his head to her breast.

Suddenly, she pushed him back. "What about Mrs. L.?"

"Getting her hair done."

"Hurry!" She tugged him down on top of her and playfully bit his lip. "I can't wait."

The front door chimed.

"The hell with them." Lockton rolled over, pulling her up on top of him. She arched back as he slipped the dress to her waist.

Her peripheral vision caught a movement on the porch. She unstraddled Lockton and yanked up the top of her dress.

A big man, at least six foot four, two hundred forty pounds, was standing outside the sliding-glass door.

Lockton realized he had left the gun out on the porch table.

The front door chimed again, followed by knocking. When Lockton sat up, the man on the porch was gone.

"Stone." Lockton sighed, checking his shirt buttons.

"Who?" Alex brushed back her hair.

Lockton stood up and adjusted his pants. He walked to the door, a little stiff-legged, then checked back to make sure Alex was ready. She nodded and he opened the door.

"Sorry if Harrison startled you, miss." Richard Stone ambled into the living room as if it were his own. Two men followed, the bear from the porch and an average-looking man in his forties, slightly overweight, with unusually large ears. The big guy sucked in his cheeks to keep from smirking as he passed Alex.

She gave Lockton one of her who-the-hell-are-these-jerks looks, then stared the hidden smirk right off the bear.

Lockton slipped his hands into his pockets, and nonchalantly adjusted himself. "Alex, this is Richard Stone."

"Alex McGuire." She extended her hand stiffly.

"Glad to meet you." Stone shook it.

"Mr. Stone is my, ah..." Lockton withdrew his hands from his pockets.

"Associate," Stone filled in. "These are my two assistants. Tom Harrison." He pointed at the bear. They nodded but didn't shake hands. "And Dick Schraeder."

Lockton was surprised by the chilly reception Alex was giving Stone. It was the big lummox, Harrison, who had caught her with her dress down.

Lockton took her arm and tried to pull her closer to the group, but she wouldn't budge.

"Alex is my neighbor," he announced, "and as of today, my fiancée."

"Really?" Stone focused on Alex.

They reminded Lockton of two boxers sizing each other up as they waited for the referee to finish his brief spiel about rules and low blows.

Finally Stone grinned and said, "Well, congratulations."

Her lips remained glued as she returned his smile. Lockton recognized the look. Pure contempt.

"I'm sure you have important business to discuss," she said. "If you'll excuse me." She started toward the porch and turned. "James?"

Lockton followed her outside and slid the door closed. "Sorry about the...interruption."

"You better do something with this." She slid the .38 up against the gym bag.

They were both aching to be back on the rug. The inner muscle of Alex's left thigh kept twitching. She ran her finger lightly down the neck of the champagne.

"Keep it cold," she said. "You owe me one."

Lockton touched her cheek. "Just one?"

Chapter 13

"HARRISON'S CHECKING the grounds," Stone said. "Schraeder's going through the house."

Lockton poured two mugs of coffee.

"Nice place."

"Who was he?" Lockton asked.

"Don't know. Maybe the dental examination will turn up something. But don't count on it." Stone sipped his coffee. "Good stuff."

"They roast it here on the island." Lockton put his mug on the dining table. "Now that whoever they are know, what do we do? Putting my family in jeopardy was not part of our deal."

"They took their shot and lost. They won't try again."

"Why do I have such a hard time believing you? Other than the fact that you said this was never supposed to happen in the first place—top secret, professional security and all that crap."

"We deserve that, I guess. Obviously there's a leak somewhere." Stone blew off the steam rising from his mug. "It'll be plugged."

Lockton did not like Stone's attitude. The smug bastard had screwed up and was trying to blame it on a leak. He watched the *Suzy Q* slow down before hitting the wake of the ferry, *Hiyu*, heading for Southworth.

"Did the police call today?" Stone took a pack of Camels from his breast pocket. "You mind?"

Lockton shook his head. He would air out the house before Nick came back. "There are some reports to make out. I have to go in later this afternoon. Alex, too."

"Are they planning to investigate further?"

"I doubt it. Seemed pretty cut-and-dried to them."

"Good." Stone stamped out his Camel in the glass ashtray on the coffee table.

"What happens now?" Lockton asked.

"We move. Everything."

Lockton had considered a number of options, but never this.

"It's not ready," he protested. "The disintegration factor still fluctuates radically." Lockton saw the top of Harrison's head pass outside the south window. "The virus shouldn't be moved until the half-life is perfected. It's too risky."

Harrison was kneeling by the steps to the kitchen, checking the dried prints in the mud. Stone watched him as he spoke. "We have no choice. You've completed the complicated aspects. I'm sure our people in Texas can add the finishing touches." Stone turned from the window. "I'll have to be honest with you. There's a few people in the Company that think you're dragging this half-life thing out on purpose. They think you're stalling."

"It's just too dangerous." Lockton emptied the ashtray into the wastebasket. "I need more time."

"We're out of time, Doc. This isn't a scientific problem open to debate. The decision's already been made."

Lockton opened the porch door to let out the smoke. Maybe it was just as well, he thought. He had fulfilled his contract. Nick's insurance would continue. The house and the lab would be his.

"What's eating you, Doc?"

The slightest hint of victory creased the corners of Stone's mouth. The boy genius had thrown in the towel.

"I have to know whether the stolen extract was incinerated or not." Lockton used his coffee mug as a prop to avoid eye contact with Stone.

"What about the decomposition factor?" Stone asked. Having checked the first and second floors, Schraeder headed down to the basement.

"Once subjected to the atmosphere, it would decompose in six hours."

"But?"

"If it was thrown out of the car, there's still the slight chance the rain could have carried it down into an underground stream. Most of our water comes from aquifers hundreds of feet down." He explained why the virus could never reach them. "But there are a few shallower water tables that also feed well systems."

Stone lit another cigarette. "And God said, 'Be fruitful and multiply.'"

Lockton glanced up from his mug contemptuously. "Sometimes you make me sick, Stone."

"You're not big on my list, either, Doc. You eggheads are more than willing to take our money, even create our weapons, just as long as you don't have to bear the responsibility for pulling the trigger."

"But you do."

"Damn right."

"That's what terrifies me more than the weapon itself."

Stone smacked his mug on the dining table. Coffee splashed over the rim onto the place mat. "You're beginning to remind me of another scientist I had the displeasure of dealing with." Just the thought of Koplenz caused the veins in his neck to bulge. Until his son's death, Stone had always been the image of control. Now it took every ounce of his willpower to keep from striking Lockton. "Somebody's got to be willing to pull the trigger, Doc. Or deterrence would have no meaning. Hell, Doc, without us, humanity would end up annihilating itself."

"You know what scares me the most?"

"No. What, Doc?"

"I don't even think you buy that crap anymore."

Stone shook his head. The Doc was right.

"We don't have to agree. Or even like each other. We just have to work together long enough to get the project moved. Then the hell with it. The hell with you. The hell with me. Okay?"

Lockton acquiesced. "I'm going to old man Follgerty's junkyard after I file the report with the police.

That's where they took the car. I already searched the area around the accident this morning."

"You don't go anywhere. I don't want you to draw attention to yourself or this lab. I'll send Harrison out tonight. After the yard's closed. How long will it take to get everything ready to move?"

"Did you bring the proper containers?"

"Harrison has everything we'll need in his Winnebago. He and Schraeder will bunk across the street, up that dirt road. I'll stay in the house. No one will get within a hundred yards of this place until everything is moved. Now, how long?"

"Two days."

"I'll give you twenty-four hours. I want to be on the ferry Monday afternoon at the latest."

"Then what? I have certain agreements with the CIA. About the laboratory, the equipment, the mortgage on the house. And Nick's medical insurance. You're not leaving with the extract until all your obligations have been met."

"I've brought all the papers with me." Harrison came up from the basement just as Schraeder walked in the kitchen door. "We'll take care of it in the morning. Right now, I have to set up security for the night. I have to protect your family, Doc." Stone smirked. "We're the good guys, remember?"

THE FUGITIVE VIRUS now numbered in the billions. Like the Mongol hordes sweeping across Europe, they had pillaged and raped their way through the underground tributaries before finally spilling into two water tables on the eastern side of the island.

The real battle would soon begin.

The battle against the multicelled creature: man.

With each quick squeak of a sink handle, the virus hordes gravitated upward through separate wells toward the water pumps that would fling them into their final assault.

3:26 p.m.

ALEX AND LOCKTON drove to the police station in her mud-splattered Trans Am. They were taken to separate rooms and questioned. It took less than an hour. The case seemed simple enough: bad guy was foiled while attempting a break-in and dies accidentally while trying to escape. Case closed.

The autopsy had been performed at Harbor View Hospital in Seattle. The man had no identification. Prints were impossible because the skin on his fingers had burned off. They were checking his dental records. He had only six teeth of his own. The rest were false and rather badly maintained. So far—nothing.

On their way home, Alex invited Lockton over to her house to finish what they had begun on his living room floor.

"And the champagne?" Lockton asked.

"Sneak in and grab it before any of your 'associates' see you."

"You didn't like Stone, did you?"

"Not really."

"Me either."

She squeezed his thigh. "You still haven't answered me."

"I can't."

"You know once we're married, you'll have an obligation, a duty, to fulfill certain, ah..." She tapped the horn in three short bursts.

Lockton laughed. "Inalienable rights?"

Alex pursed her lips. "Life, liberty, and the pursuit of the Big One."

Lockton bit her earlobe.

"Tomorrow," he whispered. "All day."

"And all of the night," she sang in time to the old Animals melody. Turning off the main highway, she started down the first steep curve on Cove Road. "So what is he doing here?"

"Stone?"

She nodded.

Lockton took a slow breath and sighed. "The project, at least my end of it, is finished. They're here to transport it to Dallas. The Winnebago is specially designed for security purposes. I've got to work straight through the night to get it ready."

"I'm glad it's finally over, James." They shared a warm glance before she turned into his driveway. "Are you going to be all right? You look beat."

"I was going to ask you the same thing." His fingers searched out hers.

"It's strange." She leaned over the console and rested her head on his shoulder. "I never saw him, only his shadow in the rain. Then his car. The chase.

The fire. It was all so impersonal. Like passing an accident on the highway.''

Lockton was relieved to hear that. It wasn't the same for him. He knew the man had violated his home. And he had seen him burning in the car. There were few smells more nauseating than burning flesh.

"I love you," she said. They kissed, gently, open-eyed, as if their lips were made of thin crystal. Lockton drank in her presence, her concern, trying to quench the parched corner of his psyche, laid barren by the break-in and subsequent death. Her instinct felt him feeding from her. She opened herself like a mother baring her breast to suckle a lost and hungry child.

9:06 p.m.
Susan Walters had almost finished correcting her sixth graders' spelling tests, folded neatly in two stacks on the desk in the living room. The George Winters tape was on its last song.

Susan was a petite, thirty-four-year-old woman. Short brown hair framed her pixielike face. She was the kind of grade-school teacher children remembered long after graduation.

John and Terry sauntered in, coated with engine grease and oil. Susan checked the wooden desk clock, carved like a clipper ship's steering wheel.

"It's past Terry's bedtime, John. Again."

"I needed his professional expertise." John elbowed his son and Terry grinned.

Susan pointed her red pen at the pair. "Don't touch a thing until you've washed up."

Terry glanced mischievously up at his father. Together, they dragged themselves toward her into club-footed zombies, grease-smeared hands outstretched. Susan bolted from the desk.

"Don't you dare." They kept coming. She grabbed Terry's toy Jedi sword and switched on its blue fluorescent blade. "I'm telling you for the last time, I won't join the Dark Side. Not if they're all grease balls like you two."

John and his son backed away, cowering from the power of the Force. Susan put the weapon down on the desk and continued correcting the tests.

"Want some instant iced tea?" John called from the kitchen.

"No, thanks," she answered.

Terry scrubbed his arms with powdered industrial soap.

"You want any?" John asked.

"Nay." Terry opened the refrigerator as he dried his hands. "I made a half gallon of raspberry Kool-Aid yesterday." He moved the pickle jar and milk carton to get at the pitcher.

John measured two tablespoons of tea into a tall glass, turned on the tap and waited for it to get cold. He let the water run for a long time before filling the glass and stirring.

"Best thing about spring-fed wells, you can always get cold water, even in summer." John followed his son into the living room. Terry immediately turned on the TV.

"I thought I said it was past someone's bedtime."

"Ah, Mom," Terry groaned. "There's a tag-team grudge match on."

John turned off the set and gave Terry his famous do-what-your-mother-says-or-else look.

"I'm going. I'm going." Terry shuffled toward the stairs.

"And don't forget to brush your teeth," Susan called after him. "With toothpaste this time."

Upstairs in the bathroom, Terry tried out a few new faces in the mirror. With eyes bugged and cheeks spread taut, he slowly pushed a mouthful of Kool-Aid out through his clenched teeth. The way it dribbled down his chin like purple blood really cracked him up. He'd have to show Nick that one.

Suddenly he heard his mother's footsteps sneaking down the hall. He quickly yanked his toothbrush out of the plastic holder glued to the wall under the mirror.

Susan peeked around the door. "Using toothpaste, I hope."

Terry grunted and kept on brushing. She took that to mean yes.

"You can watch the match in your room. But lights out at nine-thirty."

He mumbled in agreement, his lips tightly glued around the brush to keep the purple juice from leaking. When she closed the door, he spit out the Kool-Aid and gasped for air.

11:13 p.m.

FOR THE PAST SIX HOURS, Lockton had been sorting out his notes, files and computer disks. Over a thousand photographs from the electron microscope had to be cross-referenced and boxed with their coinciding literature. The hardest part was separating his personal research from project data. Up until the past six months, he had devoted a third of his time to personal research. His contract had been rewritten to allow him that privilege.

He was trying to isolate the specific gene, or genes, that when defective, caused cystic fibrosis. Until that had been accomplished, discovering a cure was impossible. He had significantly narrowed the search, however, from three million to 85,000 genes. To most geneticists, that would have been considered extremely successful progress. But not to Lockton. Not while he watched the disease slowly kill his son.

He checked the next disk. He would need to print out the last third before boxing it. He poured another cup of espresso. He needed the caffeine jolt. He was having difficulty focusing on the display terminal. When he put down the cup, he noticed he was shaking as badly as a victim of Parkinson's disease. He decided to take a break after he typed in the printout orders.

LOCKTON RAIDED the refrigerator for a glass of milk and an English muffin. He had skipped dinner. He wasn't hungry now, either, but he had to do something for his stomach. His felt as if he had swallowed a handful of aluminum pop-tops, and he still had a long night ahead.

After gulping down the snack, he went into the living room and poured a shot of Remy Martin into a brandy snifter. He swirled it around in the deep bowl, sniffed the strong, clean wood scent.

"What are you drinking?" Stone asked, entering the room.

"Cognac. It's in the cabinet." Lockton pointed with his thumb. "Help yourself."

"Can't. I'm working."

"I'm impressed," he said unenthusiastically.

"You shouldn't, either."

Headlights flashed across the cut glass bordering the front door.

"Harrison," Stone explained. "I sent him to that junkyard to check the Impala."

When Harrison entered, cold night air swirled in around their ankles. Lockton anxiously tried to read Harrison's face.

"Well?"

Harrison glanced at Stone. He nodded his permission.

"No sign of any type of container in the car," Harrison said.

Lockton grabbed his elbow. "You sure?" One quick look from Harrison and he let go. "It could have been mixed up with the shattered windshield or..."

"He knows his job, Doc," Stone interrupted.

"There wasn't anything that could identify him, either." Harrison rubbed his hands to take the chill away. It had been a cold two hours.

"Schraeder has everything set up in the Winnebago," Stone said.

Harrison nodded and headed back out. Lockton didn't appreciate being treated like an outsider. Not in his own house.

"If it was in his pocket, it should have still been in the car," Lockton said. "His clothes were consumed, so..."

"How's the packing going?" Stone undid his collar button, loosened his blue striped tie and lit a Camel.

Lockton stared at him skeptically. He'd be damned if he'd let Stone manipulate him like he did Harrison.

"Why is it you seem so disinterested in the intruder?" Lockton quizzed. "I'd have thought that'd be a major concern."

"It is." Stone returned Lockton's sharp scrutiny. "We have people working on it. My job is to get this project moved. And to retain security until it's delivered to BIOGENTEX."

"Part of the project is still out there somewhere. It's not something you can leave bits of behind."

"Doc. The damn container melted in that inferno. I only sent Harrison out to placate you. It's gone, destroyed. Forget about it. Let's take care of the business at hand."

Stone had a point.

Lockton left him standing in the living room and went downstairs. Setting the alarm on his digital watch for 2:30 a.m., he settled down on the sofa across from the pool table and covered himself with the afghan Mrs. L. had knit three years ago.

Richard Stone's footsteps creaked on the ceiling above him.

When he had first met Stone, he had known they would never be friends. But he had respected the man. He was gruff and cynical, but there had been a certainty, a purpose hidden underneath his tough exterior. He had seemed balanced—a man who believed in himself and his job, and felt they both had meaning.

Two years ago, that had changed. For two months, Stone had been temporarily disassociated from the project. He returned for a day, then Lockton didn't hear from him again for two more months. The next time Stone came to the island for a progress report, the bully had emerged.

Only his cynicism and dark sense of humor remained. The sense of purpose had died. Lockton could see it in his movements, in his eyes. He never looked at anyone anymore, just through them. His tolerance had dried up like an abused plant. Lockton had asked him why, several times, but was always rebuffed.

"The less you know, the better," Stone would say. If Lockton tried to pursue it, he'd cut him off angrily. "Mind your own fucking business, Doc. Let the dead bury the dead."

IT TOOK A HALF HOUR for Lockton to finally fall asleep. While he slept, his muscles twitched from nervous exhaustion. His mind began to fire volleys of images only bearable in the hazy world of dreams. . . .

Alex was wearing khaki shorts, knee socks and hiking boots. Naked from the waist up, she was standing on a mountain trail in the treacherous wilderness of the Northern Cascades. It was dusk and the sheer rock cliffs above the pine valley turned purple in the dying light.

Lockton walked up behind her in surgical gown, mask, cap and rubber gloves. He wanted to kiss her, but couldn't untie the mask.

Suddenly the valley echoed with the howls of wolves. Hundreds of them. He could see their red eyes in the shadows between the dense trees as they began to close in on their campsite.

Lockton tugged Alex down the mountain to a huge frozen lake. Underneath the ice, the lake disappeared into black, unfathomable depths.

The packs raced across the lake, mouths curled, teeth bared, and the ice sang out as if a thousand stones were skipping across a field of untuned violins.

They were closing in fast.

Lockton pushed Alex behind him and turned to fight. In seconds they had knocked him to the ice and covered him like wasps.

Close behind him, he heard Alex's muffled cries of agony. The wolves had her pinned on her back. Her torso was marked with bloodless bites. Suddenly one big male pushed through the pack. He was pink and furless, like a newly hatched bird. He forced himself between her legs and mounted her.

The others, all furless now, too, began to straddle her arms, legs and face. Her tortured screams pierced his ears like needles. He tried to crawl to her, but his limbs had melded with the ice, imprisoning him.

Suddenly the howling ceased. The wolves began to shrivel up like balloons. Soon there was nothing left on the ice except flat, wrinkled scabs of pink skin.

Alex slowly rolled over and gazed helplessly at Lockton. He was completely frozen in the ice.

Suddenly her belly started jerking and heaving. Moments later, dozens of tiny pink wolf pups burst through her flesh like an obscene time-lapse film of plants sprouting from the soil.

"Alex!" Lockton screamed, bolting off the sofa. His shirt was soaked with sweat.

The vivid dream left a bile-bitter taste in his dry mouth. He stumbled back into the brightly lit lab. He no longer had any desire for sleep.

11:42 p.m.

JOHN WALTERS HAD WAITED until Susan fell asleep before easing out from under the blankets. He had decided to go back to the boathouse. He had a headache, the beginnings of a prickly sore throat, a fever, and was experiencing mild attacks of nausea. If he couldn't sleep, he might as well work.

At one in the morning, he was still at it, but feeling terrible. He hoped he wasn't coming down with the flu. As he tried to concentrate on the next critical adjustment, he dropped the wrench. When it hit the engine, the clang echoed in his head like cannon fire. He shook his hand out like a wet towel. His fingers had been stiffening up on him. For a moment, he had lost all feeling in them. He cracked his knuckles and retrieved the wrench.

Now what the heck was he...?

He had suddenly forgotten which spring bolt he had been adjusting.

He sat back on the frame, confused and frustrated. The bright ceiling light hurt his eyes. The fever was causing him to sweat through his clothes. Although he felt dehydrated, he seemed to be spitting every few seconds. The reflection off the hydroplane's fiberglass blurred his vision and made his head throb. His grease-smeared eyes wouldn't stop watering.

Stepping off the boat, he poured himself a glass of ice water from the quart jar he had brought from the kitchen. For some reason, the thought of drinking the water suddenly made him sick. He put it back on the table.

Better be a twenty-four hour flu, he thought. Can't afford to be sick this week.

Chapter 14

THE CRASH, followed by a piercing cry, jarred Susan
Walters awake. She was startled to discover she was
alone in bed. Across the hall, she could hear Terry
snoring. Sleeping on his back again, she thought. She
kept listening for the clanking of dishes downstairs,
having concluded that John had been raiding the refrigerator, broken something and cussed his usual
string of bawdy superlatives.

A loud metallic clang drew her attention to the open
window. Slipping into her red-and-white striped cotton nightshirt, she looked out the window. The lights
were on in the boathouse.

The scream that followed rippled over her skin like
a swarm of army ants.

The next crash sounded as if one of the tall metal
lockers had toppled onto the cement. John's hunched
figure shuffled past the boathouse window.

"John?" she yelled out. "Are you all right?"

Suddenly the ceiling light in the boathouse exploded. The side door thudded open and she spotted
her husband slowly coming up the path to the house.
He fell into the outer edge of light from the lamp
strung in the tree above the path. His damp hair was

stuck to his grease-smudged forehead. His sweatshirt and pants were soaked with perspiration.

"John, I'll be right down."

Before she could pull her head back inside, he howled, "No! Stay there!"

His frightening plea glued Susan to the window. John dragged himself toward the lamp in the tree. Susan hadn't noticed the sledgehammer. He was pulling it along the ground like a kid pulling a wagon with two broken wheels. She could hear his wheezing attempts at inhalation. Doubling over, he vomited white bile.

Suddenly he looked up at Susan. For a brief moment, she saw the silent scream reflected in his illuminated face. Then it was gone and his eyes were burning again. With a growl, he stood up and swung the hammer at the lamp, shattering it across the bushes.

Demons, John's mind cried. Fire demons. Burning his skull. He had destroyed two Sentinels of Fire, but there were still flames licking at his eyes like dragons' tongues.

They were coming from inside the house.

John Walters, holding the sledgehammer out like a broadsword, shuffled toward the front door.

"Wake up, honey." Susan shook Terry. Before he could open his eyes, she had swept him up in her arms. Normally he was too heavy for her to lift, but her adrenaline strength carried him with ease. She ran down the hall to the top of the stairs.

The sledgehammer smashed through the wooden door, nearly snapping it in two. Another swing and half the door tumbled onto the rug. John sidestepped into the hall, hammer extended defensively.

"John. Please, stop it!" Susan pressed Terry's face against her breasts to hide his view. A long wood splinter had rammed itself into John's belly. Blood trickled out through his torn shirt.

When John Walters looked up the stairs, flames struck his eyes like lasers. His brain boiled inside his skull like molten lead. He knew then that the demon at the top of the stairs was the creator of his appalling torment.

He began to climb the stairs.

Susan backed down the hall. Something had taken possession of her husband's mind, something horrible and demented. It was not John Walters coming up the stairs. Whoever it was, the bloodlust in his eyes shone like a neon obscenity.

Susan locked Terry's bedroom door and jammed his chest of drawers under the doorknob.

"Mommy? What's the matter with Daddy?" the child cried, sobbing.

She opened the wooden box under the window.

"Mommy, I'm scared!"

"Shush. Don't talk. Listen." She yanked the window up and unfurled the rope ladder to the ground. Clutching her son's shoulders, she said, as calmly as she could, "Terry, we're going to have a fire drill."

Terry clutched her nightshirt. "What about Daddy? He's supposed to..."

"I'll get Daddy. Don't worry. Now, come on." She hoisted him up through the window. "Climb down, and run to the Berkeleys'. I'll catch up in a minute."

He stopped halfway down the ladder. "Mommy, aren't you coming?"

"Not until you're all the way down, honey. Then you hold it for me, like Daddy showed you."

As if hit by a tornado, the bedroom door blew open and the chest toppled over.

Susan spun around.

"John? Don't you know me?" She was pinned to the wall next to the window. "I'm Susan. Your wife, Susan."

John Walters had killed all the fires in the hall. The bedroom was dark and cool.

From a long, hollow tunnel, he heard a familiar voice.

"John. It's me, Susan."

"Su-san?" he stammered, fighting to hold on to the sudden burst of reality.

"Yes, John. Your wife, Susan."

Flickers of a woman's face, the mother of his child, sputtered through his brain like a badly spliced home movie.

"Susan?"

She inched to her right, slowly reaching for the bedside lamp.

"John. Put down the hammer. No one's going to hurt you. John? It's me, Susan. Here, I'll turn on the light."

John tried to focus on the moving shadow across the room. It was like trying to see through thick, silt-brown water.

She snapped on the light and he swung his forearm over his eyes.

Demon!

It had set the room on fire. Flames snapped at his flesh like hungry bats.

He screamed and charged with his weapon.

Terry had reached the ground and was holding the rope taut. Susan threw one leg out the window.

"Mommy!" Terry cried, looking up in horror at the looming shadow behind her.

The dark iron head of the sledgehammer flashed behind the window. Blood spurted out against the glass. Again the hammer swung. His mother's body went limp, half in, half out the window.

A stream of blood spilled down the rope and over the boy's clenched fist.

Mr. and Mrs. Harrison Berkeley, a retired couple in their early seventies, were awakened by the drumming on their front door. Mr. Berkeley put on his robe.

"Harry, it sounds like a child crying," Mrs. Berkeley said.

Mr. Berkeley could hear only the pounding. He was almost deaf in his right ear. He walked down the long hall of his three-bedroom ranch house, switched on the outside light and opened the door.

Terry Walters was shaking like a torn sail in a storm.

"Mommy," he whimpered, furiously sucking in air. "She . . ."

He stared down at the fresh blood on his hand.

The boy was hyperventilating. Mr. Berkeley, a retired fisherman, swept the child up into his strong arms. He cupped Terry's nose and mouth to limit his oxygen intake, before checking the boy's hands. Although bloody, they weren't cut.

"Calm down, Terry. Tell me what happened. Was there an accident?"

The boy shook his head yes, and buried his head in Berkeley's stubbled cheek.

Beyond the circle of light, a limb cracked. Mr. Berkeley cautiously stepped back inside the doorway.

John Walters emerged out of the darkness, covered with blood. Swinging the hammer out in front of him like a sword, he battled the flaming creatures only he could see as he dragged himself, one leg partially paralyzed, toward the house.

It was obvious to Mr. Berkeley that his neighbor was totally insane. He didn't want to imagine what had happened to Susan. Whatever it was the boy had witnessed it, the horror was imprinted on his face.

He slammed the door and locked it.

"Martha," he called anxiously. "Come in here. Quick!"

She ran down the hall and he handed her the boy. She was a heavyset, square-shouldered woman, weaned on a lifetime of hard work in the canneries of Alaska.

Outside, John Walters began screaming at the demons.

"Harry, what is..."

"Take the boy back to the guest room and lock the door." The look on her husband's face left no room for arguing.

Mr. Berkeley hurried into the den, unlocked the tall teakwood cabinet and loaded two shells of steel shot into his double-barreled twelve-gauge shotgun.

Outside, the porch light exploded.

A moment later, the sledgehammer struck the front door and the whole house trembled. The boy's scream from the bedroom steeled Berkeley to his task. On the fifth swing, the sledgehammer splintered the wood around the lock and the door slowly creaked open.

"Don't come any farther, John."

Like a dog unfamiliar with a new command, Walters cocked his head in confusion. Looking to his left, he saw himself in the mirror above the antique table. Growling, he jabbed the hammer into the mirror.

Harrison Berkeley edged back. "John, can you understand me?"

A mixture of blood and sweat dribbled down Walters's cheeks. His face suddenly twisted in agony and saliva spilled down his chin.

Mr. Berkeley squeezed the barrel of his shotgun to keep from shaking. John raised the hammer over his shoulder and started toward him.

"Don't, John. Stay back."

He took another step and jerked back the hammer to strike.

Mr. Berkeley fired both barrels simultaneously, lifting John off his feet and back out the door.

Terry broke free of Mrs. Berkeley's hold, unlocked the door and ran down the hall.

"Harry!" she warned. "The boy!"

Mr. Berkeley lunged at Terry, but he ducked under him.

Suddenly, the boy stopped.

His father's torn body lay six feet in front of him, sprawled backward over the doorstep.

Terry Walters's conscious mind shut down and he crumpled to the floor like a discarded marionette.

Chapter 15

THE KING COUNTY squad car arrived eight minutes after Mrs. Berkeley's call. Officer Somners quietly questioned Mr. Berkeley in the living room while his partner, Renton, went to investigate the Walters residence.

Mrs. Berkeley would not let Somners interrogate Terry.

Lying with his head on her lap, his half-closed eyes fixed on the ceiling like a drug addict, he was in no shape to answer questions. The last thing he needed was to relive the events of the past half hour.

A second squad car arrived behind the yellow rescue vehicle. Somners excused himself and went outside.

The volunteer paramedics waited until the youngest officer, Danny Glitz, finished taking photographs of John's body, before enclosing it in the black body bag and wheeling it on the collapsible stretcher to the back of the rescue vehicle.

It was not easy to get all of John Walters zipped into the body bag.

Mr. Berkeley watched them lift the stretcher into the truck. He had killed men before, in North Africa during World War II, but never someone he had known. Although he knew he had had no choice, it didn't make him feel any better, especially when he thought about the boy. He should have stopped him before he got through the hall. He regretted that as much as he did killing Walters.

A dark blue Cadillac Seville drove up behind the rescue vehicle. Berkeley recognized it immediately. It was Doc Bishop.

Although he was only fifty-seven, Bishop looked as if he was in his late sixties. His eyes had thick pouches, like pita-bread pockets, and his heavy-jowled cheeks had the puttylike thickness and varicose veins of a heavy drinker. His nose looked like a walnut. For almost thirty years he had been a general practitioner on the island. Until fifteen years ago, he had had the only clinic. It was still the closest thing Vashon had to a hospital.

"Looks a little snookered," Danny said to one of the paramedics as he set his camera in the trunk of the squad car.

The paramedic grabbed the young cop's arm and scowled. "Watch your mouth, kid. Until you know what you're talking about."

Bishop immediately walked up to Renton and Somners. Renton was as white as a bowl of flour and his breath was sour. Must have puked his guts out, Doc concluded.

He had been informed of the situation on his car phone. He knew about Terry and his father. And that Officer Renton had gone to check on Mrs. Walters. He surveyed the damage around Berkeley's door. From the amount of blood and specks of flesh, he knew Walters had been hit by a shotgun blast at close range.

Officer Somners was questioning his partner about Walters's wife.

"I hope the kid didn't see it." Renton wiped his chin. "He must have used that sledgehammer on her."

"Jesus." Somners winced and looked at the doctor. "Mr. Berkeley said he came at them like a raving maniac, Doc. Said he was already covered with blood before he shot him. I figure he must have killed his wife, then come after the boy."

Bishop hurried to the back of the rescue vehicle. The paramedic opened the body bag.

"Take him back to my clinic," Doc said, examining the mouth and eyes. The paramedic nodded and zipped the bag back up.

MR. BERKELEY WAS RELIEVED to see his old friend. Doc Bishop sat next to him on the living room sofa.

"It's not your fault," Doc reassured him. "Do you need anything?" He opened his tattered black leather case.

"I'm okay, Doc. Considering." Berkeley watched the squad car and the rescue vehicle drive to the Walterses'. "What happened to..."

"She's dead."

"I guess I knew that." Berkeley turned away from the window. "What could have caused him to go berserk like that?"

"I don't know, Harry. We'll have to wait for the autopsy."

"You're holding something back, aren't you?"

Bishop slid closer to his friend. "Tell me about it."

"He was a wild man, Doc. His eyes seemed to be on fire. He couldn't speak. Only scream. Real guttural. He looked like he was in severe pain. And he was salivating!"

"Could be rabies." Sitting back, Bishop rested his black bag up against his belly like a shield. "But if it was, he should have had preliminary symptoms severe enough to have come to see me days ago."

The two old friends sat together in silence as Doc Bishop pieced the events into chronological order. He had found it was always easier, at first, to deal with a death analytically and keep his clinical perspective as long as he needed it. Harry Berkeley was afforded no such luxury. Doc Bishop patted his friend's knee and arose from the sofa.

"How's Martha?"

"She's taking care of the boy." Berkeley looked across the room at the shotgun leaning against the wall. "He saw it, Doc. All of it."

Bishop nodded. "You did what you had to do, Harry."

The window was open in the master bedroom. Mrs. Berkeley sadly smiled as the doctor entered. Outside, two police officers were talking.

"There hasn't been this much excitement on the Rock in years," one said. "Not since old man Kronker caught the Farswell twins with his daughter."

"Three DOAs in one weekend," the other commented. "That's a record."

Bishop closed the window. Mrs. Berkeley lifted Terry up into a sitting position against her shoulder.

Bishop slowly waved his hand in front of Terry's eyes. No response. He waved again, closer to his face. The boy blinked. Mrs. Berkeley quickly glanced at the doctor.

"It's a good sign. He hasn't shut off completely." Bishop turned Terry toward him. "Terry? I want to take you to my clinic. Is that okay?"

Terry shook his head no.

"Where do you want to go?"

The boy's eyes shifted down. "Nick's."

Ten minutes later, Doc Bishop carried Terry out the back door. He kept well away from the front of the house.

"How's he doing?" Officer Somners asked quietly.

"As well as can be expected." Terry dug into Bishop's soft chest to hide from the policeman. "He wants to go over to his friend's house. A Nick Lockton. They live over on the west side."

"You're kidding." Somners was stunned. "That's the place that was..."

"I know," the doc interrupted. "I've already called Mr. Lockton. It's all set. But I'd appreciate a ride. Terry needs to hold on for a while."

JAMES LOCKTON was standing in the doorway when the squad car pulled into his driveway. Dr. Bishop gently handed Terry to him. He had given the boy a sedative on the ride over.

Mrs. L. and Nick were waiting by the stairs.

"I'll take him." Mrs. L. opened her arms.

"What's wrong with him, Daddy?"

"Tomorrow, Nick." Lockton patted his son's head.

"We'll take good care of him, won't we?" Mrs. L. coaxed.

"Sure. We're buddies." Nick followed her upstairs.

Lockton introduced Stone to Dr. Bishop and Officer Somners.

Stone thought Bishop and Somners looked shaky. But Lockton looked far worse. His face was drawn and gray. His eyes kept ricocheting from person to person, like a racquetball in volley.

Bishop addressed Lockton. "I understand John Walters was a close friend."

Lockton clenched his jaw to keep back the sickening tidal wave beating against his throat. "Yes, he was."

"I have no record of his having any mental...ah, disorders. Do you know if..."

"He was one of the most stable men I know."

Lockton looked at Stone, then back at the doctor. Stone knew what Lockton was thinking. He had the possessed look of a dying man burdened by a mortal sin.

Bishop approached Lockton. "I'm sorry about John and his wife. I liked them both, too. Very much."

Lockton nodded and turned away.

"Do you know what caused him to go—" Stone was keeping a careful watch on Lockton "—crazy like that?"

"It's difficult to say, but ..."

"But what, Doctor?" Stone prodded.

"But it could be rabies."

Lockton rapped his knuckles against the wall. Stone patted his shoulder sympathetically, but Lockton shrugged it off. He knew the gesture was only meant to impress Bishop and Somners.

The fury in Lockton's eyes was poisonous.

He was well acquainted with the kind of mental and physical suffering John must have gone through, if it was the extract. He had watched it for the past three months in the rat cages.

He prayed he was wrong.

Maybe it had nothing to do with rabies or the stolen extract. Maybe this was all just some horrible coincidence.

Realizing how much he hoped it was some kind of mental instability, and not the extract, filled him with loathing. What a horrible thing to wish. But given the alternative ...

Lockton faced Dr. Bishop. "There's something I think you—"

"How do you test for rabies, Doctor?" Stone quickly interrupted. "Can you do it at your clinic?"

Lockton glared at Stone and marched across the room into the kitchen.

Bishop couldn't help noticing the intense interplay between Lockton and Stone. There was something combustible about it, something hostile and threatening

Lockton remained in the unlit kitchen until he had regained control of himself.

"The preferred postmortem method of rabies diagnosis is the IFA," Bishop explained. "The rabies immunofluorescent antibody procedure. The skull must be opened and the tissue from the brain stem, hippocampus and cerebellum removed and sent to the state lab."

"There are newer tests," Lockton interceded, reentering the room, "that are quicker and easier. Detection of IFA-stained impressions of corneal epithelium. Or skin biopsy. Or isolation of the virus from saliva."

"I've read about some of those new antemortem techniques." Bishop was surprised by Lockton's expertise. "I didn't expect you to have such a working knowledge, Mr. Lockton. Do you have a special interest in rabies?"

"As a matter of fact, I do." Lockton met Stone's warning glance with cold disdain. "So does Stone."

Stone walked between Lockton and the others. "I don't think we need to..."

Lockton brushed him aside. "Our firm, BIO-GENTEX, has a contract to develop leukocyte interferon, to be used in conjunction with rabies antibodies as a possible vaccine. We also produce HIRG, the hyperimmune rabies globulin injected in nonimmunized bite victims. It's expensive, but we're working on ways to make it cheaper."

"You're the molecular biologist." Bishop scratched the dry skin on the edge of his bald spot on the back of his head. "I've heard of you. You got a complete genetic engineering lab here, haven't you?"

"That's right." Lockton didn't want to wait for the county or state medical examiner to perform the standard IFA test. It could take all day. He had to know what had killed his friends...*now*. If they shipped the body to the Board of Health lab in Olympia, they would only diagnose for the presence of rabies in John Walters's brain. Lockton needed a blood sample to determine whether or not it was the mutant strain. "I can perform the skin biopsy and the saliva test in my lab."

"I don't think that will be necessary," Bishop said. "The state medical examiner can take care of it. We'll need family consent or the Examiner's written request for an autopsy."

Officer Somner's radio crackled. He went into the hall and unhooked it from its belt case.

"Joe, get back over here," he was told. "Quick. And bring Doc Bishop."

The three men quickly circled around the policemen.

"What is it, Bobby?" Somners inquired, surprised by the urgency in his partner's voice.

"It's the Harpers. Two doors down. They've locked their daughter in the basement. Seems she just attacked her little brother with a carving knife."

Somners glanced over at Bishop. "We gotta go, Doc."

Lockton helped Bishop put on his coat as Stone opened the door.

"I've changed my mind. I think it's imperative we do the autopsy immediately," Bishop said to Lockton. "Are you sure you want to volunteer your lab?"

Having John's body brought to his laboratory for testing was the only way he could get a blood sample. It had to be done, no matter how much it disagreed with him.

"It's the quickest way," Lockton answered. He started to follow Bishop out to the car. "There's something else I think you should . . ."

Stone tugged him back toward the door as the two men got into the car.

"What were you going to tell him?" he asked quietly, his teeth clenched like a ventriloquist's.

"The other residents on the beachfront south of Cowley's Landing have to be warned. I know for a fact that the Walterses and the Harpers shared the same spring-fed well. I don't know how many others might . . ."

"We still don't know it was the extract."

Lockton tried to circle around him, but Stone blocked his path.

"Don't play me for an idiot," Lockton growled. "We know, all right."

Lockton caught up to the squad car as it backed out onto Cove Road. Stone ran up behind him as Bishop was rolling down the window.

"The Walterses and the Harpers had the same well system. It might be the connecting factor. Until the water can be tested, I'd suggest you contact all the houses on that beachfront. Find out who else is on the same well system. Tell them not to use their water. Don't drink it. Don't wash in it. Don't..."

"What does the water have to do with it?" The request made no sense to Bishop.

"What are the chances that they were both bitten by a rabid animal without the authorities being notified? And what about the disease's preliminary stages? The symptoms should have warranted medical treatment before now. It doesn't make sense. Something's wrong. There has to be another connecting factor somewhere."

"And you think a rabid animal might have crawled into their well and infected the water? Through its saliva?" Bishop thought the theory was a little farfetched. "Enough saliva in a small puddle could infect an animal. But an entire well system? There wouldn't be an ample concentration of the virus to..."

"It's worth checking. Something has to connect the two. If it is rabies, we shouldn't overlook any possibilities."

"All right, I'll look into it." Bishop started to roll up the window.

Lockton grabbed the top of the glass. "Send someone with water samples from the Walterses' and the Harpers'. Also, take saliva samples from all the residents who have the same well system."

"How can you possibly test water for rabies?" Bishop asked.

"With low magnification, I'll check for bullet-shaped rhaddoviruses. Once located, with the scanning electron microscope magnification at ×75,000, I can recognize the rabies virus. Like I said, I've worked with it before."

Bishop wasn't sure that was possible, but he knew Lockton's reputation and didn't feel qualified to argue.

"We gotta get going, Doc," Somners insisted.

"I'll bring over the samples," Bishop conceded. "I can assist with the tests. Somners will contact the paramedics. They'll bring the body to your lab." Bishop glanced up at Lockton. "You sure you want to do this? I know he was your friend and..."

"Someone has to." Lockton let go of the window and backed away. He did not look forward to the task ahead. As soon as the paramedics delivered John Walters's body, he would have to take a blood sample and examine it under the S.E.M. It had to be done before Bishop returned from the Harpers' with the samples. Only the mutation could travel and breed in the bloodstream.

Then he would know whether his nightmare about the wolves was beginning to come true.

Chapter 16

"I'D PUT ON MY MASK, just to be safe," Lockton suggested. Stone quickly took one from the cabinet.

"You still shouldn't have said what you did to Bishop," Stone reprimanded, slipping on the mask. He had been accusing Lockton of jeopardizing the status of the project ever since Bishop and the cop had left. Lockton was fed up with his calloused tunnel-vision. Two people had died, a teenage girl was probably infected, and all Stone could think of was project security.

"And you shouldn't have mentioned the well as the possible contaminant. Or that you had a sizable working knowledge of rabies. We don't even know if it really is the extract. What if it isn't?"

"Then you have nothing to worry about." Lockton reached toward the zipper on the body bag, but pulled back.

"And you shouldn't have volunteered the lab. The less attention we draw to ourselves the better."

Lockton took a deep breath and unzipped the bag. "It was the only way to get a blood sample."

Walters's gray, blood-spattered face stared up at the ceiling. Lockton closed his friend's dead eyes.

Stone quit arguing. He knew what it was like to examine someone you cared for in a body bag. He had insisted on identifying his son's body as soon as it had arrived back in the States. A distant chord of sympathy momentarily plucked his heart. The sudden emotional lapse irritated him. He had no pity for scientists.

As he unwrapped a syringe, Lockton kept reminding himself that this was only a lifeless carapace. John Walters no longer existed, at least not in this body. His soul, his life spark, whatever it was that had made him a unique, living individual was gone. It was not John. It was just a body.

He withdrew the blood and began preparing samples for the S.E.M. Stone gave him a wide berth. He did not want to get too close to anything that might contain the living extract.

While Lockton inspected the samples in the S.E.M., Stone paced the main laboratory. A half hour later, he returned.

"Well?" Stone asked.

Lockton walked over to the aluminum table and stared at his dead friend.

"It's the extract."

"I'll get Harrison and Schraeder. Everything goes," Stone said. "The hell with chronological order or separating your other research or coordinating photos. We can do that in Texas. We've got to get all traces of the project out of here in case..."

"You bastard." Lockton spun around and pointed a quivering finger at the body bag. "That was my friend. His son's upstairs in shock because of what he did to his mother. There's probably others who are infected and there's no antidote. Once they've ingested the contaminated water, nothing can reverse it." Lockton tore off his mask. "This could just be the beginning. Have you even considered that?"

"That's why we have to move everything," Stone said.

It was all Lockton could do to keep from going for Stone's throat with a scalpel. He ripped off his surgical garb and started for the door.

"They have to know the truth. Before more innocent people die."

Stone bounded across the room. Before Lockton could react, he had bent his arm behind his back and yanked him away from the door.

"You tell them nothing, Doc. Not one fucking thing. I'll do anything I have to, to maintain project security. Anything. Do you understand what I'm saying?" Stone's mouth was an inch from Lockton's cheek. His breath steamed against his neck. "You may be willing to risk your ass. But are you willing to risk your son's? Or Miss McGuire's?"

Lockton struggled to break free and Stone pinned him against the wall, twisting his arm higher.

Lockton grunted. "They have to be warned."

Stone added a choke hold. "You've done that already. Bishop said he'd tell the other residents on the same well system not to use their water until it was tested. You can't save anyone who's already infected. It's too late for that. The rest will be warned. That's all we can do now, anyway."

When Lockton quit struggling, Stone released him and cautiously backed away from the wall. Lockton turned, massaging his elbow. Stone's eyes were as hard and sharp as diamond drill bits.

His message had been clear. Lockton had no doubt Stone was capable of anything, even harming Nick, if he thought it was necessary to ensure the project's secrecy.

"We have to warn the residents with adjoining well systems," Lockton insisted. "If the virus has contaminated a water table that feeds a number of wells..." The thought of the ensuing holocaust overwhelmed him. "After I test the water samples from the Walterses' and the Harpers', they'll know at least one well is infected. That will warrant the continued testing of other wells." Lockton returned Stone's unblinking stare. "We have to do it."

"As far as Bishop's concerned, we don't even know if Walters had rabies yet."

"The other tests will prove it."

"Okay. I'll go along with that." Stone looked into one of the moving boxes stacked under the center table. "I'll get Harrison and Schraeder down here to move these before Bishop arrives."

Lockton took out an individually wrapped syringe, some cotton balls and a small bottle of alcohol.

"What's that for?" Stone asked. "I thought you were going to do those other tests."

"I have to do this first."

Stone began to drag the stack of boxes toward the door. "Do what?"

"Take a blood sample from Terry."

STONE MET SCHRAEDER and Harrison in the basement den and explained the situation.

"How bad is it going to get?" Harrison asked, scratching the long scar that followed his jawline.

"No way of telling," Stone answered.

"How's the doc taking it?" Schraeder looked over Stone's head at the lab door.

"Not good." Stone drew his associates together by the pool table. "I want a close eye kept on him." Stone pulled them closer. "We can't trust him. Not any more."

"What about surveillance?" Schraeder asked. "We can't move all that equipment, too?"

"The Company can take care of that later." Stone looked at Schraeder. He was glad he had persuaded him to come in with him on this. No matter what, his back would be covered. "One more thing. Keep an eye on the kid, too. We don't want our insurance policy wandering off, now do we?"

JAMES LOCKTON turned off the S.E.M.'s cathode ray tube. He had inspected enough samples of Terry's blood to have reached a definite conclusion.

When he entered the main lab, he felt as if he had just stepped into a morgue. John Walters's face protruded from the open folds of the black plastic body-bag like the head of a dead moth imprisoned in its cocoon. He lightly put a hand on the body's chest.

"Your son's clean," he consoled his friend, and himself. "Terry will be all right."

WHEN DOC BISHOP arrived at the Harpers', the para medics had already bandaged Danny Harper's arm. It was a shallow, two-inch wound that hadn't required stitches. The paramedics had done a good job. So had Officer Renton. He had already gone into the basement and wrestled the knife away from the Harpers' daughter. With one of the paramedic's help, he had been able to strap her into a straitjacket.

Mrs. Harper, however, was hysterical. Her husband had been trying to comfort her, but the sight of her daughter being led to the squad car in restraints was just too much.

Outside, Officer Renton dabbed his cheek with a bloody towel. While he had been grappling with the knife, the girl had bitten off a chunk of flesh under his right eye.

"Let me see that." Bishop pushed Renton's hand away.

"It's nothing." Renton looked stoically over at his partner.

"I wouldn't say that." The doctor took a strong antiseptic from his bag and washed it thoroughly. "You'll need shots, too."

"Not three weeks in the belly. No way."

"We're not even sure it's rabies. If it is, they have a new serum. Five shots over three weeks. In the arm."

While Doc Bishop took saliva samples from the Harpers, the Berkeleys and the residents of the four other houses on the small beachfront, Officer Somners bottled samples of their tap water. The sky was beginning to lighten as he packed the samples in the back seat of his Seville. He was worn out. The thought of retiring crossed his mind again. It did every time he was up half the night. He liked to picture himself puttering in his garden with no pressure from schedules or late-night emergency calls, and a large, cold drink in his hand.

A double vodka martini would taste good right now, he thought, wishing he'd brought his silver flask along.

"What do we do with the girl?" Renton asked.

"Someone will have to take her to the mainland. To Harbor View." He checked his watch. "They can catch the six twenty-five ferry."

"If it is rabies, will the inoculations still work on her?"

Bishop unbuttoned his lined windbreaker as he watched the ferry heading to Fauntleroy. "I doubt it."

"Then what can they do?"

"Treat her symptoms."

"But she won't live?"

"Not at this stage. Not if it's rabies."

"Poor kid." Renton opened the door for Bishop. "Jesus, some night, huh?"

"It's not over yet." Bishop sighed. "I want you to report to the clinic. We'll start you on your first shot."

"Ah, come on, Doc," Renton pleaded. "I don't need..."

"You want to end up like John Walters?"

"No, I don't think I'd . . ."

"Then stop by."

6:52 a.m.

BISHOP PULLED UP his surgical gloves and adjusted his mask. Lockton set the saliva vials on the counter. Each one was marked with adhesive tape and a name penned on. He placed the six water samples in a row behind them.

"Did you find out if anyone else shared their spring system?" Lockton asked, taking the skin samples out of the ultracold freezer. He had scraped them from the posterior region of John Walters's neck, just above the hairline. Each sample contained at least twelve hair follicles.

"Just the two. The Harpers and the Walterses." Bishop felt alien in the lab. He was a family practitioner: part psychologist, part doctor. The state-of-the-art lab techniques and testing procedures were a whole other world. It was impossible to keep up with the constant outpourings of new medical, biotechnical, chemical and pharmaceutical data. He watched Lockton closely, trying to follow the procedures. "The other four houses shared a well system, drilled down to a deeper water table."

Maybe it was contained, Lockton thought; to the one spring-fed well. If they were lucky, it would all be over soon. Quarantine the spring-fed well until the virus half-life broke down—and that would be the end of it.

"I've already prepared the skin samples and introduced the IFA serum. Normally they should be frozen for at least four hours before staining, but in emergency situations, ten minutes can give satisfactory results. We don't have known rabies positive and negative control slides for comparison purposes, but I think we can still determine infection. When we illuminate the sample with ultraviolet light, the rabies antigen in the cretaneous nerves surrounding the hair follicles should appear bright green or yellow-green." Lockton put one under the microscope. "Look."

Bishop bent over the viewing lenses. The tiny fluorescent green spots around the large hair follicles looked like distant campfires viewed from a high mountain ridge at night.

"The corneal impressions are ready as well." Lockton took the slides out of an airtight vacuum container. "I've etched around the impressions to clarify them."

Lockton exchanged the skin biopsy with one of the corneal impressions. Bishop adjusted the focus. He viewed a darker fluorescent green patch in a pitch-black background. It looked like an isolated galaxy in deep space.

"I knew it." Bishop sighed. "It's rabies. No other virus drives its host into such a fury in order to transmit itself to another host animal."

Lockton's intestines coiled like a ball of water moccasins. He did not want to ponder the inescapable pain and horror of rabies. If he let himself begin the acidic process of self-recrimination, he wouldn't be able to work. He must continue to function, quickly and efficiently, until all the tests were completed and the virus had been isolated. He owed the island that. And the Walterses. And the Harper girl.

"What I want you to do, Dr. Bishop..." Lockton led him to the saliva samples. He took out corresponding cell-culture slides and put one by each saliva sample. "Is inoculate these cell cultures with the saliva samples. We'll check for intracellular viral antigen with the IFA technique after sufficient propagation time. In other words, we'll see if any of the saliva samples are infected by trying to breed the possible rabies virus in the cell cultures."

"That could take days, couldn't it?"

Lockton knew his mutation bred at a velocity far surpassing normal clinical rabies. If any of the other residents were infected, their saliva would probably be overflowing with the virus by now. But he couldn't explain that to Bishop.

"It might." Lockton picked out the bottle of water from the Walters house. "But it might only take hours. It depends on the stage of the disease. Hopefully, none will show any signs of rabies. If you think it's necessary, we could also do skin biopsies and corneal impressions on the other beachfront residents, especially Mr. and Mrs. Harper and their son."

"I think we should. It'll be quicker."

Lockton knew it probably wouldn't be. "All right. After you inoculate the cell cultures, go back and take the samples from the residents."

Lockton talked Bishop through the procedure just to make sure he didn't miss anything.

"Good job," Lockton assured him, as he finished the last sample. "While you're gone, I'll start testing the water."

Bishop tossed his surgical garb into the disposal unit. He was impressed with this young scientist. Maybe the island rumor was true. Maybe he was a genius. The way he worked in the lab reminded Bishop of a good surgeon.

"By the way." Bishop put on his windbreaker. "I called the county Board of Health. They're sending an official out to the island. He's going to meet me at my clinic around ten."

"Send an officer over with the other samples. I can take care of the rest of the tests alone. Hopefully I'll have the results by the time he arrives."

Bishop stopped at the door. "What kind of research are you doing here, anyway?"

Lockton stiffened. He put the water sample down. "I'm working on isolating the gene or genes that cause cystic fibrosis."

"You're not involved with the rabies immunization serum your company is researching?"

"I haven't done any lab work on it for over a year."

Bishop nodded and left.

Lockton turned back to the counter. He hated lying. Lies were a sacrilege to the laboratory, to his view of Science and Truth.

Now the lies were breeding inside him and he felt contaminated.

How long? he wondered. How long before he could find and administer an antidote to the infection growing inside him?

Chapter 17

10:56 a.m., March 18, 1986

"I RECOMMENDED quarantining the Walters beach-front area," Bishop said. He had driven over to Lockton's immediately following his brief meeting with the county Board of Health officials. "We also have volunteers checking the neighborhood for reports of possible rabid animal sightings."

"Good." Lockton poured two mugs of strong Starbuck coffee and led Bishop out the front door. He did not want anyone to hear this conversation. "I tested the tap-water samples from the Walterses' and the Harpers'. They were both contaminated. The other four houses weren't."

"But how can that be?" Bishop asked, shocked. "Rabies doesn't spread in water."

"I don't know," Lockton lied. "Maybe a rabid animal crawled into one of their aboveground water tanks. But at least it appears to be contained."

"The health officials are sending an officer over to pick up all the samples and your test results. They're to be sent to the state lab in Olympia. I'm afraid they don't think you're qualified. When I told them you were testing water samples, they became extremely skeptical."

"Damn." Lockton slapped the top of Bishop's Seville. In the past three days, he had slept only an hour and a half. He was running on caffeine, adrenaline and willpower. He smelled dank and acrid, like mildewed clothes.

"I tried to explain your technique, but..."

"I've also completed the first tests on Mr. and Mrs. Harper and their son," Lockton interrupted. This was the part he dreaded. The words stuck in his throat like dry bread. "All three are infected."

The silence that followed was almost physically painful.

"Then we'll have to isolate them individually," Bishop concluded. "At Harbor View."

Lockton nodded, watching the storm front move in from the southwest. "It should be done immediately. Once they reach the furious stage, they'll become insanely violent. Like John."

Bishop scratched his head, brooding. It was still extremely hard for him to believe.

"What's wrong?" Lockton asked.

"They won't buy it. Until they've run their own tests, they just won't believe us."

"Us?" Lockton asked, grateful to have someone on his side.

"I worked with you in your lab. You know what you're doing." Bishop checked his watch. "But we're going to have a difficult time convincing the county experts that four people have almost simultaneously contracted furious rabies without any of them reporting animal attacks or earlier symptoms. They deal with postexposure prophylaxis regularly. Average a hundred possible rabies bites a year. But a multiple case, all in or near the final stages..." Bishop shook his head. When he put it like that, he became skeptical as well.

But he had seen them.

And it was true.

A squad car squealed into the driveway. Officer Somners hopped out.

"Doc, it's Mrs. Harper." He took a second to catch his breath. "She's real sick. Arms partially paralyzed. Fever. Vomiting. As soon as the sedative wore off, she started screaming. Her son's getting sick, too."

As he got into his car, Bishop glanced back at Lockton. "I guess they'll have to believe us now."

"One more thing." Lockton leaned into the window. "We need maps. Maps of Vashon's well systems, underground streams, water tables, aquifers, lakes, rivers, everything."

"That's getting a little carried away, isn't it?"

"Maybe," Lockton said.

THE OLD WOMAN had been alone for ten years. She was eighty-two. She still tended her chickens and the two goats who kept the fields around her house trim. Her three dogs, all over eight years old, were her closest companions. Four other farm mutts usually roamed with them in a peaceful, if mischievous, pack. She always kept a bag of bones from the butcher in the refrigerator, in case her dogs brought over their friends.

Seven dogs were eagerly awaiting her by the abandoned hog pen next to the barn. She gave each one a bone, so there would be no fighting, and filled the shallow trough with fresh water from the hose.

Between growls and gnawing, the dogs eagerly lapped up the cold, clear water.

12:45 p.m.

Doc Bishop's clinic was a half mile south of town, below the old Nike base on the hill above the main highway. The storm had moved over the island, but it was still clear above Seattle.

Bishop introduced Lockton to the two county health officials in his office. Lockton had just finished testing his own well water (it was clean), when he had gotten the call to come to the clinic.

Bishop had said it was urgent.

"We sent all your samples by helicopter," Mr. Roy Quincy, the taller official, with the expensive suit, announced as Lockton sat at the small conference table. "They're being retested now."

There was a plate of cold cuts and bread in the center of the table. Bishop pushed it toward Lockton, but he declined. He doubted he could keep it down.

"The state Board of Health is sending a team over," Quincy continued. "I'm afraid there's been some new developments."

"It's worse than we imagined, James," Bishop injected. The solemn mood at the table frightened

Lockton. "Two hours ago, a Vashon resident named Steve Kestler leaped to his death from a building in downtown Seattle. The people in his office said he was foaming at the mouth and acting like a madman. When they tried to subdue him, he jumped."

Lockton silently squeezed the table corner to keep from trembling.

"And there's been two incidents on the island," Quincy added, checking his notes. "The police found a Ralph and Ellen Johnson dead in their kitchen. It appears Mrs. Johnson had attacked her husband with a large pair of scissors. Before he died, he crushed her skull with a two-foot flashlight. The police were also called to Maury Island. A construction worker went berserk. Started beating a bulldozer with a lead pipe. It took four men to restrain him. They said he was screaming and trying to bite anyone who got near him."

"There was also a problem on the ferry to Tacoma," the other official filled in. "A teenage boy barricaded himself in the men's room. The police said he was acting totally insane, ripped the urinal right out of the wall."

"The dead couple's bodies have been sent to Olympia for testing." Quincy continued. "The others are in the security ward at Harbor View. Our lab has completed the test on John Walters and the Harpers. They're confirming your results, Dr. Lockton. It's rabies."

"What worries us the most is the fact that the jumper, Kestler, lived in a group of tract houses a mile south of the Walters beachfront area," the other official broke in. "And the construction worker lived east of town, a good half mile south of Kestler."

"To be honest, Dr. Lockton—" Quincy lit his pipe "—we were rather skeptical of your theory about the water supply. But now..." He slowly looked around the table. "We just don't know what to believe. There's no precedent for this. None whatsoever."

Lockton glanced at Bishop. "Did you get the maps?"

Bishop reached behind his chair. "The mayor collected these for us."

"We're sending water samples from all the areas in question to our lab." Smoke drifted out of Quincy's nose. "Our people have decided to try direct immunofluorescent antibody tests on random samples of specific organisms in the water samples. After reviewing your S.E.M. photographs, they believe the virus could somehow be breeding in the water's microorganisms."

"Rumors are already spreading," the other official said. "If we don't do something quick, a mass exodus could commence soon."

"And we can't allow that," Quincy stated emphatically.

Lockton took the maps from Bishop. "I want water samples from all the locations sent to me as well."

"We were hoping you'd say that." Quincy put his notes aside. "We've begun taking samples from adjoining areas, too. They're already en route to your lab."

Lockton stood up, walked to the door and turned. "Contact the media. Vashon residents have to be warned. Until all the water on the island can be tested, no one is safe."

Quincy's coffee mug stopped halfway to his lips. He put it aside suspiciously. "We don't want to panic the island, Dr. Lockton. Mass hysteria and all that. Bringing the media in might do more harm than good."

"Better a frightened population," Lockton stated, opening the door. "Than a rabid one."

1:53 p.m.
STONE'S WINNEBAGO was parked in Lockton's driveway, its back end facing the path that wound around the south end of the house to the basement. Schraeder handed the last box of computer disks to Harrison. Behind him, Lockton waited with the steel box containing the virus extract. He wanted to put it in the Winnebago himself, to be sure of its delivery.

As Stone slipped the box into a specially built wall cabinet, a squad car pulled up beside the Winnebago. Harrison backed up onto the grass, his thumbs looped over the back of his belt, on either side of his holstered Ruger .357.

Somners popped out of the car. "Here's the new well samples, Mr. Lockton. They're all marked."

"Thanks, Joe. How's your partner doing?"

Somners pulled Lockton away from the others. "He says he feels fine, but I keep catching him wincing. His left hand seems to be cramping up on him. And he's been sweating constantly."

Lockton gazed at the ground. Somners sensed his apprehension.

"He'll be okay, won't he?"

Without answering, Lockton took the samples to the basement. When he returned, Lockton was relieved to see the squad car was gone. He had hoped the inoculation would work on Officer Renton because he had been infected by a bite, not through ingestion of the contaminated water.

Now he knew better.

His mutation was even more virulent than he had thought.

Nothing would stop it once it was introduced into its host.

Harrison walked around the house carrying a bulging, black plastic trash bag over his shoulder.

"Here they are," he announced, swinging the bag up into the Winnebago like a sack of dirty laundry. "Individually bagged and sealed for freshness."

"Jesus, Harrison." Schraeder grimaced, jumping in to help store the dead rats.

Stone ambled over to the driver's side of the cab. Lockton followed and leaned against the open door.

"My papers," Lockton requested.

Stone unlocked the metal briefcase on the seat. "Here's the contract with BIOGENTEX." Lockton unfolded it. "We've given you a five-year extension, like we agreed. That's another half a million. The insurance policy is paid through March of 1997. It will cover all your son's medical bills. The mortgage is paid. The sales slips for all your lab equipment are in there, too. We keep our word, Doc. It's all yours now.''

Lockton put the documents into his jacket pocket. After four years, he felt there should be something said.

But he couldn't think of anything.

Except the analogy of rats abandoning a sinking ship.

Chapter 18

THE HIGHWAY wound down the hill in multiple S-turns to the Vashon Heights dock. Stone figured he would be a couple of minutes early for the two-ten ferry. There were no other cars in line for either Seattle or Southworth. Even the building at the end of the dock, a waiting area with vending machines and bathrooms, was deserted.

The wind off the Sound was chilly. It was beginning to drizzle. To the north, a supertanker was passing Alki Point on its journey to Tacoma. The white, top-heavy ferry, *Tillicum*, put its engines in reverse as it approached the dock.

A squad car suddenly pulled up in front of the Winnebago. Another parked beside the corner building at the end of the dock.

An officer approached Stone's window. "You'll have to leave, sir."

"Why?" Stone asked.

"I'm afraid the ferries are no longer in service, sir."

"But there's one docking right now." Stone pointed at it.

"That's not for public use. The State Board of Health has quarantined the island. No one's allowed on or off Vashon."

"But I've got important business," Stone objected, scrutinizing the ferry. There were two eighteen-wheel semis, four paramedic vehicles, a number of ambulances and at least ten King County squad cars parked inside it.

"Sorry, sir. But if you don't leave immediately, I'll be forced to put all of you in custody. This area must remain cleared for official use."

Cursing under his breath, Stone pulled the Winnebago around and started back up the steep, winding hill.

2:15 p.m.
"STILL CAN'T GET THROUGH," Mrs. L. said indignantly. She had been trying to call Terry Walters's grandparents. "All off-island lines have been jammed for the last two hours."

"Wonder what the hell is going on?" Alex was helping Mrs. L. tidy up after a late lunch.

"Don't ask me." Mrs. L. put Terry's uneaten sandwich back into the refrigerator. The boy hadn't spoken since he woke up at noon. "No one tells me anything. And you know how Mr. Lockton hates to be disturbed when he's down in the lab."

"Can you watch the boys for a while?" Alex looked in her purse to make sure she had her checkbook. "I have to go uptown for a few things."

"I've been watching them for years," Mrs. L. replied. "Without anyone's help."

Alex forced an insincere smile. "Do you need anything from town?"

"Well..." Mrs. L. retrieved a two-page grocery list from the drawer next to the refrigerator. "Since you're going."

The only car Alex saw on her way to town was Stone's Winnebago. He turned into Cove Road just after she pulled out onto the highway.

As she entered Vashon, she noticed there were no cars in the library parking lot or the small four-shop mall. The only vehicles on the road were police cars. More than she had ever seen on the island before. Other than uniformed officers, there wasn't a single pedestrian strolling the three-block town of Vashon.

Pulling up to the four-way stop, a policeman stepped out onto the street and waved her over. She turned right into the bank's parking lot and got out.

As she perused the empty streets, it suddenly hit her. All the stores were closed.

Except for the police, the entire town was deserted.

"What's going on?" she asked.

"Town's off-limits, ma'am," the officer said, eyeing her suspiciously, one hand tapping his holster.

"Why?"

"Sorry, ma'am." He had been warned to approach all civilians on the road with extreme caution, but this redhead was far too gorgeous to be rabid. "You'll have to return home. Vashon's closed. State Board of Health's orders."

"THAT WAS FAST," Mrs. L. chided as Alex walked into the kitchen empty-handed. Stone and his two associates were in the living room conferring in hushed voices.

Alex quickly told her what had happened. "I'm going down to tell James."

As she began to open the basement door, Stone blocked it with his foot. He pointed to the porch. Harrison slid open the glass door as Stone and Schraeder escorted her outside.

"We've got to get off the island," Stone informed her.

Harrison leaned against the glass, keeping an eye on the basement door.

"They're setting up roadblocks along the main highway," Alex reported. It was beginning to drizzle. "Two of them stopped me on the way home from town."

"Jesus Christ." Stone stared at the rusty old tugboat pulling a flat barge toward Tacoma. "You said there was a small airport on the island."

"A couple miles south of here."

"Is there a back way?"

"Down the old west-side highway and up Bank Road."

"Good." Stone glared at Schraeder. "Get the extract and the two boxes X-ed with red tape. Put them in McGuire's trunk." He looked back at Alex. "Give him your keys."

"But I have to talk to James. I want to tell him what's..."

"No time." Stone grabbed her purse and fished out her car keys. "You're to take us to the airport. Then come back and move the Winnebago. Park it up that dirt road across the street. There's a large, sealed plastic bag in the camper. Bury it in a pit of lime and store the other boxes in the surveillance room."

Alex reached for her purse. So much was happening. So much she didn't understand.

But orders were orders.

And Stone was her direct superior.

"After that, make up an excuse to stay at your house. Tell them you're sick. P.M.S. Whatever. I want continual surveillance maintained until the quarantine is lifted. As soon as it is, a team will be sent over to dismantle all your equipment."

Harrison turned from the glass. "Doc's coming up."

LOCKTON WAS SURPRISED to see Alex return from the porch with Stone and the others. She immediately began to tell him about the town and the quarantine.

"I know," Lockton interrupted. "Bishop just called. I've got to go down to the old La Fiesta restaurant by the ferry dock. The State Board of Health is setting up a control center there."

"James." Alex started toward him. "What's going on?"

"A rabies epidemic. Like nothing anyone's ever seen before." Lockton sneaked a furtive glance at Stone. "I've got to run. The meeting's already started."

A CONFERENCE ROOM had been installed in the restaurant's small banquet facility. The main restaurant had been emptied and transformed into an office network. Police officers were stationed on the dock and in the small restaurant parking lot.

Doc Bishop introduced Lockton to Dr. Thomas Green, the man in charge of the quarantine. Five other state Board of Health officials were seated at the conference table.

"I'm glad to have you with us," Green said, shaking hands. He was thin and bald, in his early fifties, with thick black-rimmed glasses that magnified his darting eyes. "As a microbiologist, I'm familiar with your earlier work. But you seem to have disappeared from the scientific arena the last four or five years."

"I've been working for a private firm."

"Doing what?"

All eyes in the room turned toward Lockton. It took him a moment to realize there was nothing accusatory in his question, only professional interest. Lockton told him about his search for the causatory gene for cystic fibrosis.

"My son has C.F.," he concluded.

That ended the conversation.

The meeting resumed.

"DOES THE EPIDEMIC have anything to do with the project?" Alex asked as they drove up the long dirt road to the airport. Stone had already called ahead and rented a small Cessna.

"I brought you in for security and surveillance, not as a technical adviser," Stone said. He glanced through the rear window as they circled around the corrugated metal hangar next to the small two-room office. Eight privately owned planes were tied down in the grass field beside the only runway.

"I think the situation warrants an answer," Alex demanded.

Stone lit a Camel. "I don't."

Six years ago, when she had first joined the CIA, she had been an ardent admirer of Richard Stone. He was a man to be emulated. And a personal friend of her father, who had been one of the best operations officers in the CIA during the height of the Cold War in the fifties and early sixties. Although he was retired now, the Agency still called her father in on special consultations.

It was Stone, after some prodding from her father, who had finally gotten her out from behind a desk and into the field as one of his security agents on the new top-secret weapons project.

Because of her gratitude, she had been able to overlook his increasing disdain toward humanity in any form. Her father had told her about Stone's son's death, and she understood his bitterness. But when he had turned against Lockton, when his disgust for the man she loved became so repugnant as to be inexcusable, she could no longer tolerate it.

What had hardened her even more was the fact that Stone not only seemed to enjoy her newly acquired animosity, but also had constantly tried to propagate it over the past year.

Alex remained in the car, while Harrison and Schraeder pushed the plane out of the hangar. In a few minutes, Stone returned from the office.

"Plane's been checked out. It's ready to fly," Stone said, climbing into the pilot's seat. Harrison opened the car trunk and carried the two boxes to Schraeder, waiting in the door of the plane.

Alex approached the wing as Stone went down the preflight checklist.

"It's the weapon, isn't it?" she insisted. "The intruder did get in."

Stone glared down at her like a maximum-security prison guard intimidating a young new convict. "You're overstepping yourself, McGuire. Leave it alone."

The plane taxied out onto the runway and turned south to face the wind. As the whine of the engines increased, Alex got back into her car.

Suddenly she spotted two National Guard jeeps and a two-and-a-half-ton truck racing toward the airport. One jeep spun in front of her, while the other two vehicles sped across the field toward the runway.

The Cessna was quickly picking up speed for takeoff, when the big truck swerved onto the runway, fifty yards south of the oncoming plane.

Stone cut back the throttle and braked as hard as he could without jamming the nose into the ground. There wasn't enough runway between the truck and the plane to either stop or take off.

"Brace yourselves," Stone cried, turning to the right.

The plane tilted up on one wheel and the edge of the right wing caught the grass. The Cessna lurched around in a sudden 180-degree turn and stopped, nose down.

Eight soldiers jumped from the back of the truck and surrounded the plane. As Stone climbed out, the man from the office came running up the field.

"What the hell are you doing?" he screamed at the sergeant in charge. "Look at my plane! Who's going to pay for this, for Christ's sake?"

"Gentlemen," the sergeant said, reholstering his .45. "By order of the governor of the State of Washington, no aircraft is allowed to take off or land from this airport, until further notice."

THE HEAVY DRIZZLE was like a low fog over the Sound. Through the picture window behind Green, Lockton kept watching the blurred outline of a supertanker heading north on its journey back to the Orient. Two hundred yards past the dock, the ferry, *Tillicum*, was starting its journey back toward Fauntleroy Dock, on the mainland. It had just discharged a full load of National Guard vehicles. Lockton figured there had to be at least a hundred and fifty troops seated in the metal-ribbed, canvas-hooded beds of the passing trucks.

"The legal statute 43.20.050," Green continued, addressing Lockton, "gives the state Board of Health supreme authority over all official personnel, including local, county or state police." Green noticed that Lockton's attention was still being diverted by the onslaught of National Guard personnel and equipment. "Dr. Lockton? You asked about the chain of command during a quarantine?"

Lockton glanced over. "Sorry."

"The governor has the authority over the National Guard, however. They're considered state militia under the Fourth Amendment. However, Governor Bunano has assured me he will cooperate in any way necessary. As you've noticed, one of the two companies from the First Battalion 150th Infantry out of Auburn has arrived. Roughly 240 men will be at our disposal. The other half arrived from Tacoma forty-five minutes ago. They've already moved up from the south end. They're setting up an operations center at the old Nike base. We'll also be using that facility as our emergency hospital and security ward." Green rose from the table abruptly. "I guess that's it for now."

Lockton remained seated. He was still stunned by what he had heard at the meeting.

Six more residents had been taken into custody as possible rabies victims. Three others had been reported, but not confirmed. There was also a number of reports about a possible rabid dog pack running loose on the island. At least two attacks had been confirmed. A family's poodle had been killed, as well as two sheep on the east side, a mile north of the KVI tower. The heads of the dead animals were now en route to the state lab.

More reports of possible victims—sudden bizarre behavior of neighbors or family, violent outbursts, strangers seen lurking in the woods—were coming in all the time.

The island's in a state of siege, Lockton surmised. Like a medieval castle facing the plague.

One of the officials carried a cardboard box to the table.

"One more thing," Green announced before Lockton and Bishop could get out the door. "These are reflective stickers." He handed two to Lockton and Bishop. "Put one on your back window, one on your windshield. They'll give you official status so you can get through the roadblocks."

Green walked to the parking lot with the civilians. "I want to thank you for opening your lab, and your expertise, to us. I'll send over two lab techs to help you with the testing."

Lockton nodded. "When will your lab finish its tests on the first two water samples?"

"Soon, I hope." Green turned up his coat collar against the rain. "If they do confirm your theory..." He wiped his glasses off with a handkerchief. "And I hope they don't. But if they do..." He glanced up the steep hill toward town. "All hell will break loose."

Suddenly a jeep came squealing down the road and pulled up in front of Green.

"Sir?" A sergeant got out. "We apprehended four civilians at the airport. Three men—a Mr. Stone, Harrison and Schraeder. And a woman, a Miss

McGuire. The three were attempting to take off in a rented Cessna. The woman drove them there.''

"Excuse me," Lockton interceded. "But those three men are associates of mine from Texas. Miss Mc-Guire is my neighbor. I doubt they even knew the island was quarantined."

"We've kept them at the airport," the sergeant said. "Colonel Smith ordered me to report to you."

Green looked at Lockton. "I think we'll let this one incident slide, Sergeant."

As Lockton put the stickers on his Mazda, he couldn't help wondering why Alex would have volunteered to take them to the airport.

It had seemed obvious, from the second they met, that Alex couldn't stand Stone.

Maybe she just wanted him the hell out of the house and off the island, he concluded.

Chapter 19

2:45 p.m., March 18, 1986

NICK TURNED the television channel to an old movie Mrs. L. had said was wonderful. It was called *Gunga Din*. Nick didn't recognize any of the stars she said were quite famous. He was willing to give it a shot because she said it was very similar to Spielberg's *Indiana Jones and the Temple of Doom*. With a cult of bloodthirsty murderers, the British Army, elephants and an Indian bugler, it might be all right—for an old black-and-white movie.

While Nick and Mrs. L. tried to interest Terry in the upcoming movie, Alex drove into the driveway with a National Guard jeep escort.

As soon as the jeep left, Stone ordered Schraeder to take the extract and the box containing the most vital computer disks to the wall safe in Alex's basement surveillance room. He and Harrison were to guard it in alternate eight-hour shifts.

"We were lucky," Stone said, as he and Alex walked around the house to the porch. It had stopped drizzling, but the sky was still dark and threatening. The wind had picked up and it was getting chilly.

"I bet James had something to do with it." Alex leaned against one of the supporting poles under the porch.

"Your good old fiancé to the rescue," Stone said sarcastically.

"I told you two months ago, I wanted out of this assignment," she reminded him. "But you refused my request."

Stone returned her cold, challenging stare. "You hadn't finished your assignment."

"That wasn't the reason." She pushed off the pole. "You just couldn't stand the fact that I fell in love with him. A scientist. Like the man you blame for your son's death."

Stone flinched inside, but didn't show it. He hadn't known she knew.

"Don't flatter yourself," he said, watching Lockton's buoyed boat rock against the waves. Suddenly he slapped his thigh. "Jesus, why the hell didn't I..." He walked under the porch and pulled Alex toward him. "Get Harrison. Tell him to pick up Schraeder and the boxes."

"Why?"

Stone grinned triumphantly. "We're going for a cruise."

"THIS OLD FLICK'S pretty good," Nick announced. Terry was sitting on the floor next to him, staring at the TV like a pyromaniac possessed by a newsreel of a forest fire.

Nick nudged his best friend. Terry swayed, but kept staring. He still wouldn't speak.

Nick understood why his friend had chosen to go away for a while. But if he stayed away too long, could he come back again? That was why Nick had decided to keep talking to him, no matter what.

He didn't want Terry to get lost on his journey back.

"It was originally a poem," Mrs. L. told the boys.

"They made a movie from a poem?" Nick was flabbergasted. It was the craziest thing he had ever heard of.

"What do you think of it, Terry?" Nick asked. His friend remained mute. Mrs. L. set a tray of home-made chocolate-chip cookies on the coffee table behind them. They were still warm from the oven.

The movie was suddenly interrupted by a local newscaster. "We interrupt our regular programming to give you a special announcement. The State Board of Health has quarantined Vashon Island," the newscaster declared. "I have been requested to inform the residents of Vashon not to drink, wash, or in any way use their water. Do not eat any meats or fresh produce grown or purchased on Vashon. Bottled water and food are being distributed by the National Guard at this very moment."

Nick looked up as his father came in through the kitchen. "What's quarantine mean?"

"In a minute, Nick." Lockton sat on the arm of the sofa. The two lab technicians watched from the hall.

"Because the number of off-island calls have jammed the system, the State Board of Health has closed all long-distance capabilities in order to ensure open lines for official use. If you have any questions, or if you want to report any unusual situation in your neighborhood, or if you are feeling ill, please dial this emergency number."

The phone number flashed on the bottom of the screen.

Mrs. L. sat down in her favorite leather chair, stunned. Nick was enthralled with the drama of it all. The movie had resumed, but no one was watching.

"Quarantine means you have to stay where you are and not leave," Lockton explained. "Which means don't leave the house. Got that?"

Nick wasn't impressed. "I guess, but..."

"No buts about it."

"What about Thor?" Hearing his name, the dog trotted over to his master's side. He had been lying by the porch door, watching the crows on the lawn. "He's got to go to the bathroom sometime."

"Don't let him wander beyond our property. As soon as he's done his business, he's to come back in. Okay?"

"Okay." Recognizing the seriousness in his father's commands, Nick knew better than to argue over details.

After showing the two techs to the lab, Lockton walked outside to the back porch. He needed to be alone. His mind kept rewinding mental tapes of his laboratory rats tearing each other apart. A wave of nausea turned his belly inside out. He tried to stabilize the attack with a series of deep breaths.

Everything he had wanted to do for humanity, all his idealistic dreams as a brilliant, if naive, young biologist had now been crushed. In the past three days, he had felt as if he were being slowly buried alive, stone by stone.

It had all seemed so logical four years ago.

They had promised him the best medical attention money could buy for Nick. Being able to work at home, he would also have considerably more time to be with his son. Not knowing how long Nick had on this earth, that had been extremely important to him.

It was the only decision he could have made, he told himself; the only realistic option left open to him.

And now innocent people were dying.

Lockton leaned over the railing and vomited.

The boy genius—a mass murderer by proxy.

When the dry heaves shook him again, he felt two warm hands hold his shoulders. He held his breath, but couldn't control the spasms. Alex stationed herself directly behind him to block any possible view from the living room.

"What is it, James? Please? Talk to me?"

His body convulsed again. She pressed herself against his back and hugged him. Tears rolled off her chin onto his neck. They felt like the first cold drops of rain from the approaching storm.

"Let me help you, James. Please?"

He curled down over the railing, and gagged. Cocking his head, he looked up out of the corner of his eye at her.

"I just need to eat something," he said. "Lack of sleep. Too much coffee."

"I told you before you're a terrible liar," she said, stroking his hair.

Suddenly he saw Stone and his men emerge from the woods by the beach. They were carrying the extract and another box. Harrison unclipped the dinghy's line from the cement block.

Lockton forced himself to stand erect. "What the hell do they think they're . . ."

"James." Alex clutched his arm and pointed north. "Look!"

Three gleaming white Coast Guard cutters plowed around the north end of the island and headed south. One ship, a sixty-footer, veered off to the west and circled back. The other two stayed on course, following the island's coastline.

A few moments later, four police vessels followed. As they passed the cutter, one turned east toward Lockton's boat.

Harrison tugged the dingy back up the beach to the cement block. Schraeder quickly disappeared back into the woods with the two boxes.

The police vessel pulled alongside Lockton's craft and one of its men hopped onto the bow. Unhooking the boat from its buoy, he tossed the line to the stern of the police vessel.

"My God, they're towing your boat away!" Alex exclaimed.

Stone and Harrison started back up the hill at Lockton's house.

Lockton tucked in his shirt and wiped his chin. "Do I look all right?"

"A little pale, but . . ."

"Be back in a second."

He went into his study and called Bishop.

When he returned, Stone was on the porch with Alex.

"They're blockading the island," Lockton announced. "To enforce the quarantine. All private vessels on the coastlines are to be towed to the harbor and anchored."

All along Vashon's coastline, residents were watching the official armada encircle the island. Like a mechanized chain strangling their last lifeline to the mainland, the twelve-ship blockade began to tighten its noose around the island. Lockton thought there was something absolutely terrifying about the ships' smooth, impersonal precision.

Vashon had suddenly become an island prison.

"We've just been sent to Alcatraz," Stone muttered contemptuously.

Chapter 20

AFTER ALEX HAD MADE Lockton some canned chicken noodle soup, using bottled water, he rejoined the two technicians in his lab. Within an hour, they had tested seven more water samples. The first three, taken from the Kestler, Brighton and Johnson residences, tested positive. Lockton had expected that. To his relief, the samples brought in from the four systems in closest proximity to the three infected wells all tested negative.

While the technicians prepared the next group of water samples for the electron microscope, Lockton called Green. He hoped that the virus was contained in the four infected water systems, all located on the northeastern to eastern third of Vashon, within a seven-square-mile area.

"Perhaps the Walters spring is linked to an underground source that feeds a tributary leading to the other three sites," Lockton told Green. "Either that, or an entire water table is contaminated. None of the infected wells have been from one of the two main aquifers. That's something positive, at least."

"Why do you think they have to be connected?" Green asked.

"It's the only logical conclusion. If a rabid animal somehow got into the water system, through a well, a stream feeding an underground source, whatever, and that system fed into others..."

"I see what you mean, but..." Green paused, trying to figure out a way to phrase his next statement without insulting Lockton. "My people don't think your tests can be considered conclusive."

"They're wrong," Lockton argued. "I know what I'm doing. Even if it is unorthodox, I'm telling you we're finding the virus, in quantity, in those well systems."

"Hold on," Green said, "I've got a call on the other line. It's the lab in Olympia."

Green switched lines and Lockton waited.

"Lockton?"

"I'm still here."

"They've completed the IFA on a specific cluster of one-celled organisms in the water samples from the Walterses and the Harpers wells."

"And?"

"They found granular clusters of immunofluorescent antigen among the cells. In other words, you were right. The water is contaminated with the rabies virus."

"Then we've found the cause."

"Yes, but how did the water become contaminated in the first place? And how does the virus sustain itself in that environment?"

"At least we know what we're up against now."

"But what if it's not limited to those four sites? What if it's still moving underground? How do we stop it?"

"I'm not sure we can."

"I'll be honest with you, Lockton. I was hoping my people would disprove your theory. This entire situation has us completely baffled. I'm afraid we're going to have to start treating this as if it were an entirely alien virus."

"Got to get back to my testing," Lockton snapped. "Sorry I was right."

"So am I."

4:06 p.m.

"I WANT OFFICIAL STATUS," Stone said.

Lockton was sitting at his desk in his study. He had just locked the pistol Alex had given him in the top left drawer. The last time he had shot a pistol was out in a farm field in eastern Washington. He was nineteen, popping a tin can with a .22 until it was out of range.

"It's not up to me." Lockton put the key into his pocket.

"And I need a car. Your Subaru station wagon will do. But we'll have to get those reflective stickers." Stone examined the small brass sculpture, coiled like two snakes making love, on the corner of the desk. Lockton had bought it because it reminded him of the DNA double helix.

"We'll have to go to Control and ask Dr. Green." Lockton was relieved when Stone put his sculpture back down. He didn't like him touching anything he loved.

"I'm a colleague of yours from BIOGENTEX. I'll need official status to transport samples, check water systems, et cetera." Stone smiled confidently. "He'll buy it."

Lockton had gone to the study to be alone after his conversation with Green. He was extremely annoyed at Stone's intrusion. "What have you done with the extract?"

"It's in a safe place."

"Where?"

"Secured at our agent's."

It was the first time Lockton had heard there was another agent on the island. "I didn't know you..."

"Since the day you moved in."

"Where was he when the lab was broken into?"

Lockton was hoping that would dissolve Stone's smugness. He knew he had to be worried. Stone wanted off the island and he was stuck. Like everyone else, the extent of the quarantine had taken him completely by surprise. And he knew Stone found it personally contemptible to be like everyone else. He had to be seething under that shell of complacency, Lockton thought.

Stone closed the door and returned to the desk. "How long will the water remain contaminated?"

"I'm not sure. I told you the half-life wasn't completely developed yet."

"Estimate." Stone was in no mood for ambiguities.

"If we're lucky. Three to five days. If not, two weeks. Three and a half—maximum." Lockton slowly twirled his ivory letter-opener in front of his mouth like a cob of corn. "Samples of the water and from infected victims, both deceased and alive, are en route to the rabies laboratory at the Center for Disease Control in Atlanta. Green's chartered a Lear jet."

Stone's eyes tightened. He walked around the window behind Lockton. "Will they be able to determine whether or not the virus has been...tampered with?"

"It would be almost impossible to prove, beyond a shadow of a doubt, that the genetic alterations were laboratory induced." Lockton put down the letter opener. "Some might suspect. If they're good. And I know the people in Atlanta are. The big question, however, is how did the water become contaminated in the first place?"

Stone looked across the street at the Winnebago parked in the dirt road. "So let's give them an answer."

"How?"

Stone walked back to his chair and sat down. "With one of the rats."

LOCKTON INTRODUCED Richard Stone to Thomas Green. Stone said he was a molecular biologist from BIOGENTEX. Green told him he was glad to have him on board.

"We're going over to Colman Road," Stone said as they walked out of the control center to put two official stickers on Lockton's Subaru. "We traced two of the infected wells back to a possible underground source." Stone spread a map out on the roof of the car. "They seem to converge here, on the west side."

"You think another tributary might be the original source of contamination?" Green asked, following the water routes Stone had pointed out.

"It's worth looking into." Stone folded up the map.

"I want you to take two guardsmen with you."

"That won't be necessary," Stone said.

"There's been a confirmed sighting of a possible rabies victim in that general vicinity. Male. Six feet. Approximately 180 pounds. Dark hair. In his forties. A patrol spotted him from the road, but lost him in the woods."

"We'll be careful," Stone assured him. "No need to take two of your men from their duties just to baby-sit us."

Conceding the point, Green asked one of his assistants to bring out a two-way radio.

"It's on the right frequency. If you see anything, call in immediately. And get the hell out."

4:52 p.m.
STONE AND LOCKTON were stopped by two National Guard roadblocks on their way to Colman Road. The late-afternoon light was quickly waning. The wind had died down. The woods were still and silent. Nothing moved. Even the birds seemed wary of the approaching darkness. The trees, the vegetation, the rocks—all seemed unnatural, like plywood props on a huge movie set, waiting for the cameras to give them life.

It began to drizzle again. They parked the station wagon by the mud slide where the fatal accident had occurred. The crater below looked like the aftermath of a volcanic eruption.

As he descended the steep cliff, Lockton could swear he smelled the stench of burned flesh again. He chewed a piece of sugarless spearmint gum to take away the sudden sickness in his belly.

Stone hauled a large briefcase out of the car and carried it down the muddy hill.

"I've already combed every inch of this area," Lockton called up to him.

"So comb it again."

Standing in the spot where the car had burned, Stone carefully scanned the ground. The drizzle quickly turned to rain. Neither had brought any rain gear. Stone watched the thin rivulets begin to flow down the hill.

As Lockton checked the unburned woods below the wreckage, Stone climbed back up the cliff and traced each small river's descent, looking for breaks or a sudden unexplainable end to the stream's course. He saw nothing that would suggest an opening to an underground pool. He decided to focus his search around the impact areas where the car had flipped.

Just below the second indentation, a large split stone jutted out of the slide area. Stone climbed up onto its precipice and watched the rain. The open fissure acted like a funnel. He squatted down and took out his flashlight.

Shards of clear plastic reflected yellow-blue against the gray rock. Stone put on a pair of rubber gloves and began collecting all the broken pieces with a pair of tweezers. He sealed them in two extra-strength Ziploc plastic bags, one inside the other.

"Hey, Doc!" he called from the precipice. "I got it."

Lockton was in the woods, kicking aside long-leafed ferns. Stone's voice startled him. The patter of rain in the silent primordial forest had been hypnotic. He edged around a thorny ridge of blackberry vines and stepped out into the clearing.

Something snapped behind him.

When he heard the swish of branches, he ducked and spun around.

Something ran behind a big red alder to his left. Lockton kept his eyes pinned on the tree as he backed up the clearing.

"Come on, Doc," Stone called impatiently.

Lockton put a finger to his lips and pointed down at the alder. Stone reached inside his jacket for his P220 SIG-Sauer .45.

"Did you see him?" Lockton whispered as he reached the rock.

Stone checked the clip. "He's keeping low to the ground, using those big ferns as camouflage." He took the radio out of his jacket. "I'll notify Control."

Green told Stone there was a jeep patrol less than two miles away.

"They should be here in about five minutes," Lockton estimated.

"Good." Stone knelt on the rock and opened the briefcase. "That should give us enough time."

He opened a double-sealed plastic bag. The stench of rotting meat suddenly permeated the area. Wheezing in disgust, he removed the decaying, gray-white rat and laid it on the rock. Holding it down with the sole of his boot, he clenched the back left leg and snapped the bone in two. Lifting it up by its pink, wormlike tail, he lowered it into the crevasse.

"There." He peeled off the rubber gloves, put them in another plastic bag and stuffed it into his jacket. "The rat was rabid. Broke its leg when it fell into the crack. Got wedged in and couldn't get out. The rain washed over it into the pool underneath it." He showed Lockton the waterline on the rock. A pool was slowly beginning to rise around the rat. "That must lead down into some kind of underground stream." Stone grinned. "Now they have their answer."

Lockton had to admit it was ingenious. Taken from his lab, the rat was infected with the identical virulent mutation—the perfect solution.

How the rat became rabid and what caused the virus to mutate would probably remain unanswered, questions the medical profession would debate for years to come.

A National Guard jeep pulled up behind the Subaru and three soldiers descended the hill. Stone quickly slipped his pistol back inside his jacket and pointed down at the alder. The freckle-faced, redheaded corporal nodded and led his men along the wooded perimeter of the slide area.

"I think we might have found the source of contamination," Stone radioed Control.

"Don't touch anything," Green said. "I'm coming out."

Stone glanced at Lockton. He was watching the guardsmen. They were approximately forty feet from the alder. Thick underbrush, ferns and blackberry vines stood between them and the tree. The corporal directed one man uphill and one down past the tree.

Suddenly a hollow cry, like a bobcat's, shattered the soft drumming of the rain. The man stood up. His face was bruised and muddy.

"Come on out," the corporal coaxed. "We won't harm you."

Only the man's head and shoulders were visible. The corporal checked his men's positions. They were approximately thirty feet from the tree. The corporal's position marked the apex of the 120-degree triangle they formed around the alder.

The man ducked back into the ferns.

"Sir? Please step into the clearing. This is not a request. It's an order."

The corporal slowly approached the tree. He could tell his men were nervous, so he moved with restraint. His men kept their M-16s aimed at the spot where the man had disappeared.

Suddenly he popped up again and his face contorted.

"Sir, we . . ."

A shotgun blast blew a hole through the underbrush and lifted the corporal back off his feet. With their M-16s on automatic, the two privates sprayed the man with a barrage of lead, cutting him apart as if with a chain saw.

Lockton ran down the hill. The two guardsmen approached the tree with new clips in their rifles.

The corporal was still alive. His blurry, startled eyes searched Lockton's face.

"I didn't...see it," he gurgled as blood poured from his mouth. "I should have... seen it."

He died just as Green's car pulled up to the cliff.

The guardsmen gently laid the corporal by the side of the road. The younger soldier was crying in his comrade's arms. Green, Lockton and Stone walked to the edge of the cliff to let them mourn in private.

A yellow rescue truck arrived less than a minute after Green. Two paramedics took a stretcher down to retrieve the other body. They had to bag it before strapping it on the stretcher. The left arm and leg were completely severed.

Lockton watched as they loaded both bodies into the back of the truck. Numb, empty coldness swept through him like an ice storm.

"What did you find?" Green asked as the rescue vehicle and the jeep pulled away.

Stone had seen Lockton turned inside himself. He was used to him looking like a caged animal—sharp-eyed, agitated, ready to leap at the first opening. This new look—calm, detached, empty—made him wary. Stone lit a cigarette and led Green down to the rock, never letting Lockton escape his peripheral vision.

"There's an underground stream here that leads back to a water table on the east side. Look at this." Stone aimed his flashlight at the partially decomposed rat, then pointed out the pool rising around it. "It could be nothing, but I think we should test it."

Green stood up, still breathing through his mouth. "Rodents can contract rabies, but it would be extremely unusual."

"This entire situation is extremely unusual," Stone argued.

Green gazed down at the crevasse. "I'll take it up to the Nike base. There's a chopper there that can fly it to Olympia."

Chapter 21

NICK STOOD IN THE GARAGE as Thor trotted across Cove Road into the woods. Since he was a puppy, the dog had refused to defecate on his own property.

It was raining steadily.

Suddenly a deer dashed across the dirt road up the hill. Thor shot after him like a hawk swooping down on its prey.

"Thor! Come!" Nick yelled, dashing out into the rain.

Thor was already long gone. When it came to chasing deer, the dumb mutt was deaf, Nick thought.

He hurried across the street and started up the muddy road. Dad had warned him about letting Thor out of his sight and now he was probably halfway up to the main highway.

Just better find him before Dad gets home again, he told himself, increasing his pace to a slow jog.

5:08 p.m.
TWO TWO-AND-A-HALF-TON National Guard trucks parked on Cove Road between Lockton's and Alex's. Four soldiers hopped out of the lead truck and walked down to the beach. Alex watched them from the liv-

ing room as they split into two two-man teams and marched off in opposite directions.

Shore patrols, she surmised. Taking Lockton's binoculars, she scanned the point four miles to the south. Every mile or so, she spotted another two-man patrol, walking the beach.

Not much fun during high tide, she thought. When there was no beach at all. They'd have to battle their way through the dense foliage, laced with blackberry thorns, above the shoreline.

The doorbell chimed and Alex headed for the door. Mrs. L. got there first. Two guardsmen were standing in the rain, boxes of food and bottled water in their arms. Mrs. L. told them to put them in the hallway.

"We'll need more than this," she estimated. "I've got ten people to feed, you know!"

"Yes, ma'am." One guard tipped his helmet as they started back to the truck for more supplies.

"Nick!" Mrs. L. called up the stairs. "Come down and help put this food away."

As she began to sort through the cans and boxes, Alex began putting the bottled water in the cabinet under the kitchen sink.

"Nick?" Mrs. L. called again.

"I'll get him." Alex bounded upstairs, only to find Terry alone in Nick's room. She checked the first floor, then the basement. "He's not in the house."

"And neither's Thor," Mrs. L. added. She hurried out to the driveway, with Alex close on her heels. "Have you seen a little boy out here?" she asked the two guardsmen returning with more boxes.

"No, ma'am," the polite one answered. "Better not have wandered off, though. There's patrols out in those woods. Been a reported sighting of a possible rabid victim, a female in her forties, somewhere in this vicinity. Word just came that Corporal Stokes was killed. The patrols are pretty jumpy now."

"He's probably gone after the dog," Alex said, trying to soothe Mrs. L.'s anxiety, after what the guard had said. "You know how he likes to chase anything that moves."

The guardsman put down his boxes and adjusted his belt. "Hope he ain't with the dog in the woods. Patrol's got orders to shoot stray animals on sight. 'Cause of that dog pack."

"I'd better go after him." Alex started up the driveway, but the other guardsman blocked her path.

"Can't do that, miss," he said. "All residents are to be confined to their homes. Anyone found wandering around outside will be arrested. State Board of Health orders. Sorry."

"THERE'S SOMETHING up there by those rocks under the cliff," the point man reported, wiping the rain from his face.

Corporal Riggins waved in his other two men. "What is it?"

"Not sure." The point man snapped a twig off the bush between them and began to peel away the bark. "But I think it's a dog."

"Spread out," Riggins ordered, taking his M-16 out from under his parka.

The patrol began to approach the small cliff.

Suddenly they heard the low, warning growl of a large dog. The patrol halted. Two knelt, rifles aimed toward the sound.

Thor stepped out from the rocks into a small clearing. The thick forest was heavily shadowed in the darkening twilight.

"There it is," the point man whispered.

All rifles immediately zeroed in on the target as they waited for the order to open fire.

Suddenly another shadow flickered through the tall fir trees on the south side of the clearing.

"Jesus, it's the whole pack," one of the soldiers cried, stepping back.

Nick emerged from the shadows. "Darn you, Thor. I've been calling and calling and you . . ."

"Hold your fire!" Riggins screamed.

Nick spun around. Thor ran to his side and began barking at the intruders.

"Jesus," the point man muttered, rising from his knees. "I was this close to blowing the kid away."

WHEN LOCKTON AND STONE arrived home, Alex and Mrs. L. were pacing the garage.

One of the guardsmen had volunteered to go look for the boy and had just returned.

Stone waited for them to clear a stall before driving into the garage. Before Lockton could open the door, Mrs. L. had begun explaining the situation. Before she could finish, they heard Thor barking.

Nick was perched on the point man's shoulders. Thor was leaping in circles around him. The entire patrol was laughing uproariously as they crossed the street.

"Told you it drives him nuts," Nick said.

When he saw his father's stern look, Nick swallowed his laughter and asked to get down. Thor happily trotted into the garage beside his master.

"Dad, Thor took off and I . . ."

Before he could finish, Lockton snapped, "Go to your room! Now."

5:53 p.m.

"ARE YOU STILL UPSET?" Alex asked, walking across the porch behind Lockton. Mrs. L. was upstairs with Nick. His father had confined him to his room until further notice.

Stone and Harrison remained in the living room. Stone did not want to let Lockton out of his sight, especially after this latest incident.

The rain had let up and night was quickly approaching. The blockade vessels' lights shimmered white across the purple water.

Lockton turned from the Sound to face her. "Seven people are dead," he said suddenly. "Five are locked in security cells up at the old Nike base. Five others are dying of rabies at Harbor View in Seattle. Renton, the officer who was bitten by the Harper girl, has already reached the final stages of the disease. There are also three confirmed reports of rabid victims still at large, and what the hell do I discover when I get home?" He was almost screaming now. "Nick out wandering in a woods full of trigger-happy weekend warriors! You're damn right I'm upset."

"I'm sorry, James." She leaned against his chest. "I should have watched him more closely."

He wrapped one arm around her shoulder. Just feeling her against him was soothing.

"It wasn't your fault." He brushed the wet strands of hair back off her face. "Nick should have known better."

"Don't be so hard on him. He didn't . . ."

"Let me deal with Nick, okay?"

She nodded. "I was scared for him, too."

"The whole damn island's starting to go berserk." He hugged her closer. "An hour ago a farmer took a shot at a patrol across his field." He proceeded to tell her about the rat. He had just heard that Green had sent a well-drilling team to the accident site. Twenty feet below the rock, they found an underground stream. "Jesus." He stroked her hair. "It's going to be a long night."

"So what's the good news?" Smiling, Alex brushed his cheek with her forefinger.

"We've almost completed testing all the main water systems on the island. Those two lab techs are good. So far, only those original four sites, which we've already isolated, have tested positive. The rest are clean."

"Then it's not spreading."

"I hope not. We'll have to keep retesting though."

Alex was relieved that he was finally talking about it now. He had kept it bottled up far too long. She wanted to tell him that she knew the epidemic wasn't his fault. It was the man who stole the extract, and the people who had sent him, that were responsible.

But she couldn't.

She wasn't supposed to know.

It was becoming increasingly difficult to draw James out of his shell without giving away her true identity.

Suddenly she heard the sound of a small craft smacking across the waves. Spotlights from the blockade vessels crossed the water.

A twenty-foot pleasure boat, built for waterskiing, was illuminated in the spotlight's cross hairs. There were a man, woman and two children aboard.

"For God's sake, they're trying to run the blockade." Arched out over the railing, Alex watched in disbelief.

A bullhorn from the sixty-foot cutter blared, "Turn back. Cut your engines and turn back toward the island."

Stone and Harrison ran out onto the porch.

"Thought they towed all the boats away," Harrison said.

"Must have been in a boathouse. Not buoyed in the water," Lockton decided.

"They don't stand a chance in hell against those Coast Guard twin diesels," Stone said.

"This is your last warning," the bullhorn declared. "Turn back. And cut your engines."

The man steering the boat leaned over the wheel and increased speed. The bow shot up and the vessel started slapping across the waves like a skipping rock.

Two sailors armed with M-16s ran out onto the bow of the cutter. Automatic weapons fire echoed across the Sound. A line of waterspouts burst in front of the boat.

The vessel tilted into a hard-angled starboard turn and the two children tumbled across the narrow deck. Sinking into the trough of a wave, the boat slowed to a crawl.

A police vessel pulled up alongside it and herded it back toward the island.

"What would they have done if they hadn't turned back?" Alex asked, still shaken by the sudden burst of gunfire.

"Green said the Commander of the 13th District, a Rear Admiral Kelsey, is in charge of the blockade. The state Board of Health has no authority over it," Lockton said.

"But what would they have done?" Alex repeated

Stone slid open the porch door and glanced back at the water. "Anything necessary to incapacitate the escaping craft, I imagine."

"In other words—" Alex looked at the children spotlighted in the boat "—blow them out of the water."

Chapter 22

TAKING HER FLASHLIGHT from the kitchen drawer, the old woman walked outside and rang the bell hanging from the porch roof. Her dogs were trained to come when they heard it. She had already rung three times tonight and still the dogs had not returned. Disheartened, she walked out past the barn and shone her flashlight across the meadow into the woods near the creek.

Past the furrowed unplanted soybean field above the meadow, she heard the faint sound of barking and smiled.

Her family was finally coming home for supper.

One of the old woman's dogs momentarily recognized her scent. A sudden sharp pain in his head shattered the memory like glass. The insatiable craving for blood spilled into his veins like a shark homing in on a feeding frenzy.

The pack broke into an attack run across the field, down toward the barn.

The old woman happily waved her flashlight to direct them in.

6:22 p.m.

THE QUARANTINE MADE the national news on all three networks. Dan Rather described the situation as a severe outbreak of rabies. A body count followed: six dead, nine infected. No names were given until the state Board of Health could contact family members. It was unequaled in the country's history. There were unconfirmed reports that the virus was a completely new strain of rabies believed to have contaminated an underground water table by an as-yet-unknown source. The state Board of Health would only confirm the fact that it was rabies, nothing more.

During the news, Mrs. L. had made dinner for ten. She used only canned, bottled or packaged items brought by the National Guard to concoct a huge pot of spaghetti.

Leaving the dinner on simmer so her guests could eat when they wanted, she carried two sets of bedding from the upstairs hall closet down to the basement den. After making the beds, she knocked on the laboratory door to let them know dinner was ready when they were.

Lockton came out alone. "They still have to retest a couple of samples," he explained, slumping down onto one of the cots. "They'll be up in an hour or so." His head hung down on his chest like a dead weight.

"You've already made yourself sick once," she scolded, feeling his forehead. "You need to eat. You also need a shower. Desperately."

Her mothering was appreciated. Lockton smiled weakly. "Getting pretty rank, huh?"

"Like a wet mule."

He started to laugh, but his throat blocked with phlegm. He bent over and coughed until it cleared.

"You can't keep working like this." She wiped his cheek. "Look at you. It's cold down here and you're sweating."

"I'll be all right."

"I won't have it," Mrs. L. threatened. She yanked him up off the cot. "You're going to sit in the kitchen and eat. And I'm going to watch to make sure you do. After that, since you said our water is clean, I'm taking you to your room and running a hot bath. And if I have to, I'll toss your naked behind in the water myself."

8:25 p.m.

"YOU TAKE HAN SOLO." Nick placed the rubber toy replica of the *Star Wars* character into Terry's hand. Terry looked down at it uninterestedly. "I'll take Darth Vader. We'll pretend I've just found you on this planet." He ruffled the quilt into mountains. "Now you . . ."

The toy dropped from Terry's fingers. Nick glanced back at Alex. She was sitting on the corner of his bed. Thor watched from the floor. Everything he had tried today had failed to evoke the slightest response from his friend.

Terry was staying away too long, he thought. But he could hardly blame him. When he had tried to imagine his own life without Daddy, Mrs. L. or Alex, he had cried. And that was just pretend.

Earlier that day, before the quarantine, a policeman had brought over the Walterses' address book so
they could call Terry's grandparents. Terry's father's
parents had died three years ago. His mother's parents lived in northern Minnesota. Alex got through to
them, and they said they would take the next flight out
of Minneapolis. By the time they landed at the Sea-Tac
airport, the island had been quarantined and all un-
official long-distance calls to Vashon had been dis-
continued.

When Alex had told Lockton this, he had called
Green, who had one of his people page the airport.

They had left twenty minutes earlier, after calling a
reporter from the Seattle *Times*. When Green was informed of the reporter's struggle to get a call through
to the island, he realized the mistake he had made. He
shouldn't have allowed his people to page the airport.
There were hundreds of other concerned family
members all over the nation who were also trying to
get through to their loved ones. If Green made one
exception, he would have to let them all through.

Rumors and innuendo would spread through the
press and the public like food poisoning. And the
long-distance lines would be jammed again. The last
thing the governor or the State Board of Health
wanted was to panic the large urban populations surrounding Vashon. The hysteria that would ensue
would make the chaos on Vashon seem like a minor
family squabble.

Luckily, Alex and Lockton had decided not to let
the boys know about the call until they were sure the

grandparents could get through. That way Terry wouldn't be disappointed.

Nick put his *Star Wars* figures back into the toy chest by the closet. Terry walked over to the fish tank. He seemed mesmerized by the shimmering movement of the Congo tetra. Alex studied him curiously. It was the first time today he had moved on his own, without being led.

"That's one of my new ones," Nick announced, anxiously sliding next to his buddy. "Awesome, huh? Want to feed it?"

Terry pressed his face against the glass, absorbed by the fluid motion and the bright colors of the assorted fish.

Nick opened the Tetra-min box and sprinkled a pinch of food onto the water. "You remember how to do this?" Nick tried to hand the box to Terry, but he remained glued to the glass, as if his future was being foretold within the depths of the aquarium. Thor stretched and stood up to see what was so intriguing.

The serenity of the tank was broken by the introduction of the food. The feeding became more frenzied as the fish competed for the last few flecks.

Terry stepped back from the aquarium. His entire body started vibrating like an old washing machine. His jaw slackened.

It was not his future he was watching, but his past.

"Daddy!" he shrieked, covering his face. "Don't!"

Nick hugged him tightly. "It's okay, Terry. It's only fish."

Alex wrapped herself around both of them. What she had just seen in Terry's eyes had lanced her heart with anguish. As the boy shook violently against her breast, Thor tried to nuzzle in, but Nick pushed him away.

The scream had brought Mrs. L., Stone and Lockton running. Alex looked up at the crowd in the doorway.

"He was just watching the fish," she said.

Lockton squeezed through. "Doc Bishop left a bottle of sedatives, Mrs. L. They're above the refrigerator."

"And how am I supposed to reach them?" she asked, annoyed. Stone said he would get them.

Alex tried to put Terry to bed, but he wouldn't let go of Nick. Nick understood his insecurity and crawled into bed with him, their arms wrapped around each other like sleeping lovers. When Stone returned, Lockton retrieved a bottle of water from the hall bathroom. Stone shook out two pills and gave them to Alex.

Fifteen minutes later, Terry was asleep.

"You can let go now, Nick." Lockton gently ruffled his son's hair. Nick unraveled Terry's arms, and slid off the bed. Thor hurried to his side.

"It's time for you to hit the hay, too," Lockton said. Nick crawled under his own covers, grateful that the mist tent was still in the closet. He hadn't needed it for over a week. Alex remained on the corner of Terry's bed. The child seemed so peaceful, so serene in sleep. She hated to imagine what his dreams might bring.

"Daddy, why'd the fish scare him?" Nick fluffed his pillow into a small nest.

"I don't know, Nick." Lockton kissed his son. "I'm very proud of you. You've been a good friend to Terry."

"I don't know what to do, Daddy." Nick rolled on his side and looked at Terry. "I keep trying, but I can't get him to... notice anything."

"He needs time. It may not seem like it, but you're helping. You really are."

"I don't think so. The only time he's said anything was when he screamed."

"It may be a good sign, if it cracked the shell he's built around himself," Lockton conjectured.

Nick rolled over on his back, trying to understand. He couldn't quite fathom how, but if his dad said he was helping, he knew it was true. He sat up and hugged his father. "Daddy?"

"Yes?"

"You should get some sleep, too."

Lockton laughed as he laid Nick back down. "I will."

"Promise?"

He held up three fingers in a Boy Scout pledge. "I promise."

Alex joined Lockton at the door. "Sleep well," she said. "I love you."

"Me, too, Nick." Lockton smiled and reached for the light switch.

"Daddy?"

"What?"

"Could you leave the light on? Just for tonight?" He hated to seem like a baby, but he couldn't help it. "In case Terry wakes up and gets scared," he amended.

Lockton smiled. "Of course."

Chapter 23

SERGEANT MATT PATTERSON, normally a computer programmer employed by Boeing, led his fire team southeast across the open farm field. Intermittent blue-black clouds tumbled high across the night sky. Stars constantly flickered in and out of view. The silver-green quarter moon grinned at the island like a half-hidden psychopath watching his future victim.

Patterson scanned the edge of the woods with his infrared scope. He had joined the National Guard for the added income and the relatively safe excitement of part-time military excursions. One weekend a month wasn't much and the men he worked with in the First Battalion, 150th Infantry, were a good bunch. Not embarrassingly gung ho. Besides, as his wife often pointed out, he enjoyed playing soldier. When alone with her girlfriends, his wife described the inconvenience another way: "Once a month, I have my period," she would say. "And once a month, Matt has the National Guard."

This time, however, it was real.

His patrol's orders were to search out and destroy the rabid dog pack. Not an assignment any of the fire teams had relished. And certainly not a game. Especially at night.

His point man traversed the field toward the big barn behind the red farmhouse at the end of the long, tree-lined driveway. A light was on in the kitchen. Outside, a bulb above the barn entrance lit the area between it and the screened porch. From the field, they could hear the porch door flapping in the wind.

As Sergeant Patterson scoured the area through the orange glow of the scope, he rechecked the hill just north of the barn. There was something there. It looked like an upturned basket of laundry.

He directed his troops toward it. As they drew closer, he noticed the stench drifting up the field.

"Over here, Sergeant." One of his troops pointed at a muddy ditch in the middle of the field. A number of paw prints were embedded in it, all going the same way. "They were running, all right. See how far between the prints. How the back paws extend to the front. Six, seven dogs. Maybe eight."

The patrol cautiously marched across the field to the hill. The point man reached the north corner of the barn first.

"Sergeant, come quick!" he cried, sickened by the sight.

It was the old woman.

Or what the dogs had left of her.

9:15 p.m.
ALEX ENTERED the guest bedroom on the main floor across the hall from Lockton's study.

"Where's the doc?" Stone asked, closing the door behind her.

"Back in the lab." She walked over to the window. With the bedside light on, there was no view. Only blackness.

Having just showered, Stone was sitting on the corner of the bed, shirtless. A year ago, there wasn't an ounce of fat on his body. Now he had a considerable paunch.

"So what did you want to report?" he asked, putting on his socks.

"Over the last month or so, Nick has been seeing what he thought were neighborhood kids playing at the old Hobbit House up the hill."

Stone went to his suitcase and retrieved a turtleneck sweater. "So?"

"I don't think it was kids," she said. "I'm going up there tomorrow. Whoever broke in, had to have had the house under surveillance for quite a while." She waited until he had the sweater on before turning from the window. "He knew this place inside out. The alarm systems. Floor plans. Everything. And he had to have had keys, which he could only have gotten from inside the Agency."

"We're looking into that." Stone tucked in his sweater. "Personally, I'd rather know how he got through your surveillance in the first place."

"James asked me to marry him. I said no. We had a fight. I wasn't monitoring the house for the next hour or so, and..."

"I warned you not to get involved."

Alex crossed her arms. "We've already been through that."

Stone shook his head. "There's no need to go up there. He's dead. The extract's been moved. We'll find the leak from the inside."

Alex was surprised by his lack of interest. In her estimation, it was of the utmost importance to discover who the intruder was and who he worked for.

"I don't understand," she chided. "It seems to me..."

"That's right," Stone growled. "You don't understand. So let me explain. The last thing we need is to draw any more attention to ourselves. Especially after the airport incident. There's patrols all through these woods. I don't want you going anywhere. Your job is to stay here and keep the doc from going bonkers." Stone smirked. "Make him happy, so to speak."

The innuendo was obvious. Alex gritted her teeth and walked to the door. There was nothing more she wanted to say to him. Not after that.

"Remember who you work for," Stone warned as she opened the door.

She turned. "I'm trying to."

No matter what Stone said, she was going to the Hobbit House tomorrow.

She had the distinct feeling Stone knew more about the intruder than he let on.

But what?

What was the connection?

What was he hiding?

9:40 p.m.

PRIVATE MURPHY, the point man, kept a hundred feet ahead of Sergeant Patterson and his patrol. Murphy was a pipe fitter. His only love, besides his family, was hunting. He had been hunting the mountains of Washington, Utah and Montana since he was eight years old.

Now he was hunting a rabid dog pack that had killed an old woman.

Kneeling with his flashlight, he studied the chunks of fur caught on the broken underbrush in the forest south of the tree nursery on the knoll above the fishing dock. They were still damp with blood.

Suddenly he heard growling to the south. He flicked his light back at the patrol.

For the first time in his hunting career, Murphy was hoping to lose the quarry he was tracking. Stooping behind a bush, he peered toward the growling through his infrared scope.

The dog pack was devouring the carcass of a sheep in a clearing about forty yards directly east. He listened for his patrol. He would have felt more secure if he had heard them closing in behind him.

The big German shepherd—at least 140 pounds, he figured—suddenly tilted his snout up. Its bloody face snapped toward the bushes. He could see its eyes glow in the lens of the scope.

The point man felt as if he had on a shirt full of insulation dust as he watched the rest of the pack trace his scent. When he backed away from the brush, the pack's ears perked up like a dozen periscopes.

Starting at a trot across the clearing, the dogs soon broke into a gallop. Murphy began running and blowing the whistle for his patrol.

He knew they would be on him in seconds.

Still tooting the whistle, he turned, squeezed the trigger of his M-16 and fanned the rifle. The two lead dogs flipped backward as if the ground had been jerked out from under them.

Coming in from his right, the German shepherd leaped at Murphy's neck, knocking him to the earth. In an instant, the other three were upon him, ripping at his flesh like a school of piranha.

The patrol broke through the trees.

"Fire," Patterson ordered. "Dammit, open fire."

"But we'll hit Murphy," a guardsman objected, horrified.

The dogs formed a half circle in front of their kill to defend it from the intruders. Patterson's flashlight beamed across the point man's upper body. His neck had been eaten away to the spine.

The patrol opened fire. Bunched together, the pack was an easy target. The shepherd sidestepped around and charged the sergeant. Its teeth cut through his shirt. He batted it away with the barrel of his rifle and sprayed it with half a clip, rolling it across the ground.

As the patrol checked the bodies, Sergeant Patterson peeled back his torn shirt sleeve. Blood oozed from his arm. Stepping away from the others, he quickly tied a handkerchief over the wound.

He did not want his patrol to know.

Chapter 24

GREEN DRAINED the last of the coffee into his mug. It was cold. Doc Bishop stared at the eight red flags dotting the map on the conference table in the operations center. Each signified a civilian's death. Within the past hour and a half, two more had been added. The old woman and the unidentified body of a middle-aged male, also killed by the pack.

Officer Somners entered the conference room and walked over to Green. "Sir, a Sergeant Patterson just called in. They destroyed the dog pack. All of them. But they lost their point man."

Green waited until Somners left. "We'll have to isolate the point man's body with the other deceased victims."

"At least they took out the pack," Bishop said.

Green walked up to the big map. He wished they had the luxury of being able to mourn the death of a brave soldier, but they didn't have time.

"What are these yellow flags?" Bishop asked, studying the map.

"They represent confirmed sightings of suspected rabid civilians."

"Then there haven't been any new sightings confirmed," Bishop injected, hoping to add another note of optimism to the lugubrious mood, "for over three hours. As long as everyone adheres to the rules of the quarantine, maybe these three—" he tapped one yellow flag "—will be the last."

10:38 p.m.

LOCKTON WAS LYING on his bed fully clothed. His body ached for sleep, but his mind was whirling like a revolving door. At nine o'clock, he had dismissed the two lab techs. They had gratefully adjourned to their cots in the basement.

Once alone, he had begun the tedious and complicated process of monitoring the infected water samples. He had been hoping to discover the first signs of the virus's half-life—the beginning of the breakdown within the virus.

At 9.58 p.m., he had isolated a viral cluster in a water sample from the Walters well that looked promising. When viewed under the scanning electron microscope, his suspicions were confirmed. The virus was becoming brittle. Ten percent had already broken apart. He could not calculate the exact rate of disintegration from such a small, random selection, but it was a good sign.

The virus would self-destruct in a matter of days, not weeks.

The beginning of the end, he thought, staring up at the bedroom ceiling. Alex removed his shoes and socks. After she unzipped his pants, he arched his hips and she slid them off.

"It's easier to sleep if you close your eyes," she advised, unbuttoning his shirt.

He continued to gaze at the ceiling. He reminded Alex of a fresh cod on ice at the market in Seattle.

"Mrs. L. said if I didn't do this, she would." Alex lifted him up under the arms and led him to the bathroom. She had already drawn a hot bath. He sank down into the steaming water and was instantly soothed. Alex began shampooing his hair.

"I don't suppose this is a good time to open the champagne?" she asked.

God, he thought despondently, what a way to ruin the confirmation of a marriage proposal. I'll get back to you about this wedding thing, he parodied without amusement, after this killer virus thing blows over...okay?

"It wasn't supposed to be like this," he said, languishing. "I'm sorry."

"So you can speak." She began to soap his chest and arms. Her continual massaging took away the terrible stiffness that had encased him like an ill-fitting suit of armor.

After a long soak, Alex toweled him dry and tucked him back into bed. Outside the blanket, his left thumb kept tapping his thigh like a broken metronome. She took his hand and sat beside him.

"It's all connected, isn't it, James? The attempted break-in. The epidemic. Your research."

He turned to face her. She had never seen such painful resignation in a man's face before. It reminded her of the empty-eyed looks in the photos of the Nazi concentration camp survivors when they first set eyes on their American liberators.

The last thing he wanted to do was answer that question.

"Whatever it is, it's not your fault. I know it," she consoled him. He rolled his head over onto her thigh. "When it's all over, we'll go to the ocean. Just you and me . . . and the champagne. I'll make love to you until all the pain is gone." She leaned over and smiled. "No matter how long it takes."

His fingers dug into the taut muscles of her upper thigh. He shut his eyes.

She knew he couldn't talk about it even if he wanted to. She understood the rules completely.

She had secrets, too.

Secrets that had kept her from giving herself completely to the man she loved more than all else.

Secrets, she feared, that would eventually destroy what had taken them so long to build together.

Love.

And trust.

Chapter 25

5:08 a.m., March 19, 1986

Alex awoke before dawn. Lockton was sleeping fitfully. But at least he was sleeping, she thought.

He had screamed himself awake a little after three, mumbling something about a wolf pack. She had cradled him in her arms until he had finally drifted off again.

Easing out of bed, she gathered her clothes and her purse and quietly tiptoed to the hall bathroom to dress.

The house was as still as a mausoleum. She slipped out the porch door and hurried around the house to the road. It was cold. A heavy, rolling fog clung to the land like a damp wool sweater.

After checking on Schraeder in the surveillance room, Alex went up to her bedroom and flopped onto her bed.

She had hoped to put off any question about marriage until after her assignment had ended. She had had only a month to go. It wouldn't have been so complicated then. The lies wouldn't have seemed so grotesque. It might even have been an amusing anecdote over dinner.

I'm not really that rich, James. Actually I don't even have a trust fund. I work for the Company.

Yes, that's right.

I'm an intelligence officer for the CIA. I was assigned to protect you and maintain laboratory security. When I started falling in love, I requested a transfer, but it was denied.

What's that?

Well, yes... your entire house is bugged.

But at least someone who loved you was monitoring your life, your work, your family. Not some stranger.

Don't you understand?

The more I listened to your life, the more I loved you, James. It was like a wonderful obsession.

My surveillance room was an umbilical cord between us. I was never alone because of it, never truly separated from you.

For the last year and a half, I have shared every little hurt, every fear, every moment of tenderness and passion in your life. It only served to draw us closer, James. It wasn't really like spying.

Who was she kidding?

She tossed some clothes into an overnight bag, zipped it up and headed back to Lockton's.

Maybe she should quit the Company.

Bury the lies with more lies.

Tell him her lawyer squandered the trust fund. They could get married and she'd find another job—they'd start fresh and no one would ever know....

And how long would their life together last before the roof tumbled down over the lies?

It was all a joke—love, getting married, being Nick's mother—a terrible, cruel joke, she thought dolefully.

But no one was laughing.

Dropping her suitcase by Lockton's garage, she started up the road to the Hobbit House.

5:41 a.m.
WHEN ALEX RETURNED from the Hobbit House, everyone was still asleep. She tiptoed to the guest bedroom and woke up Stone.

Sitting up in bed with the quilt tucked around him like a sarong, Stone watched Alex dump the contents of a paper bag onto the small round table by the reading chair. Cigarette butts—all Marlboros—matches, sandwich wrappers, gum wrappers, a few cans of Pabst beer.

Alex lifted up a Baggie containing a cracked lens cap from a pair of binoculars. "I doubt the neighborhood kids are Peeping Toms." She brushed through the pile of butts. "Or chain-smokers."

"I told you not to go up there."

Alex carefully began to put the different pieces of evidence in plastic bags. "We could get prints from something here."

Stone picked the sleep from the corners of his eyes. "You disobeyed a direct order."

"But I was right." She pointed at the evidence. "This could tell us who he was. Once we know that, we'll be able to trace him back to the one who gave him the keys and the blueprints to the alarm systems."

"This will go in your files, McGuire," Stone threatened, scratching his chest. Alex started to put all the Baggies back in the paper bag. "Leave all that here. I'll take care of it."

Alex glanced across the room at him. She'd never last in the field, Stone thought. You could read her like a book. It was obvious she didn't trust him and was reluctant to abandon the evidence.

And she was right, Stone deliberated. If they had a set of prints, they could identify Haskell from his military records. Given enough time, they would trace his records back to their involvements during the war.

She had done her job well. She'd stopped the intruder. Driven him to his death. Then found the evidence needed to identify him.

Too bad it would never reach Langley.

"Why?" Alex suddenly asked.

"Why what?" Stone grumbled.

"Why don't you want to identify him?"

Stone's eyes narrowed like a cobra's. "Don't try to turn it around, McGuire." He tugged up the quilt. "You disobeyed orders. And that's that."

"You already know, don't you?" Alex wouldn't let him intimidate her. She lifted her head and returned his stare. "You know who it is."

"Straws, McGuire." He shook his head. "You're grasping at straws to cover your own mistakes."

"Add a little mud to the straw," Alex stated. "And you can build a damn pyramid."

Too smart for your own fucking good, Stone thought.

But you made one critical mistake.

You gave away your hand.

Now you've got nothing to bluff with.

While I'm holding a pair of aces.

Schraeder and Harrison...

5:55 a.m.

ALEX WAS HAVING COFFEE in the kitchen when Mrs. L. wandered down in her favorite green terry-cloth robe.

"You're up early," Mrs. L. commented, getting a cup for herself. "Don't think there's enough for all the guests." Because of the quarantine the two women were maintaining an uneasy truce. Although Mrs. L. knew about the marriage proposal, she had never mentioned it. Not even a curt congratulations.

Mrs. L. retrieved the dented blue coffeepot from the bottom cabinet next to the stove. It could hold over a gallon.

"Is Mr. Lockton up?"

Alex had checked on him before her talk with Stone. "Still sleeping. He had set the alarm for five-thirty. I moved it to six-thirty."

Mrs. L. took two half-gallon bottles of water from under the sink. "They don't know how to take care of themselves," she baited. "Never have. Never will."

Alex decided to bite. "Who?"

Mrs. L. put three big frying pans on the stove. "Men."

Alex smiled to herself. It was too early in the morning to argue about sexual stereotypes, let alone how much coffee should have been made. It was still dark outside, for God's sake.

"How 'bout we make a big breakfast for everyone?" Mrs. L. took two dozen eggs from the refrigerator. "They hardly touched their dinner."

"Good idea."

Maybe if they worked together and shared a common chore like cooking breakfast, it would open the door to friendship, Alex speculated. Married life with a live-in, surrogate mother-in-law on your back was not a pleasant view of the future.

At six-thirty, breakfast was ready. Lockton mumbled something about the alarm clock being broken as he placed extra boards in the dining-room table. To Alex's surprise, Mrs. L. didn't snitch on her. Either her concern for Mr. Lockton's health took precedence over her feud with "his neighbor" or she was finally beginning to accept her into the family.

"No one leaves the table until they've finished their plate," Mrs. L. dictated as the lab techs, Stone, Harrison, Lockton and the two boys sat down. It was a heartland-of-America breakfast: scrambled eggs, toast, jelly, soybean sausages, bacon, pancakes, orange juice and all the coffee they could drink. Mrs. L. stacked Lockton's plate herself before joining the table.

He peered down at it, intimidated. "I'm not that hungry."

Mrs. L. pointed her fork. "Eat."

Like a kid hoping his sister would intervene on his behalf, Lockton glanced across the table at Alex. She ignored him. He was getting no pity this morning. The women in his life were going to keep him healthy, whether he liked it or not. After forcing down one heavily syruped pancake, Lockton discovered he was actually hungry. So was everyone else. Except Terry. Alex had to continually coax him into taking the next bite. But at least he was feeding himself now.

After breakfast, Nick helped Mrs. L. clear the table. All leftovers were dumped into Thor's dish.

The room began to lighten with the first gray tint of morning. The island was entombed in heavy fog. Moisture droplets speckled the windows. Stone left the table and hunted for a news broadcast on the radio. Every half minute, the burly, resonant groans of the blockade vessels' foghorns called to each other like lost cows.

"Green wants all water systems tested again today," one of the lab techs reminded Lockton.

"They'll be doing those in the lab they set up at the operations center." Lockton spread homemade blackberry jam on another piece of toast. "We've got more important tests to run here. I discovered something in the lab last night. Something that—"

The sudden cackle of automatic weapons fire stopped him in midsentence. Two short bursts were followed by an extended barrage of multiple weapons.

Terry screamed and dived under the table. Mrs. L. gently pulled him out to console him.

They were close, Stone estimated. Within a half mile. He glanced at Harrison.

"If you'll excuse me." Harrison closed Lockton's study and called Alex's house to make sure Schraeder was all right, then he went out to check on the Winnebago.

Alex angrily arose from the table. It just wasn't fair. She had hoped the breakfast would create a brief air of normalcy for them all, especially James and Terry, but the gunfire had ruined it.

Lockton phoned the control center from the kitchen and reported the incident. When Green was told Lockton was on line three, he took the call. He had just received radio confirmation from Operations. A fire team patrolling the western coastline had found one of the three suspected victims at the abandoned quarry a half mile south of Lockton's property. A resident had reported seeing the elderly man hurling rocks from the top of the quarry's east wall. Unfortunately, he had attempted to bury the patrol in a landslide when they approached the foot of the cliff and they had been forced to defend themselves. The man's body was being sent to the operations center for postmortem tests.

Each time Lockton was informed of a rabies-related death, he felt as if another layer of his skin was being peeled from his body, leaving him even more exposed and defenseless. Alex's brief but heartfelt reassurance last night had been kind, but . . .

She was wrong.

It was his fault.

He had created it.

It didn't matter if his fingers had never actually touched the trigger, it was his weapon.

And when it killed, he was responsible.

Lockton listened in silent bewilderment as Green recounted the night's events.

An eight-family religious group called the Church of New Israel had armed and barricaded themselves in their new church. At 2:12 a.m. they had opened fire on a patrol passing by in the woods. They believed the outbreak was the beginning of the Second Coming and that the patrol was part of the legions of Satan, suddenly unleashed upon the world.

A firefight had ensued and three of the congregation had been wounded. But none seriously. When reinforcements arrived, the entire congregation was taken into custody and put under guard in the high-school gym.

At 4:15 a.m. a nervous father had fired a couple of warning shots at a patrol crossing his backyard. No one had been hurt. The man was taken into custody and delivered to the operations center's security ward.

At 4:56 a.m., another of the three confirmed rabies victims had been captured alive and was now locked in Security.

Overall, Green felt they had been pretty lucky, considering what could have happened, especially at the church. The best news was, there hadn't been any new reports of rabies victims since late yesterday. Now that they had located the man at the quarry, there was only one victim still missing.

Her name was Clarisse Beckman, a single, thirty-three-year-old blonde. Lockton had met her at Ray's, a pizza parlor in town that had an amateur night every Thursday. Accompanying herself on a guitar, she had sung two old Joan Baez protest tunes fairly well, if unimaginatively.

Now she was wandering the island, rabid and insane, while armed soldiers hunted her down like a wounded and dangerous animal.

Green told Lockton he had to get off the line. One of the governor's aides was calling.

"Wait a second," Lockton protested. "I found something interesting last night." He told him the virus had a possible disintegration factor. "I don't know how long it will take, but I think we can calculate a final annihilation time. That is, if the sample I found last night is typical."

Green was ecstatic. "Are you telling me it's starting to die off?"

"Exactly."

"What's causing it?"

Lockton was about to explain his built-in decomposition factor, but caught himself. "I don't know, really. But it's happening. At least in one water sample."

Alex and Stone had been listening to the conversation from the hall.

"Thank God," she sighed.

"Don't thank Him." Stone pointed at the ceiling. "Thank the doc."

Alex glared at him contemptuously as he sauntered into the living room. A Coast Guard cutter's foghorn bellowed like a sick moose.

"My opinion exactly," Alex said.

She couldn't shake the feeling that they were no longer on the same side.

If that were true, she couldn't think of a more dangerous adversary than Richard Stone.

Chapter 26

AT SIX FOOT THREE, Sergeant Patterson had to bend over in order to look through the small square window in the door at the end of the long gray corridor of the operations center's security wing. The door had been reinforced with two horizontal steel bars. Muffled by the thick cement walls of the Nike base's underground bunker supply rooms, he listened to the pathetic cries of the rabid locked in isolation.

His fire team had been off duty since the battle with the dog pack. After they had brought in Murphy's body, the four-man team had met in the small chapel next to the lab for a short service. After everyone had left, Patterson had locked the door and taken off his shirt to examine his wound.

The German shepherd's incisors had cut into the upper muscle of his left forearm, just below the elbow. The wound was smeared with the rust tinge of iodine. He had soaked it back at the jeep while his patrol had carried up Murphy's body. Patterson had remained in the chapel for the rest of the night, praying.

They had been briefed about Renton, the cop that had been bitten by the rabid teenage girl before going on patrol. All the troops knew that Renton had been inoculated and the serum had proven useless.

If you were bitten, they'd lock you up.

To die.

He was in there somewhere, Patterson thought, looking down the empty corridor. Patterson removed the steel bars. His left arm was stiff. It felt as if ants were crawling under the skin on his hand. He couldn't stop sweating. Fighting back another wave of nausea, he opened the door.

The hallway echoed with the pathos of the condemned; tearful whimpers of unending mental agony interrupted by fierce howls of terror or spine-jolting physical pain.

They recognize me, he suddenly thought, edging along the wall. They know I'm one of them.

As he shuffled down the long corridor, it seemed to shrink and elongate, as if he were looking through the wrong end of a telescope. The victims' cries stabbed at his eardrums like needles, upsetting his already tenuous balance.

"They won't," he muttered aloud. "They won't lock me up." He glanced into the square wire-meshed window in the nearest door. "I'm not one of you."

A middle-aged woman was sitting on the bare floor, wrapped in a straitjacket stained with saliva and vomit. Their eyes met and she smiled. He felt her diseased soul tugging him closer to the window.

"No!"

He kicked the door and her warped shrieks of amusement filled the hallway.

Three doors down, he found the police officer. Renton was also wrapped in a straitjacket. He kept pounding his head into the padded cement wall.

Suddenly his face snapped toward the door. Blood dribbled out his nostrils. The stench of vomit overwhelmed Patterson, twisting his stomach like a dirty washrag.

The eyes, he thought.

Just like the woman's.

Windows to their diseased souls.

The longer he stared, the more Renton's eyes seemed to grow. At first they were like fresh eggs spreading out on a hot skillet, but soon they were so huge, they began filling the room like two inflatable rafts.

They're trying to escape, Patterson thought. Trying to break open the door.

To devour me.

And make me . . .

One of *them*.

Patterson fled up the corridor. The hallway started to tilt and roll, as if he were in the belly of a storm-tossed ship. He stumbled out the door and slapped the steel bars back in place.

He shook his head like a wet dog. Suddenly everything was still.

Too hot in here, he thought. Have to get out.

He started running up the corridor. A door opened and he slid to a halt, almost tumbling over the double-decker medical cart Doc Bishop was wheeling out of the examination room.

"Slow down." Bishop laughed. "Or I'll ticket you."

Patterson exhaled, relieved. His mind was becoming lucid again. The hallucinations were only a hazy memory now. He was still feverish and sick to his stomach, but his skin no longer felt as if it were on the verge of boiling over.

"What do you got here, Doc?" Patterson tapped the metal tray containing six hypodermic needles and six vials.

"Human diploid-cell vaccine," Bishop replied. "The immunogenic rabies vaccination."

"Oh." Patterson walked with him down the hall. "One vial per shot?"

"Five, actually." Bishop turned the cart around to back into the laboratory door. "Over a three-week period."

"Let me help you." Patterson grabbed the other end. "You hold the door, I'll push."

Bishop thanked him and opened the door.

"No problem, Doc." Patterson eased the cart inside and left.

One of the medical technicians grabbed the cart handle. "I'll take it from here, Dr. Bishop."

Doc nodded and turned to go.

"Hey, Doc," the technician called out. "I thought we ordered six."

"You did. They're right..." Bishop squinted at the cart in surprise.

There were only five syringes and vials on the tray.

8:15 a.m.

THE OLD NIKE SITE had been built on the highest spot on the island. From its vantage point, you could view the entire south half of Puget Sound and both mountain ranges. Dr. Bishop was waiting for Green in the parking lot.

There was no view now.

Only fog.

A dark green sedan drove up the hill. Passing three ambulances and two rescue vehicles in the east corner of the parking lot, the car pulled up next to Bishop.

"Now what's the problem?" Green asked, getting out.

"Sergeant Patterson," Bishop said. He quickly told him about the missing serum.

"Have you put him in isolation for testing?"

"That's the problem," Bishop sighed. "He's gone. And he took a jeep."

"What about the roadblocks?"

"No one's seen him." Bishop stared down the hill. "But with this fog, who knows?"

8:22 a.m.

"MAYBE HE'D LIKE TO HEAR the Beatles," Nick suggested. He put on his father's old *Sergeant Pepper's Lonely Hearts Club Band* album. "This has a lot of songs from the cartoon we saw, Terry."

"'Yellow Submarine,'" Alex said. She had remained with the boys since breakfast. After Terry screamed, he had completely closed into his shell again. For the past hour, Nick had been playing various records for him, sometimes accompanying them on his flute. The music seemed to soothe his friend.

At least he had stopped trembling, Nick thought, wishing he could help Terry more than he was.

Across the hall, Mrs. L. was praying for the boy in her room. After the gunshots, Nick had said a silent prayer, too. The prayer hadn't stopped Terry from trembling, so Nick had tried what he thought was the next best thing—music.

"I wish we were over at your house," he told Alex. "Then we could both play for Terry."

"We could sing along," Alex suggested. The three of them were sitting on the floor, leaning against Nick's bed. Terry was cradled in the middle.

"You know I can't sing." Nick put his arm over Terry's shoulders. "Terry, here, is the one that can sing. Mr. Bartlett, our music teacher, always has him lead the class."

The compliment had no effect on Terry. Nick kept his arm around him anyway. He really hadn't thought it would, but he wasn't about to quit trying.

"I suppose it wouldn't hurt, even if I sing off-key," he decided, willing to embarrass himself in front of Alex if it might help his friend.

The album was playing a song about a lovely meter maid named Rita. Alex remembered the words and started them off. Nick joined in while Rita was standing by a parking mee-tah.

Suddenly Terry stood up. A puzzled expression distorted his face.

"Uh-oh," Nick warned, leaping up.

"What is it?" Alex asked. "What's he . . ."

Nick grabbed Terry's hand. "Got to go pee," he said, leading his friend out the door.

Alex walked to the window, amazed at Nick's sense of responsibility. His unselfish concern was a rare gift, especially in someone so young and physically handicapped.

And whose life was probably half over, she suddenly thought.

Hooking her fingertips on the ledge above the window, she leaned against the glass. Patches of trees shimmered in and out of the floating grayness like distant mirages on a heat-blurred desert.

A jeep bounced out of the fog and turned left onto Sylvan Beach Road, disappearing into another curling, gray bank.

Funny, she thought. Only one soldier. Considering the situation, it didn't seem strategically proper to send one man out alone on patrol.

In fact, it seemed militarily inane.

Chapter 27

SERGEANT PATTERSON turned up a dirt access road used by lumber trucks thirty years ago to haul their logs out to the Sylvan Beach Road. A second generation of fir trees dotted the hill. He drove the jeep up the steep trail until the wheels dug into the mud.

He knew they were hunting him now. He took his pack and supplies from the back of the jeep. They'd have to kill him. He wouldn't go back. He wasn't going to die like that cop, Renton—arms bound, pounding his head against his cell like a caged animal.

Suddenly he heard a tiny voice calling his name. It sounded oddly mechanical. He put a clip in his M-16 and pointed at the trees.

"Don't come any closer," he warned the unseen intruder. Fog tendrils slipped in and out of the forest surrounding him. Within the wooded shadows, the head of the German shepherd slowly materialized. Its bloody, bullet-riddled face kept growing and growing, until it was almost as large as the trees. He crouched behind the front fender. His left hand cramped as he squeezed the cold barrel of his rifle.

"Sergeant Patterson? I know you can hear me. Please reply."

The words seemed to puff out of the shepherd's torn mouth like smoke plumes. Sweat stung his eyes. He wiped his face with his forearm, keeping both hands on the M-16.

"Sergeant Patterson, this is Dr. Bishop. Please reply."

The hallucination in the fog disappeared. Patterson dropped to his knees. His mind had cleared again. He was okay, he reassured himself. He wasn't sick. He was okay. The fog was just playing tricks on him.

"Sergeant Patterson? Matt? Can you hear me?"

Patterson pulled himself up on the fender, reached across the passenger seat and picked up the radio. "Doc?"

Green and Bishop huddled around the radio in the communications room at the operations center.

"Sergeant? Is that you?" Bishop glanced hopefully back at Green.

"Yeah, Doc. It's me. Thanks for the shots."

Green took the mike from Bishop. "Sergeant? I want you to report back here immediately." His voice softened. "We can help you here. We have drugs. We'll do everything in our power to..."

"Lock me in a cell," Patterson finished for him. "To die."

"Patterson, how do you feel right now?"

"Fine, Doc."

"Tell me the truth... please?"

"Really, I'm..."

The extended pause that followed alarmed both men.

"What?" Bishop asked. "What were you going to say?"

Patterson groaned, "Oh, God."

Green glanced at Bishop. "Patterson? Are you still there?"

"It's coming! Oh Jesus, God. It's coming!"

"What is? What's coming?"

It was the dog's head again. Even bigger now, crawling along the ground like a huge slug.

"Where are you?" Green pleaded. "We'll help you. Just tell us where you are?"

Bishop sadly shook his head. "He's hallucinating. Could mean he's entering the final stages."

Green hunched over the mike. "Patterson? We want to help. We..."

"It's coming!"

The stark terror in his voice unnerved Bishop.

"Stay with the jeep," Green implored. "We'll send a patrol. They'll protect you. Just tell us where you are."

"It's still alive!" Patterson screamed. "As big as a house."

"It's not real, Patterson. You're hallucinating. That's one of the symptoms." Green slapped the side of the radio. "Patterson? Patterson, are you there?" He waited, then slowly looked up at Bishop. "I think we lost him."

3:00 p.m.

"HOW'D YOU DO IT?" Lockton asked excitedly.

"I sent a letter to a colleague of mine at the lab in Olympia. Put it in with the samples flown out yesterday," Bishop explained. "If he did as instructed, Terry's grandparents will be waiting at this number on the mainland. Green said he would connect us himself. As long as we keep this to ourselves."

You lovable old bastard, Lockton thought. Sending sentimental notes out with legally restricted body samples.

Lockton escorted Bishop into the living room. Alex, Mrs. L. and the two boys were waiting by the phone.

When it rang, Bishop answered. He had written a brief psychological profile in the note to his colleague. Terry's grandparents were prepared to be met with silence when the child was put on the line. Bishop handed the phone to Nick, who held it for his friend.

Terry didn't show any signs of recognition. Nick looked at Alex, disappointed. His friend's eyes still reminded him of glass marbles. Bishop had hoped this would open a channel of communication between Terry and his environment. He checked his watch. Green had told him they would only be allowed five minutes.

"Grandma?" Terry suddenly asked.

No one moved. Radiating with excitement, Alex gratefully squeezed Bishop's hand. A spark of understanding flickered in Terry's eyes.

"Grandma? Wh-where's Daddy?"

Tears began to stream down Mrs. L.'s face. Terry took the phone from Nick and cradled it against his cheek like a security blanket.

"Grandma? I...I want to go home. Take me home, Grandma."

Bishop nodded at Alex. The five minutes were up.

Alex gently nudged herself between the two boys and reached for the phone. She could hear Green interrupt Terry's grandmother. He hugged the phone tighter as she tried to slip her fingers around it. The obnoxious drone of the dial tone suddenly caught everyone's attention.

"Terry? Time to hang up now," she coaxed. Finally he loosened his grip.

After she replaced the receiver, Terry slipped down off the wicker chair. Nick followed him through the hall.

"How're your grandparents, Terry?" Nick asked.

Terry stopped by the stairs and looked back at the others.

"Gotta get ready," he explained. "Daddy's coming over to take me home."

3:11 p.m.
"THE RABIES LABORATORY at the Center for Disease Control in Atlanta called in their results a half hour ago," Bishop explained. He and Lockton had gone down to the basement to talk in private. "The virus is definitely a mutation. They tested the rat, too. It was definitely infected. They've discovered that this mutation can breed in fresh water and perhaps even a

host's bloodstream. The theory is, the mutation might have been caused by a second, yet undetermined, viral infection in the rat, which somehow transferred genetic material into the rabies virus while both were breeding in the same host cells.''

"So they think the rat caused the contamination in that underground stream.''

"They're skeptical, but it's the only theory they have.''

Lockton sat on the corner of the pool table, rolling the eight ball around in his palms. "I've calculated the viral breakdown. It's the same in all four infected water systems. It's incredible. By six o'clock tonight, all the wells should be clean.''

"You're kidding?'' Bishop was astounded.

"I've been monitoring it for almost twenty-four hours.''

Bishop laughed. "Hallelujah. This calls for a little drink.'' His grin broadened. "Maybe a lot of little drinks.''

Lockton called Dr. Green from the lab phone and told him about the breakdown. Green was ecstatic.

"What happens now?'' Lockton asked.

Green quickly filled him in. A patrol had located Clarisse Beckman a few minutes ago. She had locked herself in an old bomb shelter in a cow pasture next to her house. She was dead when they found her. Apparently she had locked herself in to keep from hurting anyone.

That meant there was only one rabid victim left unaccounted for. Sergeant Patterson.

"I think we should continue testing all water supplies for at least another forty-eight hours," Green said. "Just to be sure. We'll maintain all patrols for the same period."

"Then you're not going to lift the quarantine."

"Not for at least two days. The governor wants to be absolutely sure that whatever happened here, doesn't spread to the mainland."

Chapter 28

4:41 p.m., March 19, 1986

TERRY BOUNCED the rubber handball to Nick. They were playing keep away. Thor was always it, but that was all right with him. He had been shut up for two days and was overflowing with pent up energy. On the other side of the room, Alex was playing pool and Mrs. L. was reading a *National Geographic* on the sofa.

Lockton had just left, having insisted on driving Bishop home after the good doctor had thrown down three more double Scotches with water. Stone had gone to the Winnebago, parked up the dirt access road, to check on Harrison.

Mrs. L. excused herself to take a nap before starting dinner. Having all those strangers in her house was making it impossible for her to keep the place tidy. Her reputation was at stake, so she had to work overtime to keep up. That, plus worrying about Terry, had finally drained her. She hated to admit it, but she couldn't keep up with Alex. She would have to watch the boys alone for a while. As much as it irritated her, she was beginning to appreciate having "their neighbor" around.

"I'm hungry. How 'bout you?" Nick asked, after Thor intercepted his toss.

"Yeah," Terry agreed, trying to peel the ball out of Thor's mouth.

"Can we have a snack?" Nick asked Alex.

She hit the six ball into the corner pocket. "I guess. What do you want?"

"Peanut butter, crackers and orange soda."

Alex started to put her cue in the wall rack.

"We can get it," Nick said.

Thor led the boys up to the kitchen. He had recognized the word *snack* immediately. They took the Triscuits, peanut-butter jar, knife and cans of orange soda into the living room. The fog had completely cleared and the sky was rimmed with high white clouds. Above the Olympics, the sun speared through the clouds in long dusty streaks.

"Boy, are they neat," Nick said, watching the two white Coast Guard ships patrol the northwest coastline.

"Where are they going?" Terry asked.

Nick thought it best not to explain. "I gotta go take the big one, Number Two. Be back in a minute. Okay?" Thor trotted behind Nick toward the bathroom.

Terry put down his can of soda. He was feeling homesick again.

Why hadn't Daddy come yet?

He should have been there by now.

He felt a deep aching in his chest.

Something had happened.

Something terrible.

Suddenly he saw his mother in his bedroom window.

She was yelling something.

"Mommy?" Terry glanced around the room, frightened.

A sledgehammer glinted above her head.

Run, Terry...

Blood exploded across the glass.

Run!

Terry yanked the sliding door open and fled down the porch stairs.

Run, Terry! Run!

He dashed across the lawn to the path in the woods. Something awful was behind him, he remembered.

Tall fir trees loomed above him, dark and sharp and trembling. The narrow path twisted up the hill and he kept running. He didn't know where he was or where he was going, only that he had to run.

Something moved in the woods to his left and he stopped. Pieces of Sunday night were bursting through his mind like fireworks. He heard the scratching of bushes being pushed aside.

Slowly he turned to face the noise.

A soldier stepped out onto the path.

"Daddy?"

The soldier stretched his head back and screamed.

Run Terry!

Run!

4:45 p.m.

NICK ZIPPED UP HIS JEANS as he sauntered back into the living room. As soon as he saw the open door, he knew.

"Thor." He bent down. "Find Terry. Get him! Get him!"

The dog scampered down the porch stairs and raced to the path. Nick hobbled after him. Taking care of Terry had begun to take its toll on him as well.

"Terry?" he yelled. "Where are you?"

Hearing Nick's cries, Alex looked out the basement window just as Nick disappeared down the path.

TERRY BACKED UP THE TRAIL, never taking his eyes from the soldier in the tattered camouflage uniform. His mind kept blinking back and forth between reality and the memory of his father emerging out of the darkness toward the Berkeleys', swinging a blood-stained sledgehammer.

His fragile consciousness wasn't able to cope with the attacking images. His body shut down and his legs became rooted to the path.

All he could do was whimper.

The soldier shuffled up the path, dragging his stiff left leg as if it were made of wood. Spit oozed out through his teeth.

The child heard his mother's voice again, telling him to run, but his limbs wouldn't react. He closed his eyes to make the apparition disappear.

Sergeant Patterson snapped a thick limb off the dead alder beside the path. Terry could hear his grunting, wheezing breath edging closer.

With the last of his strength, the last of his dwindling sanity, Terry screamed.

"Mommy!"

NICK'S LUNGS ACHED. He was having trouble expelling air, but he pushed himself forward as fast as his trail, skinny legs would go. Thor had kept ahead of him on the path, but when the dog heard Terry's piercing scream, he ran back to his master.

There was a strange, odious scent ahead in the woods. A human scent unlike any he had smelled before. Thor's fur prickled across his back and shoulders.

Nick knew he was getting close.

He could hear Alex behind him, calling, but he couldn't wait.

Not after Terry's scream.

Passing the boulder on the hill, Nick started limping down the incline toward the gully. The air was growing thick and heavy. It was becoming increasingly difficult to breathe, like trying to inhale molasses.

As he rounded the corner to the gully, he almost tripped over Terry's body. The boy's neck was broken, his flesh riddled with bites.

Thor sniffed around Terry's dead body. The human that smelled of decay and death was near. He quickly backed up toward his master, snarling.

Nick saw a figure flicker between the trees to his right. Thor pushed up against his master's leg, forcing Nick back across the bridge.

Sergeant Patterson kicked through the underbrush and stepped onto the path. He was now between the boy and his house.

There was no retreat.

The virus in the neurons of the limbic system of his diseased mind had completely taken control. He was, in essence, a walking corpse, a slave to the virus's only need . . .

Propagation.

To accomplish this, it had to create furiously violent aggression in its host in order to introduce itself into its next victim.

The virus commanded the body of Patterson toward the boy and his dog.

It needed them in order to survive.

Alex called again, but Nick didn't dare answer. It would only irritate the madman.

Suddenly Thor sprinted to the bridge.

"Thor, no!" Nick screamed.

Patterson lifted the club above his head and started across the bridge. Growling, Thor coiled to spring.

When Patterson reached the middle of the bridge, Thor leaped. The sergeant protected his throat with his free arm. Thor's teeth dug through his flesh, hit bone and tore.

With an inhuman howl, the club descended.

Thor flipped off the bridge and dropped into the gully. His limp body lay in the mud, blood dripping from his nose and mouth.

"You bastard!" Nick shrieked, tossing a rock at the soldier.

It struck Patterson above the right eye. With one arm nearly chewed off at the elbow, Patterson started toward the boy. His paralysis was spreading up through his left leg into his spine and he was losing a lot of blood. Nick was able to increase the distance between them as he fled down the path to Alex's house.

When he reached the basement door, he could hear Patterson crashing through the low-hanging branches.

It was locked.

Nick picked up a red brick from the stack Alex had bought to build an outdoor barbecue, broke the lower left window pane, reached in and unlocked the door.

Once inside, he tried to push the sofa up against the door. In his weakened state, it felt like a block of granite. He couldn't budge it.

Backing up from the sofa, Nick tripped over the coffee table. Too weak to pull himself up, he crawled across the room and squeezed behind the green recliner chair.

As Patterson entered, Nick quietly reached for the iron-tipped brass poker beside the fireplace.

Suddenly a section of the paneled wall to his right swung open.

As soon as Schraeder saw the mangled guardsman, he went for his SIG-Sauer 9 mm. Patterson charged, swinging the club backhandedly.

It cracked the side of Schraeder's skull, killing him instantly.

Nick jammed his fist into his mouth to muffle his scream. Patterson spun toward the fireplace.

As the killer approached, Nick stood up and got into his batter's stance.

Patterson kicked the recliner aside.

Totally exposed, Nick waited for the attack, ready to pop the soldier's head into left field if he had to.

Suddenly glass exploded across the floor.

Patterson lurched back, as if punched in the chest. Another shot slammed him against the paneling and he slid to the floor.

Alex poked her face through the shattered window. "Don't move, Nick. Just close your eyes. He can't hurt you now. I'm here."

Nick fainted.

4:55 p.m.
STONE WAS STANDING by the door when Alex picked Nick up off the floor. He stepped aside as she carried him out of the basement, then immediately went to work.

Alex stopped by the window. The asshole hadn't even asked how the boy was.

Lifting Schraeder by the ankles, Stone dragged his body back into the surveillance room.

"The boy's all right," Alex announced, repulsed.

Stone used the towel, draped over the desk chair in the surveillance room, to mop up the blood around the hidden door, then wrapped Schraeder's skull with it. After securing the surveillance room, he studied Patterson's blood trail. His arm had pumped a path of blood from the basement door to the fireplace. With the door closed, no one would know a second man had died there. After the patrol came to take Patterson's body, he would be safe where he was and security would be maintained.

Alex walked up to Cove Road. She did not want to take the trail past Terry.

Stone caught up with her halfway to Lockton's. He tried to check the boy's pulse.

"Don't touch him," she hissed, pulling away.

As soon as he had arrived at the basement door, Stone had assessed the situation. He could see the boy hadn't been hurt—physically, at least.

So he had taken care of business.

Schraeder had to be moved and the surveillance room resealed to protect the project.

But he saw no reason to explain that to McGuire. Her opinion was of absolutely no consequence. If she thought of him as ruthless or inhuman—fine. It could work to his advantage, as it did with the doc.

"Did he see it?" Stone inquired.

"See what?" Alex knew full well what he meant.

"The room."

Alex tugged Nick tighter against her breast. "You leave him out of this. If you even think . . ."

"The boy doesn't know what he saw," Stone predicted. "You were there. You didn't see any door. Or another man. If the kid tries to say otherwise, you deny it. He was out of his mind with terror. He doesn't know what he saw."

Alex shook her head. "Got it all figured out, huh?"

"Would you prefer the alternative?"

Alex felt as if a handful of snow had just been dumped down her back. She halted. Her entire being focused into the threat. "I'd kill you first, you fucking bastard."

Stone continued walking as if he hadn't heard her.

As soon as she had said it, she regretted it. She knew there were no shades of gray in Stone's way of thinking. Only black and white. Either you were his ally or his enemy.

She had just crossed the line.

Chapter 29

TWO NATIONAL GUARD JEEPS followed the squad car into Lockton's driveway. Stone led one of the fire teams back up the road to Alex's. The other patrol headed down the path.

Lockton arrived a few moments after the rescue vehicle. He pushed his way through the paramedics, the police and his lab techs and ran upstairs.

Alex and Mrs. L. were waiting in Nick's room. The boy was in bed. Lockton tried to read Alex's face.

"The man didn't..." He couldn't bring himself to ask. He quickly began examining his son.

"He never touched him, James," Alex reassured him.

Lockton still checked every inch of Nick's body. "Tell me exactly what happened."

After Alex's summation, he cupped her face. "You saved his life." He didn't know what else to say. Tears welled up in his eyes. "Thank you."

Alex buried her head into his shoulder. After finding Terry's body, saving Nick had been her only thought. Now the realization of how close Nick had come to death overpowered her.

As Alex wept in his arms, Mrs. L. quietly sneaked out of the room.

5:14 p.m.
THE FOUR GUARDSMEN stepped off the trail as the paramedics carried Terry up the path on a stretcher. Three of them had children of their own. After they passed, one guardsman quietly sneaked off into a thicket to vomit.

They waited for their sick comrade to return before starting up the trail to the gully. They found a large amount of blood on the bridge and a puddle of blood down in the ravine.

But no dog.

The sergeant picked a ball of fur out of the blood puddle. "It must have attacked him in the middle of the bridge," he called up. "To protect the kid."

"So where is it?" the soldier who had been sick asked.

The sergeant followed the trail of blood east, up the bank of the ravine into the underbrush. "Crawled up this way."

"Maybe it was only wounded."

"We've got to find out." The sergeant looked woefully at his men on the bridge. "If it is still alive, we have to shoot it."

5:15 p.m.
POLICE SERGEANT Harold Fitz waited patiently in Lockton's living room. Mrs. L. had given him a Diet Pepsi and told him Mr. Lockton and Miss McGuire

would be a few minutes. They were still upstairs with his son. The sergeant had five children himself and understood completely.

"Sorry for the delay, officer," Alex apologized. Her eyes were swollen from crying. Lockton held her around the waist.

"That's all right." Fitz put down his drink. "That was a hell of a brave thing you did." He flipped open his notepad. "I know this isn't easy, but I'd like to ask you a few more questions."

"I understand." Alex recounted the events leading up to the shooting.

"And when you got to the window, you saw Sergeant Patterson about to strike the child?" Fitz asked.

"That's right." She dabbed her eyes with a handkerchief. Lockton rubbed her lower back for encouragement. "I fired twice."

"Do you usually carry a .38?" The sergeant hadn't meant it to sound accusatory. "I mean, is it your habit to . . . ?"

"Because of the situation on the island, I've . . ."

Fitz smiled reassuringly. "It was a good thing you did." He had heard about the car chase from Officer Somners. She was one tough lady, he thought, respectfully. "Is there anything else you want to add?"

Alex pictured Stone dragging Schraeder into the surveillance room. "No."

Fitz's partner entered the house and waved the sergeant into the hall. He had just finished getting a statement from Stone. They compared notes before returning to the living room.

"Would it be all right if I talked to your son, Mr. Lockton?" Fitz asked.

"He's still unconscious," Lockton said. "Is it really necessary?"

The two officers glanced at each other. Neither had the heart to pursue it. The boy had been through too much already. Stone had verified Alex's statement. The evidence seemed clear.

"I guess not." Fitz put away his notepad and they all walked outside. "Sorry about your son's friend. And his dog."

Both jeeps were still in the driveway. It was quickly getting dark. As the squad car pulled away, the patrol came back from the ravine.

"Sir?" The sergeant approached Lockton. "May I speak with you a minute?" Lockton walked him to his jeep. "Sir, your dog's still alive."

Alex was watching them from the doorway. Lockton's shoulders deflated as the sergeant spoke.

"We followed the trail of blood as far as we could. Then we lost it." The sergeant put his M-16 on the seat and lit a cigarette. "We don't have our night patrol equipment here, so we had to come in. The dog could be anywhere by now. I'd advise you to lock up your house tonight. Until we find him and—" the sergeant flicked his cigarette away and grimaced; he did not like the job ahead "—take care of the matter, you should be very careful. He could try to come home. It's an instinct, I think . . . coming home to die."

5:42 p.m.

LOCKTON POURED COFFEE for himself and his two lab techs in the kitchen.

"We've been told to report back to Operations," one of the techs said. "To help at the lab there."

"Mrs. L. said you weren't to leave until after dinner. She's thawed a roast," Lockton told them as he refilled their mugs. Neither tech was in a hurry to go. Hard, dormitory-style metal bunks and military chow held no appeal at all.

The phone rang and Lockton answered it.

"Green told me what happened. How's Nick?" Bishop asked.

"Still sleeping."

"He's lived with pain all his life, James," Bishop said. "And death. It's given him an inner strength most of us never develop. He'll pull through this all right."

"Thanks, Doc. You're right."

"How are you holding up?"

"As well as can be expected."

"Get some sleep tonight. Doctor's orders."

Lockton smiled to himself. Amid all this turmoil, he had gained a real friend. "I will, Doc. Thanks for calling."

Lockton filled an ice bucket and put it on the counter. "Gentlemen, the booze is in the cabinet. Help yourself. I'll be in Nick's room."

6:31 p.m.

LOCKTON AND ALEX were sitting on the floor in Nick's room, their backs against the guest bed. Mrs. L. was downstairs, cooking and chatting with the lab techs. When the front door creaked, Lockton cocked his head.

"Stone," Alex said.

"Everything I did. This house. The lab. The project." He looked up at Nick. "Was all for him. I wanted him to have as happy a life as he could. For as long as . . ." His eyes drifted to the rug and he sighed, crossing his arms to comfort himself. "Didn't seem like much to ask. A few good years together. On the island. With the water and the dog and . . ."

The painful irony of it all welled inside him like a massive boil pushing up against his solar plexus. His chest felt like an overinflated basketball. If he didn't let some of the pressure out somehow, he was going to burst.

"If anything had happened to Nick." He could barely chisel out the words. "Oh, Jesus, Alex." She curled up against him and he unwrapped his arms. "He was that close to death. Because of me."

It was the first time he had admitted to Alex that his research was related to the epidemic. The blanket rustled and Nick rolled over.

His eyes fluttered open. "Daddy?"

Lockton swept his son up into his arms. "I'm here, Nick. Everything's all right. You're safe."

"Thor saved me, Daddy."

"I know." He kept rocking his son as he petted his hair. "I know."

Alex decided to stay where she was. Seeing her two men together, both so full of pain inside, trying to talk out the confusion, the hurt, the love, made her both proud and a little scared. How could she ever hope to be as close to them as they were to each other?

"He sacrificed his life for me, Daddy." Nick squeezed his father closer and began to cry. Lockton saw no reason to tell him that Thor was still alive.

When his tears had subsided, he laid the boy down and wiped his nose.

"Are you hungry?" Lockton asked.

"No." Nick pulled his stuffed dolphin against his cheek. "I just hurt."

Alex got up and kissed Nick on the forehead. He hugged her passionately. It was the most wonderful gift he could have given her. She suddenly felt a part of the family, not a loving outsider. She kissed them both and walked to the door.

"Daddy?" the boy whispered.

Lockton lowered his head. "What?"

"Who was that other man?"

"What other man, Nick?"

"The one that came out of the wall."

"Shh. Don't keep going over it. Sleep now," Lockton cajoled.

"Is he . . . dead, too?"

"I don't know who you're talking about, Nick."

"The man in the room," Nick insisted. "Behind the wall. The one who got hit on the head."

Lockton glanced back at the doorway.

Alex was gone.

6:45 p.m.

LOCKTON'S BEDROOM WAS UNLIT. From the doorway, he could see a knee and shoulder in the pale green hue of the moonlight. The rest of Alex was hidden in the shadows.

He walked to the reading chair by the west window and flicked on the table lamp. The sudden illumination made Alex cringe.

"Is it true?" he asked. Alex had been waiting in the darkness while Lockton finished his conversation with Nick.

She crossed her legs. "Is what true?"

"Where's Schraeder?" Lockton's voice was as brittle as a detective's interrogating a murder suspect.

"I don't know."

"Don't lie to me, Alex." He closed the bedroom door.

"What do you want to know?"

"Is it true?"

"What Nick said?"

"To start with."

There was no point avoiding it any longer. "Yes."

"You didn't mention it to the police."

"I'm not the only one that's lied to the police lately."

"You work for them, don't you?"

"Yes."

Lockton slowly sat down on the edge of the bed. Nothing seemed real any more. He felt as if his soul was being siphoned from his body through a hose. His guts, his blood, his tears, poured out over the rug.

Without looking up, he asked, "Was it all a lie?"

"No." She started to get up from her chair.

"Stay there!" he warned, pointing.

She slumped back down. "I love you, James. I asked to be taken off this assignment a month ago. And again when you asked me to marry you. I told them I didn't care about procedure. I was going to marry you anyway. James, I do love you. That's not a lie."

He punched his thighs with his fists and stood up. "So who's listening now?" he snarled, kicking the reading chair against the wall. Its leg snapped and the chair tipped over on its side. Alex flinched each time he ripped a drawer from his dresser and flung it across the room. "Where are they? Is the whole house bugged?"

His questions slashed her like razors.

"Yes," she muttered, ducking as a drawer flew past, denting the plaster wall.

Lockton yanked the dresser over and it crashed onto the floor. His rage was insatiable. "And when we made love? Who was listening then?"

Alex rose. "That's not fair, James. I was the only one..."

Lockton recoiled from her. "Not fair? Not fair? The woman I love has been spying on me for over a year. My son was almost killed today because of what

I created. What *we* created." He fell back against the wall and doubled over. "What the fuck has 'fair' got to do with it?"

Alex started to put her arm around his shoulders. "I wanted to tell you before, but..."

Lockton knocked her backward. "It was all a lie!"

"No, James. Please, believe me."

"Believe you?" He rolled off the wall, grabbed the lamp off the bedside table and heaved it across the room. "Why the hell should I do that?"

"James, I..."

"God, it must have given Stone a good laugh." He stepped into the center of the room and began turning in a circle. "And whoever the hell else is listening!" he screamed.

The bedroom door suddenly opened. Lockton's head snapped toward it.

"Take it easy, Doc." Stone stepped over a broken drawer. Alex was braced against the far wall, arms tightly intertwined.

"Go fuck yourself!" Lockton snarled.

"Doc." Stone made his way through the scattered piles of clothes. "The techs are worried. They asked me to come up and see if you were all right."

"I'm not! Now get out!" Lockton ripped the sculptured glass lamp from the reading table and the room went dark.

"You're making a fool of yourself, Doc."

"I had a lot of help!"

Like a bat diving for an insect, the lamp flew through the blackness and exploded against the wall.

Stone jumped over the dresser to restrain him. Lockton caught him with an elbow, turned and struck him in the eye with a right cross. Covering up like a boxer, Stone ducked, caught Lockton's wrist, twisted his arm over his shoulder and flipped him onto the floor. Jamming his knee into the middle of Lockton's spine, he tugged his head back by the hair.

Alex side-kicked Stone in the ribs. "Let him go, you bastard!"

Stone released him and stood up. Lockton pulled himself to his knees, gasping for breath.

He looked up from the floor. "Get out! Both of you!"

"James, please . . ." Alex bent down beside him. "I love you. It's not what . . ."

"Get out," he groaned, shoving her away. "Now!"

Chapter 30

"WE CAN'T JUST LEAVE HIM in the Winnebago. If we have to wait two more days before we get off the island, you'll be able to smell him halfway to Seattle." Harrison finished washing the blood out of the surveillance room and squeezed the mop into the bucket.

"We'll bury him," Stone decided. "In the woods."

Harrison dumped the bucket into the aluminum utility sink beside the dryer in the basement washroom. Stone listened to the ceiling creak. When the toilet flushed and the basement pipes gurgled, they both looked up. It was Alex. "You'll have to do it tonight. And watch out for patrols. The area's thick with them, all looking for the kid's dog."

Harrison started to mop the tile floor, from the hidden doorway back toward the fireplace. The fresh bucket of water quickly turned pink.

Stone deeply regretted Schraeder's death. He was a good agent, a man you could count on when it got rough. And a friend. The last one he had had.

Schraeder was not the type to make mistakes. They were too costly in their business. If a madman could get Schraeder, anything could happen.

Although he was not superstitious, Stone couldn't avoid the feeling that his luck was slowly being chipped away by the dementia that possessed the island.

8:48 p.m.

"WHAT'S HE UP TO?" Stone asked.

There wasn't a sound coming in over the monitors in the surveillance room.

"Same thing he's been doing for the last couple hours. Nothing. Just sitting in his room."

"Be quick with Schraeder." Stone took the earphones as Harrison got up from the chair. "I need you here."

"Why? What's the . . ."

"McGuire. I think we'd better watch her as closely as the doc. I have a feeling they've both . . . defected."

9:42 p.m.

A POWERFUL NIGHT WIND was blowing in from the southwest. It shook the glass door to the balcony off Alex's bedroom. Standing in front of her dressing table, she studied the photographs that encircled her makeup and hairbrushes. She picked up the gold-framed photograph of her and James standing in front of the two-story A-frame condominium in the Cascade Mountains. It had been their first weekend alone together. The first time they had made love. It was supposed to have been a ski weekend, but they never left the condo.

There had been nothing shy about him in bed, she remembered fondly. Or on the living room floor. Or the kitchen table. Or the stairs. Or in the hot tub... It was as if their bodies had purposely been sculpted to fit together, like connecting pieces of a jigsaw puzzle. That wonderful aching she felt the first time they had touched had never left.

It was still with her now.

The largest photo on the table was shot when she was twenty-two. Her father had taken her on a three-month tour of Europe. For the first time in her life, he had treated her as an equal. It was one of the few fond memories she had of her father. He knew important people in the diplomatic and political arenas of the Continent. They had been wined and dined in places and styles she had only seen or read about in magazines. The photograph showed them standing in front of the Berlin Wall. Back in the States, she had had it blown up and her father had written a note in the corner: "Congratulations to the new graduate. May each generation be stronger." The trip had been his present to her for completing her CIA training.

She picked up the Berlin photo and walked out onto the balcony. The cold wind pricked her face. The trees creaked and moaned like old men bent in hard labor. To the north, the lights on the ferry docked at Southworth shone like a torch-bearing funeral procession.

Something was nagging at her. Something besides James, her father or the Agency. Something bitter and out of sync, lurking just under the surface of the night.

Peering over the balcony, she saw Harrison sneak down to the basement with a pick and shovel over his shoulder. When he looked up, she backed away from the ledge.

The cold spring wind cut through Alex's sweater. She was suddenly shivering. She closed the balcony door and sat at the head of the bed.

Turning the digital alarm-clock radio around, she pulled out the four loose screws and removed the back. Inside was a small monitor. Its corresponding transmitter was hidden in the electric baseboard under the wall-length table in the surveillance room. She always turned it on when she went to bed, as an added security measure.

No one knew about it except her.

She had installed it the day she moved in.

Individual initiative, she could hear her father lecturing. Trust no one but yourself.

She switched on the monitor.

"How'd it go?" Stone asked.

"No one should find him. I used some of the lye in the garage. He won't take long to decompose."

Stone lit a Camel. "I've been thinking. When we get to Texas, Courser will need at least 5 cc of the extract. No one knows how much of the extract was stolen, except . . ."

"The doc," Harrison said.

"Exactly." Stone took a deep drag of his cigarette. Smoke tunneled out both nostrils as from a sleeping dragon.

"What about McGuire? If anything happened to him, she'd..."

"I know." Stone blew on the end of his cigarette until it was bright orange.

"Wait a minute," Harrison objected. "Her old man's powerful. He'd insist on an investigation."

"Not if they were to die from the disease. The doc has been working closely with the virus, calibrating the breakdown of the infected wells. And McGuire has been sleeping with him. As his fiancée, I'm sure they've exchanged bodily fluids recently. If he became infected while working with the virus, she would too. The virus can be passed through saliva."

"But how do we..."

Stone looked back at the wall safe where the extract was hidden.

"I'm glad I'm on your side," Harrison said, stamping out the cigarette Stone had just flicked onto the floor.

10:18 p.m.

JAMES LOCKTON WAS SITTING at his desk in the study, listening to Debussy. He had never heard of the composer until he met Alex McGuire. The strong, haunting music beat against his disillusioned heart like ocean waves ripping down the walls of a sand castle. He felt old and tired and foolish.

He had given his love to a lie, as he had his career, and both had crumbled down around him like badly structured card houses.

Some genius, he thought mockingly.

He opened the screen on the window and poured the glass of Scotch outside, as if it were his own sacrificial blood. Even it tasted bitter to him now. The low, distant churning of the blockade vessels' diesel engines washed in with the wind.

An hour ago, Mrs. L. had come into his room and sat on the floor beside him for a while. The two techs had left right after Alex and Stone. He had half expected some kind of I-told-you-so, knowing how she felt about Alex.

Instead, she had said simply, "She loves you. I know she does. I don't know what the fight was about, but don't lose her now."

He unlocked the top left-hand drawer and put the key in his pocket. Removing the snub-nosed .38, he pointed it at the Aztec mask on the bookshelf.

Her giving him the pistol made sense now. And why she chased the intruder instead of calling the cops. And why she didn't have to work for a living. And why she had been so reluctant to go out with him in the beginning.

But he had kept pushing, he thought ruefully. Just wouldn't let go, like a damn monkey with its arm stuck in a clay jar, too greedy to drop the piece of fruit inside.

It's 0 for 2, he concluded with chagrin.

One death.

One betrayal.

But they felt the same.

He closed the window. Three quiet knocks interrupted the music. For a second, he thought it was a scratch on the record. Then he saw Alex standing in the doorway, an overnight bag slung over her shoulder.

Her dark red hair was windblown and tangled. Everything she was wearing was black. In the unlit hall, all he could see was her pale face framed in wild red hair. She adjusted the tight waistband of her black corduroy jeans and smiled. He could not take his eyes from hers.

"How did you . . ."

Alex pressed a finger to her lips and waved at him to follow.

Her sudden presence made him feel as though he had just swallowed a live grenade. Any second now, he would explode, splattering pieces of himself all over the room.

She pressed her hands in mock prayer and waved at him again. He followed her out to the back porch.

"They're monitoring you. I didn't want them to know I'm here."

"Why are you here?" he asked coldly.

She flipped her jacket collar up, turned her back to the wind and told him everything she had just heard.

"You think Stone sent the burglar?" he asked.

"I know he did."

It made sense to Lockton. That, in itself, made him suspicious. He had been taken for a fool once too often.

"Why should I believe all this?"

Alex walked to the railing. "Because it's the truth. And if you don't believe it, you'll be dead."

Killing him seemed the only logical alternative . . . if what she said about Stone was true. Now that they had the extract and all his files, Lockton was no longer valuable. Stone would be only too happy to watch the doc die of his own disease. Poetic justice, so to speak.

"James, why would I lie? What possible good would it do?"

"To get me to overreact and run. Stone calls Control. Tells them we're missing. That I was showing the first signs of infection. Paranoia. Delusions. Hallucinations. After he finds me, with your help, he gives me an injection of the virus, waits until I'm totally insane and calls in the National Guard!"

"You don't believe that?" Alex desperately searched his face, deeply hurt by the speculation. "You can't. James, I love you. You know I love you."

He stiffened. "I don't know shit." He circled around the glass table to the railing.

"James, you can't really think I could ever hurt you."

"You already have."

"Please, James. There isn't much time. I'm trying to save our lives."

He slapped the wooden railing and a splinter cut into his thumb. "Prove it."

"How?"

"Tell me where they've hidden the extract."

"James, it's too dangerous. We'd never . . ."

He stared at the lights of the Coast Guard Cutter, *Plymouth*. "It's the only way, Alex."

10:35 p.m.

LOCKTON PACKED a small suitcase for his son before waking him up. If what Alex said was true, he had to send Nick to a safe place, a place where Stone couldn't get to him. Alex was across the hall helping Mrs. L. pack. He could hear Mrs. L. complaining as she dressed. Wrapping a blanket around Nick's shoulders, he carried the boy and his suitcase downstairs. Mrs. L. and Alex joined them in the garage.

"Daddy?" Nick was still half asleep. "Where are we going?"

"To the old Nike base. Where all the soldiers are."

"If you don't tell me why you got me up in the middle of the night, I'm not going anywhere," Mrs. L. said, refusing to get into the Mazda.

"There's no time to explain, Mrs. L." Lockton opened the door to the driver's seat. "I want you to drive to the Nike base. You're both to remain there until I come for you. Is that clear?"

Nothing was clear, not to Mrs. L. First Mr. Lockton had kicked Alex out of the house. Now she was back and he was kicking her and Nick out.

If nothing else, however, she was sure of one thing: whatever his reasons, he was doing it to protect them. She had no idea why, but obviously it was serious. Otherwise he wouldn't send Nick away at a time like this. She took the keys from him and got into the car.

Lockton laid Nick in the passenger seat.

"Aren't you coming with us, Daddy?" he asked.

"Shh," Lockton soothed. "Go back to sleep. I'll see you soon."

Nick poked his head out of the blanket. "But I don't want..."

"I'll meet you there later, Nick. I promise. I just have to do something first." He closed the door and peered in the window at Mrs. L.

"You won't have any trouble with the roadblocks. You've got official stickers. Just go slow approaching them."

Mrs. L. backed out the car and Lockton followed in her headlights. Nick looked out the passenger window. He was starting to feel abandoned and it scared him. Lockton ran up to the car and Nick rolled down the window.

"Just you and me, kid," he whispered.

"All the way." Nick grinned.

Chapter 31

10:31 p.m., March 19, 1986

STONE AMBLED DOWNSTAIRS with a sandwich in one hand and a beer in the other.

"She's over at the doc's," Harrison called out. "They've just sent the kid and the housekeeper to Operations."

"What?" Stone flipped the plate onto the table by the sofa. He had just checked on McGuire. Her bedroom door had been locked, but he had heard the shower going. He had assumed she . . .

They ran upstairs and began searching her room. Harrison noticed one of the screws sticking out of the back of the radio and opened it.

"She knows," he announced.

Stone searched her tall mahogany dresser and found an empty ammunition box in the back corner of her lingerie drawer.

"I underestimated her." Stone tossed the box onto the floor.

"How much do you think she heard?" Harrison asked.

Stone glanced at the photograph of Alex and her father. "We'll have to assume the worst."

"Think they'll go to Green?"

"No." Stone sat down in front of the dresser mirror and picked up the photograph taken in Berlin. Old man McGuire was as smart as they come. And as dangerous. But he couldn't worry about that now. He suddenly found himself wishing Harrison had bought it and not Schraeder. He would have felt more confident. "They've probably gone into hiding."

"The doc grew up on this island," Harrison said. "How the hell will we find them?"

"We won't." Stone put down the photograph. "The National Guard will."

"How?"

Stone stomped across the room and pushed Harrison. "Hit me."

Harrison backed away. "What?"

Stone closed in again. "Hit me. I'm sure there's been times you've wanted to. Especially in the last few days. Come on." He poked Harrison in the chest. "Hit me."

10:54 p.m.

GREEN SCANNED the laboratory results recently delivered to the control center. All water systems on the island had been retested again, including the four previously contaminated systems.

Green smiled. Clean. Every damn one of them. Clean and pure and drinkable.

He started to dial the governor when one of his assistants told him he had a call from Operations on line three. It was one of the two lab techs that had been assigned to Lockton.

"Sir, Mr. Lockton just sent his housekeeper and his son over here. Mrs. L. said they were told to remain here until he came for them. I asked her why he sent them. She doesn't know. She just said he seemed extremely anxious and she did as she was told."

"Did you try calling Lockton?"

"Yes, sir. Twice. No answer."

"No answer? They're supposed to remain at home like everyone else. Someone should answer."

The restaurant door banged open. Stone stumbled inside and tripped over the front desk.

"He...he went berserk," Stone stuttered, lifting himself off the desk. Blood dribbled out of a gash in his left eyebrow. The eye itself was badly swollen. His right cheek was bruised and his lower lip was cut.

He had told Harrison to make it appear convincing. From the looks on their faces, he had done a good job.

"I'll get back to you." Green hung up and hurried to Stone's aid.

The state Board of Health official at the front desk quickly soaked a towel in cold water and gave it to Green. He gently patted the blood off Stone's cheek and eye. Two other officials were supporting him by the arms.

"Who went berserk?" Green exchanged the bloody towel for a clean one. Stone bent over, holding his ribs, and exhaled, trying his best to sound like a half-plugged bicycle pump. He was playing his role to the hilt.

"Lockton," he gasped, momentarily rolling his eyes up into his lids.

Green glanced at one of his people. "Call Operations. Get Larson, the lab tech, back on the line." A woman handed Green a towel packed with ice. He pressed it over Stone's left eye. "Go on."

"He had exploded earlier. Literally tore his bedroom apart. Anyway, I came up from the basement. As soon as I walked into the hall, he came at me, screaming. McGuire was with him. I finally made it to the bathroom and locked myself in. He was screaming like a madman. I pushed out the screen window, escaped to his car and drove here."

"We have Larson, sir," Green's assistant announced.

"Hold this against that eye." Green gave the ice pack to Stone and went to the phone. "You didn't mention anything about an earlier ruckus. What happened?"

"I was going to tell you about that but you cut me off," Larson said. "A couple of hours ago, Lockton went berserk. We could hear him from the living room. He even hit Mr. Stone. That's why I called when I heard he'd sent his son and housekeeper over here."

"He just attacked Mr. Stone again," Green informed him. There was a long pause on the other end. "Larson, did you hear me?"

"I'd hoped I was wrong," Larson said.

"What do you mean?"

"Think about it. Why would he send his family away? Especially after what happened to his son. In the last few hours he's had two violent episodes. The second much worse than the first. I keep getting the feeling he knows."

"Knows what?"

"That he's showing the first signs...of the disease."

"If that were the case, why wouldn't he have sent his fiancée away, too?"

"Maybe she's infected, too. If they've exchanged bodily fluids..."

"I want everyone that's worked in the labs to be tested immediately. The boy and the housekeeper, too."

"Yes, sir."

Green handed the phone back. "You'd better go up to the operations center for a test as well," he said to Stone. He signaled the guardsman at the radio. "Call the patrols near Lockton's house. There's at least four fire teams looking for that dog. Tell them to be on the alert for Mr. Lockton and his fiancée, Miss McGuire. There's a possibility they may be infected, so they're to proceed with extreme caution. And send a patrol to search Lockton's house. They have to be found. *Now!*"

11:08 p.m.

THE CLOUDS had finally blocked the moon, but the air was dry. It didn't feel like rain. At Alex's suggestion, Lockton had changed into a dark sweater and jeans.

He buttoned the top of his lined, blue jean jacket and pulled his navy blue stocking cap down on his forehead.

They were standing on either side of her unbroken basement window. The other window and the door had been boarded up by the National Guard.

"You think he's in there?" Lockton asked, peeking at the paneled wall.

"Stone wouldn't have left the surveillance room unguarded. I'm sure they heard you send Nick and Mrs. L. away. They know something's up."

"So why would Stone leave?"

"Doesn't make sense to me, either."

They crouched down under the window.

"Maybe it's a trap," Lockton said. "Maybe Stone hid the car and came back."

"Maybe."

Alex slipped her arm through his. Lockton did not draw away. She was grateful for this first, tangible sign of trust.

Keeping close to the house, the pair sneaked under the deck to the north wall. There were no lights on in the house. The darkness was comforting.

Alex pointed at the window in the guest bedroom. "That's the one with the broken latch."

She took Lockton's lawn clippers out of her shoulder bag and handed them to him. He snipped the screen and unhooked the two stays. After lifting the screen out, he slid the window up.

Using his hands like a stirrup, he boosted Alex up through the window. She checked the hall as he climbed in after her.

Keeping to opposite walls, they crept down the hall, checking all the rooms on their way to the living room.

The main floor was empty.

Lockton searched upstairs while Alex waited by the door to the basement.

"If Stone's here," he concluded as they walked back to the guest bedroom, "he's in the surveillance room with Harrison."

"Maybe he did come after us. He could have been driving to your house while we were walking down the path."

"Alone?"

"Not being able to handle both of us would never enter Stone's mind. Believe me."

Lockton's heart was tapping against his sternum like a hungry woodpecker. "Give me the gun."

Alex took her Smith & Wesson .38 special out of her purse. "I really think I should be the one to go in."

Lockton shook his head. "No way."

"James, I've been trained for this."

He walked to the window and offered her his hand. "We've been through all this. Now let's go."

After he helped her back out the window, he picked up the stainless-steel pistol and stared at it. He had promised her he could use it if he had to, but he had no idea if he really could or not. He just hoped he wouldn't have to find out.

Lockton made it to the basement without a noise. Keeping against the paneling, he inched toward the false light switch. Outside the window, Alex pointed at his jacket. For a moment, Lockton didn't understand. He had been too busy worrying about the racket his heart was making. She raised her hand, thumb and forefinger extended at a right angle.

He nodded and took out the .38.

When he glanced back at the window, she was gone. A second later, she reappeared with a brick. He pressed his back against the paneling. She had told him the door would open up toward him if he stayed to the left of the switch.

She held up one finger. Then two.

The brick shattered the glass and thudded against the sofa.

The wall cracked open.

A thin line of light cut across the floor like a laser beam. The barrel of a Ruger .357 peered beyond the door like the angry head of a snapping turtle.

Lockton stepped back and kicked as hard as he could. The Ruger clanked against the wooden floor. Harrison shoved the door back and dived for his weapon.

Bouncing off the wall, Lockton leaped onto Harrison's shoulders and swung the butt of his pistol against his jaw, just below the ear. Harrison went limp.

Alex crawled in through the window and quickly checked his pulse. "Better roll him on his stomach. He could drown in his own blood, lying on his back like that."

Lockton bent down and examined Harrison's face. He had a deep gash in his jaw. Blood was trickling out of the corner of his mouth.

"His pulse is good."

Lockton entered the brightly lit surveillance room. For four years, this electronic wall had been spying on his family. The longer he stared, the angrier he became. He picked up the central monitor and smashed it on the floor. Then he ripped out the headphones and started beating them against the wall.

Alex stepped over to the wall safe. She knew better than to interrupt. She was an integral part of this destructive rampage. As the surveillance equipment crashed around her, she concentrated on opening the wall safe. When she swung the thick steel door open, Lockton stopped.

Alex pointed into the safe. "Do you believe me now?"

11:21 p.m.
WITH THE EXTRACT CONTAINER and the key computer disks in his backpack and a five-gallon can of gasoline in his hand, Lockton followed Alex up the muddy road to the Winnebago. With the crowbar Alex brought, it didn't take long to snap open the aluminum doorframe.

They piled all the files, printouts and disks into the center of the Winnebago. While Lockton doused them with gasoline, Alex pocketed the two-way radio that was on the counter by the sink.

Hopping outside, Alex tied one of the camper's kitchen towels around the end of a broomstick. Lockton unscrewed the vehicle's gas cap and tossed it into the woods. Alex soaked the towel in gasoline and chucked the can into the back of the camper.

"Ready?" she asked.

Lockton lit a match and Alex held out the makeshift torch.

"Say goodbye to four years of my life," he sighed.

11:49 p.m.
HARRISON AWOKE FACEDOWN in a puddle of blood. He felt as if a bass drum had been implanted inside his right ear. With each heartbeat, the drum pounded against his brain. As he pushed up onto his knees, an excruciating pain shot up through his jaw into his skull.

Standing up dizzily, he surveyed the damage to the surveillance room. It was beyond repair. Once he looked inside the open wall safe, he understood why he had been attacked. Turning off the light, he stumbled back into the den and closed off the room.

It was no longer of any use.

Harrison now two lights flashing outside the broken windows. Mopping the blood from his face with his jacket, he zigzagged to the boarded-up door. Harrison hit it with his shoulder and the nailed boards popped out.

"Hey," he called to the lights. "Over here."

One of the soldiers shone his flashlight on Harrison's huge figure. The other aimed his M-16.

Harrison shaded his eyes. "Move that fucking light, asshole."

The soldier lowered his flashlight and approached the basement. His partner kept back by the path, prepared to blow the man away if he made a sudden move. The two other members of the patrol were running down from the road.

"What happened?" Corporal Ashby asked, looking in the basement.

"Dey attackee," Harrison mumbled painfully. He could barely move his jaw.

"What?"

"Lock-on. Ahackee."

"Lockton attacked you?" the corporal repeated. The man's face was a mess.

Harrison nodded very slowly. "And dgirl."

"McGuire? She was with him?"

Again Harrison nodded.

"Why?"

Harrison shrugged. "Ee's kazy."

"Crazy?" The corporal waved to the private with the radio. "Did he seem ... rabid?"

Harrison nodded.

"Call Operations," the corporal told the radioman. "Tell them Lockton and the woman attacked ..." He glanced back at Harrison.

"Har-is-on."

"They attacked a man named Harrison at McGuire's house. He said Lockton was rabid. The attack took place ..." He looked back again.

"Aff ... our."

"A half hour ago. Tell them to send a medic. We're going to search her house now. Alert all other patrols in the area."

As he was relaying the message, Dr. Green broke in. "Put the corporal on."

Ashby grabbed the radio. "Yes, sir?"

"I'm sending a platoon to your location. Remain there until they arrive."

"Yes, sir."

Suddenly there was a tremendous explosion.

"What the hell was that?" Green barked.

"I don't know, sir."

Chapter 32

12:21 a.m., March 20, 1986

ONE OF THE FIRE TEAMS in the woods east of Cove Road spotted the burning Winnebago moments after the explosion, when the fire inside the camper had set off the vehicle's gas tank.

As soon as the patrol had radioed Operations, Green knew the pair was within his grasp. They couldn't have traveled very far in those dense woods at night. He immediately ordered twenty jeeps to cruise the two-mile stretch of road on the main highway directly above Cove Road. Four jeeps were sent to traverse the Corbin Beach road just south of Cove Road. Three others were driving south from Vashon Point along the beach roads north of Lockton's house.

The platoon arrived at McGuire's in two two-and-a-half-ton trucks. After picking up the fire team there, the trucks split up, one to either end of Cove road. The other patrols in the woods had been ordered to meet them at either point. Lieutenant Merrick was the platoon leader. He commanded his troops to spread out down the road at fifty-foot intervals.

"Sir, the platoon is in position," he radioed his colonel.

"Good." The colonel stood up in his jeep and looked down the main highway at the second platoon, also fifty feet apart. His troops were illuminated in the continual line of jeep headlights patrolling the two mile stretch of road.

When the sergeant gave the signal, the entire platoon clicked on their flashlights and started into the woods. Every fourth guardsman, a squad leader, was equipped with a radio. They were to report to the platoon sergeant every five minutes as the line descended west down the hill.

"Move it, Lieutenant," the colonel radioed Merrick. The platoon on Cove Road advanced east into the woods.

12:45 a.m.

WHEN JAMES LOCKTON and Alex McGuire climbed out of the ravine, fifty yards from the main highway, they saw the wall of lights bouncing directly toward them and ducked behind a rotting log.

After they had torched the Winnebago and traversed the hill to the ravine, Alex had used the two-way radio she had found in the Winnebago to monitor Corporal Ashby's message to Operations and the National Guard's movements.

Stone had set them up.

Attacking Harrison had sealed their fate.

They were now considered rabid and dangerous.

"Nice night for a stroll in the woods," Lockton muttered, looking for an escape.

Alex slid up against him, staring at the beams of light spearing through the forest. They both knew the guardsmen would open fire as soon as they spotted them. They had been warned not to take any chances because of Lockton's past violent behavior.

"Where do we go from here?" she asked, trying to sound calm.

"Up."

By the second radio check, the two platoons were within a quarter mile of each other. Neither line had seen any evidence of the two fugitives.

"I can't hear them any more," Alex said, balanced eighty feet up in the fir tree.

Lockton looked around the tree trunk at the two lines of lights down the hill. "We've got to get across the highway before they meet."

They carefully climbed down the tree, blindly feeling with their feet for each lower branch. It took twice as long to descend as it had to scale it.

Lockton had been timing the jeeps on the highway during their ten minutes in the tree. They seemed to pass by the bus stop approximately every ten seconds. All the vehicles kept within headlight distance of each other. There wasn't a blank spot in the chain of light.

"He's got the road lit up like a Christmas tree," Alex said. They were hiding in the ditch beside the road, under the half-enclosed bus stop's short bench.

They watched the procession of jeeps for another five minutes, trying to detect a flaw.

Neither could find one.

Suddenly a jeep, fifty yards south of the bus stop, skidded to a stop. On the opposite side of the road, another jeep slammed on its brakes. All down the highway, jeep tires began squealing. Caught in the cross fire of headlights, a dog froze on the yellow no-passing line.

The chain was broken.

They darted across the road and leaped into the gully.

The dog began barking at the two stationary jeeps.

"It's Thor!" Lockton crawled up to the edge of the highway.

A guardsman stepped out of his jeep and aimed his M-16. Thor hunched his shoulders and growled. Flames spewed from the barrel. As chunks of road blew up around the center line, Thor bolted into the trees.

Alex turned on the radio.

"Sir, we spotted the dog. Williams fired, but missed. He's heading west down toward..."

"The hell with the fucking dog, mister!" the colonel screamed. "You've broken our chain of light, you shithead!"

"But, sir, we..."

"Get moving, soldier! If those two got through because of this, I'll personally see that your ass..."

Alex switched it off. "They never would have gotten him. Not Thor."

Lockton pushed her back into the trees. "The deer trail's right up there. Let's put some distance between us and those platoons."

Like Alex, his immediate reaction had been to root for Thor's escape.

Now he wished the guardsman had hit him.

He didn't want his dog to go through the slow, torturous death of rabies.

1:03 a.m.

THE LIGHTS of a four-man patrol bobbed across the open terrain between a row of view homes and the eastern cliff behind them.

"The lines just met," Alex whispered, as they huddled in the underbrush to wait for the patrol to pass. When the patrol turned west, Alex stepped back onto the deer trail. "There can't be many patrols here on the east side. From what we've heard, the colonel pulled about everyone up for his pincers movement."

"Let's hope so."

Below the cliff, the trail leveled off by the northwestern perimeter of a six-acre horse pasture and followed the cross-planked wood fence east. It was easier to walk in the dark with the fence as a guide.

A loud snort caused the pair to drop behind a fence post.

To Alex's amazement, Lockton tore a handful of long, wet grass from the ground, stood up and reached over the fence.

"Hey, Joey," he called softly. The big gray gelding trotted over. "What are you doing out of the barn? It's not safe out here. Not with all these trigger-happy kids playing soldier."

The horse eagerly munched the grass. Laughing, Alex rose and gently scratched his jaw.

"James, we'd better get going."

"It's not like Sarah." Lockton could barely make out the outline of the barn and the trailer home. "She loves old Joey as much as her kids. She wouldn't leave him out. Not during this."

"With everything that's happened, maybe she..." Alex stopped when she felt his back stiffen.

"She shares the same water system with those tract homes south of here." He remembered from the maps. He slapped the top of the fence post. "Where Kestler lived."

"James." She tried to tug him away from the fence. "We've got a couple of miles to go. They'll be sending patrols."

He climbed through the fence. "I'm going to put Joey in the barn."

"There's no time."

He picked another handful of grass and looked back.

"I have to, Alex. For Sarah."

4:43 a.m.

RICHARD STONE WAS STANDING at the bay window, legs V-ed, hands cupped behind his back, staring at the lights of the peninsula when Harrison opened Alex's front door. He ambled over to the dining table and sat down.

"They insisted I wait at Operations until they could fetch the dental surgeon," he spit through clenched teeth. "He wired my teeth shut. The doc broke my jaw in two places."

Stone finally turned. He looked like a man who had just spent the past three days gambling away everything he owned.

"They took you out. They fucking took you out!" Stone grabbed the hardwood African bust of a Guro tribeswoman and heaved it across the room. Harrison ducked. It punched a hole in the plaster wall behind him. "What the fuck were you doing, jerking off?"

The words struck Harrison harder than the pistol Lockton had broken his jaw with. "I screwed up. What do you want me to say?" Harrison was getting angry now, too. He didn't need to have it rubbed in.

Stone kicked Alex's coffee table over, snapping its two front legs. "We've got nothing! We had it all, and now we've got nothing!"

Harrison was still woozy from the anesthetic. He decided to keep quiet and let Stone get it out of his system. If he opened his mouth now, which would be impossible without wire cutters, they could end up trying to kill each other. They were that angry.

Stone paced around the piano. "Ten million dollars! Some candy-assed scientist gets the best of us and we burn ten million bucks."

At least he said "us" this time, Harrison thought, watching Stone rap his knuckles along the edge of the piano.

He decided to chance it. "He'll still have the extract. We can get it back."

"He'll destroy it." Stone stopped pacing. "Just like he did all his files. He's got a lot more balls than I gave him credit for." Stone sat on the piano stool. "If they could get through two platoons, we sure as hell won't be able to find him. Not within six hours."

"Why six hours?" Harrison was relieved to see that he was planning again, instead of raving.

"The decomposition factor," Stone explained. "If the virus is left in the open air for six hours, it will be destroyed. That's his plan. Hide somewhere safe, somewhere where he can open the extract and wait until it has decomposed."

Harrison pushed away from the table, still a little dizzy. He waited until he regained his balance before standing. "What if he does? What do we do then?"

Stone slammed his fist on the piano keys. "If we can't give Courser the extract, we'll have to give him the next best thing."

"What's that?"

"It's creator."

"What if he refuses to make it again?"

"He won't." Stone grinned. "Not if we have his son."

Chapter 33

4:51 a.m., March 20, 1986

THE BOBBING LIGHTS of the two National Guardsmen on beach patrol faded around the point north of the Walters boathouse. Alex kept watch by the door. There was a permanent guard post at the end of the road, a half mile north near the La Fiesta restaurant. All the houses on Cowley's Landing had been evacuated Monday afternoon. Except for the roving beach patrols, they were alone.

Alex understood, now, why Joey's safety had been so important to James. He had dated Sarah, the horse's owner, two years ago. They had remained friends ever since. Because the horse hadn't been in its stable, Lockton had assumed Sarah and her two children had either been evacuated or had succumbed to the disease.

Returning Joey to the barn was the only thing left he could do for them.

Alex checked her watch. The beach patrol had passed the boathouse at exactly 5:17 a.m. It was now 5:29 a.m. If they were under the same half-hour schedule as the patrols on the west side, another patrol should pass, going south, in about eighteen minutes.

While she was timing the patrol, Lockton quietly cleaned up the wreckage in the boathouse.

Another atonement, she thought.

The room had been in complete disarray. Tools were scattered everywhere. One of the big metal lockers was lying upside down in the water between the hydroplane and the cement wall. A workbench straddled the *Suzy Q*'s fiberglass stern.

They both knew how much that hydroplane had meant to John Walters. After looking at what he had done to the boathouse, it was easy to understand the demented fury that had caused him to murder his wife. As soon as they had arrived, Lockton had nailed a grease-smeared blanket over the window in the door, then lit two candles. When he had seen the carnage, he had recoiled like an acrophobic from the edge of a skyscraper.

It had been a long and difficult journey across the island, but Lockton had refused to take a break until the boathouse had been completely put back into working order—the way John always left it.

Alex sat beside him on the edge of the cement walk-around. Just below their feet, the water gently splashed up and back against the walls under the boat ramp. Lockton hadn't spoken since he had lit the candles.

"One more thing to do," he stated, as if addressing the hydroplane.

"James?" She stopped him before he could get up. "I love you. More than anything. I love you."

Suddenly he was seeing her for the first time. He studied every feature of her face, as if, in the soft glow of the candles, he was looking at a perfect work of art. Like a young, tormented painter, staring in fear and wonder at Van Gogh's last self-portrait, Lockton felt his battered soul pour out into the living canvas.

Seeing his own pain slowly fill her eyes, he looked away. After unstrapping the backpack on the workbench, he removed the airtight metal box containing the extract and unlocked it. That terrible sinking vortex that had been sucking at his belly since he had lit the candles was almost gone.

Somehow she had taken it from him, as if she had willed it, without regard for the suffering it contained, into herself.

From the backpack's front pocket, he removed a pair of surgical gloves and rolled them onto his hands. Slowly, so as not to tilt the individual test tubes, he opened their rubber stops. Carrying the metal box like a tray of champagne glasses, he climbed the short stepladder and hid the box amid the gloves on the top shelf behind a case of STP motor oil.

Lockton removed the three, heavy green army-surplus blankets covering the hydroplane's hull, spread two out on the concrete near the side door, and rolled the third up into a pillow. He blew one candle out and brought the other over to their new bed.

Alex snuggled in under the blanket next to him. "Am I forgiven?"

He kissed her. "I'm the one that needs forgiving."

She slithered underneath him. "They didn't arrest any scientists at Los Alamos as war criminals, James. Don't condemn yourself. You didn't steal it. Stone did. The spill was his fault. He caused the outbreak. Not you!"

She drew his mouth to hers and kissed him deeply. Her body writhed beneath him.

He needed her now.

All of her.

She had felt it in his eyes, before he had stood up to hide the extract.

And she needed him.

They had to take away the pain and the death that had enveloped them since they entered the boathouse.

"Let it go, James," she whispered, tugging his sweater up. "Please..." Her breasts pressed up hard against his ribs as her knee slipped between his thighs "Love me. Now. Please!"

"I'm sorry," he said.

"James, please!" Her hand tugged his shirt up and slid across his belly. "Quit blaming yourself. It's not fair. Not to you. Not to me." She pushed her hips up against his. "And not to the children."

Lockton arched back to look at her. "What children?"

She tugged him down. "The ones you're going to give me."

6:33 a.m.

THE TWO GUARDSMEN posted at the end of the road to the old Nike base did not like each other or their assignment. They'd been stationed at the entrance to the operations center since midnight. A week earlier, they had come to blows over a girl. Not a word had passed between them all night.

The cloudy sky was turning amber in the premorning light. A southbound car crested the hill and slowed as it approached the entrance. The two guards blocked the road.

Richard Stone rolled down his window. The guard on the driver's side checked the official sticker on the Subaru's windshield. He remembered the driver as soon as he saw the bandage above his swollen eye. He was the scientist that had been beat up by that Lockton character. Everyone had heard about it. The colonel had blown a gasket after Lockton and his fiancée had eluded two of his platoons. All the soldiers at Operations had been walking on glass all night.

"Any news about Lockton?" Stone asked.

The guard bent down by the door. "None of the patrols have seen a thing." He looked in at Harrison. "Looks like someone punched the hell out of you too, fella."

In his rearview mirror, Stone watched a jeep slow down as it approached from the south. The other guard waved to let them know everything was okay. The jeep passed by.

"Don't he talk?" the guard asked, looking at Harrison. He'd had a lousy night and was happy to hassle a couple of college-boy scientists.

Harrison spread his lips into a sneer, revealing the steel fence across his teeth.

"Wired shut," he grunted.

The guard leaned in farther. "You're the guy they jumped." He glanced at Stone. "Just after they got you. Couple of tough cookies, eh?"

"That's right." Stone was having a difficult time remaining polite.

"You're one lucky son of a bitch they didn't off ya," the guard said, pointing at Harrison.

The look Harrison gave the guard could have parched a rain forest.

"Dumb bastard," he hissed, as they sped up the hill to the Nike base.

The majority of the parking area was occupied by three rows of two-and-a-half-ton trucks. A Cobra helicopter was perched in the field north of the main building complex. The colonel had requested one as an added security measure. Harrison admired the gunship's 40 mm cannon as he got out of the car.

"We've come for supplies," Stone informed the two soldiers guarding the main entrance to the operations center. The guards recognized the two men and opened the glass doors.

Inside the lobby, there were three military personnel, one at each corridor entrance. Stone knew the layout. The corridor to the right led to the hospital area and security wing. The one to the left housed off-duty guardsmen. It also contained sleeping quarters for the state Board of Health's medical people, plus the cafeteria and kitchen. The center corridor led to the storage rooms. Bunks had also been set up in one of its two small utility wings. That was where Nick and Mrs. L. had been given quarters after their antemortem rabies tests had shown they were not infected.

"Need some supplies," Stone repeated to the guardsman stationed by the center corridor. He was half asleep on a chair next to the door, his M-16 casually laid across his lap. He nodded, barely opening one eye.

Stone checked the first room in the next wing past the supply rooms. It was filled with boxes of medical supplies and laboratory equipment. He tried the next room. One wall was stacked with green army blankets, pillows and folding cots. In the back was a pile of empty cardboard boxes.

"Grab that big box," he said, pulling three blankets off the shelf.

They walked to the far end of the hall. Stone slowly turned the door handle to the last room on the left and cracked it open. Mrs. L. was lying on a cot, snoring. He eased the door closed and checked the room on the right.

Nick had heard a voice in the hall and was sitting up on his cot when Stone walked in.

"Where's Daddy?" he asked.

"He sent me to get you. He's busy." Stone put down the box and Harrison dumped the blankets inside it.

Nick jumped off the bunk and backed up against the wall.

"He wouldn't send you," he argued.

Stone stopped at the corner of the bunk. "He had to. He was in the lab."

"He said he'd come himself. He told me to wait until he came."

Harrison pushed around Stone. "He's busy, kid."

Nick ducked under Harrison's arms and scrambled over the cot. Stone blocked the door. He was trapped behind the cot. He tried to roll under it, but Harrison caught his leg and yanked him out.

"Mrs. L.!" Nick cried.

Harrison's big hand gagged his mouth. He kicked the huge man's shins with his bare feet as he watched Mr. Stone sprinkle something on a gauze pad.

An awful smell filled the room. It reminded Nick of the hospital.

Stone gave Harrison the gauze and he pressed the chloroform-soaked pad over the boy's face. Nick held his breath as long as he could, but he finally had to inhale. He felt as if he had just rolled down a steep hill. Everything was spinning.

The guard at the corridor entrance heard the two men walking up the long hall. He had no intention of getting up off his chair now. In five more minutes, he could either go to chow, then hit the sack, or hit the sack first and eat when he awoke. To him, it was the only problem worth worrying about.

Stone opened the door for Harrison, who was carrying the large cardboard box.

"Blankets," Stone said. Harrison tilted the box so the guard could look inside without getting up.

"Okay." He leaned his chair back against the wall, uninterested. That was where he'd be soon, he thought, his eyelids iron heavy. Under a blanket, bagging ZZZs. He decided he'd go to chow afterward, not before.

11:14 a.m.

FOR THE FIRST TIME in what seemed like months, James Lockton woke up feeling rested. His back and neck were a little stiff from sleeping on the concrete, but other than that, he felt pretty good.

Brushing Alex's hair from his shoulder, he studied her sleeping profile. God, she was beautiful. He pulled the blanket up over her shoulder. Her warm, naked thigh curled up across his hips and he felt himself stirring beneath her.

He had never made love with such frenzied abandon as he had last night. It was as if he had been struggling to crawl outside of himself, to burst through his agonizing cornucopia of conflicting emotions for one brief moment of pure, physical communion.

The earth hadn't just moved, he thought, it had completely stopped. For one eternal, climactic moment, time itself had stopped.

Looking past Alex, he noticed the midday light under the automatic door facing the beach. There was no water in the boathouse now. Slipping his arm out from under her head, he sat up.

"What's wrong?" Alex asked sleepily.

"It's late." Lockton started to dress. He was concerned about Nick. He did not like the thought of his son remaining any longer than he had to in the same building complex with the victims of his disease. Last night, there had been no alternative.

Now that his goal had been accomplished, it was time to get his son.

Alex pulled her jeans on under the blanket. It was damp and chilly in the boathouse.

"Is the virus . . . dead?" she asked, zipping up.

"Totally decomposed." He slipped on his sweater and checked his watch. "At least it will be in a few minutes."

Alex rose, naked from the waist up. "Then we've done it. We've destroyed it all. The virus. The files. Everything."

Yes, he thought, we've destroyed it. But that won't bring back the dead.

"I have to call Nick," he said, lacing his hiking boots.

"Are you sure that's a good idea?" She fastened her satin bra.

"All they'll know is I had access to a phone. They won't know where I called from. When's the next patrol?"

"They'll pass by in ten minutes."

"After I make sure Nick's all right, I'll call Green at Control. Tell him we're coming. He'll probably send some people to meet us. As long as we act calm and don't make any sudden moves, we should be all right. After they test us, everything will be fine. We'll stay at Control. Stone won't be able to get at us there. Once the quarantine is lifted, you can alert your people and that will be the end of Stone."

Alex watched the beach from the side door. Above the hill behind the boathouse, the sun appeared between the clouds and lit the water like a thousand tiny campfires in a brown desert. The patrol from the north marched noisily down the beach. She checked the time.

"They've passed," she said.

"Just two calls and we'll be home free," he reassured her.

11:27 a.m.
ONE OF THE PHONES installed at the front desk in the lobby of the old Nike base buzzed and the corporal on duty answered it. "Operations center. Corporal Walsh speaking."

"I'd like to speak to Nick Lockton, please."

"Who?" The corporal asked the three guards stationed at the corridor doors if any of them knew a Nick Lockton. They all shook their heads no.

"Nick Lockton," the caller reiterated. "The boy who was brought in last night. With his nurse, an older woman that . . ."

"Oh, right." Walsh quickly put his hand over the phone and yelled at the guard by the door that led to the strategy room. "Get the colonel. Fast!" Then, to the guard by the supply corridor, "Go get the kid. And hurry!" He took off his hand and cleared his voice. "Who is this, please?"

"I'd like to speak to Nick Lockton," the caller repeated.

"Yes, sir. We're getting him now. Who shall I say is calling?"

James Lockton didn't answer.

One of the guards rushed out into the lobby. "Sir, he's gone. His nurse says she's been looking for him all morning."

Lockton couldn't make out the muffled conversation. He glanced at Alex nervously. He could sense the tension on the other end of the line.

The colonel took the phone. "Is that you, Mr. Lockton?"

"I want to speak with my son."

"Where are you?"

"Put my son on."

The corporal had already told him about the missing boy. "He's coming, Mr. Lockton. He's ah…in the bathroom."

James Lockton covered his phone. "They're stalling."

"Can they trace the call?" Alex asked.

"They don't have that kind of equipment." He took his hand off the receiver. "Where's my son?"

"Mr. Lockton, we're all very worried about you here. Why don't you tell me where you are?"

Lockton hung up the phone.

Alex watched his gray-green eyes blend acute panic with an almost malevolent loathing.

"He's not there," he said.

"But where could he have..." It suddenly hit her like an avalanche. "Oh, God, no!"

Lockton stared at the wall phone as if it were the electronic trigger mechanism to a pipe bomb planted in the same room with his son. He jerked off the receiver and dialed his own number.

"Stone?" He paused. "I want to hear his voice first." Suddenly his face softened. "Nick? Are you..." Lockton flinched. "If you harm him in any way, I swear I'll..."

Lockton flinched again, then slowly lowered the receiver. Alex took it out of his clenched fist and hung it up.

"He wants to make a trade," Lockton stated.

"For the extract?" Alex clutched his arm excitedly. "It's decomposed. We could..."

"He knows about the decomposition factor." Lockton leaned over the sink.

Alex glanced back at the phone. "Then what does he want?"

"Me."

Chapter 34

"IT CAN STILL WORK," Stone said, pouring a glass of Johnny Walker over ice. He offered one to Harrison, but he declined.

"Isn't good to drink with your teeth wired shut," he said. "The doctor said if I tied one on, I could drown in my own puke." Harrison crushed two aspirin-codeine tablets on the coffee table with the back of a spoon. After dissolving the powder in water, he drank it down. "So where do we make the trade?"

Stone packed a Camel on the back of his hand. "He said he'd call back in a half hour. I think he needed time to get control of himself."

Nick was sitting on the toilet in the guest bedroom, one wrist handcuffed to the pipe under the sink. Harrison had brought him a baloney sandwich and a can of Pepsi, but he was still too sick from the chloroform to eat.

"Once the quarantine is lifted, what then?" Harrison asked, fetching a quart of milk from the refrigerator. He hadn't eaten since his jaw had been broken and his stomach burned from the aspirin.

Smoke filtered out Stone's nose in quick, short puffs. "We'll collect on our old debt with that Mexican arms dealer, Varez. After we pick up our new identities in Texas, we'll head across the border. Varez can get us a plane. Hell, for ten grand, Varez would shoot his firstborn. Then we'll fly to Argentina. They'd be more than happy to shelter two unobtrusive Canadian millionaires. As long as they get their percentage."

"But how do we get the doc to the Persian Gulf?"

"I've worked with some of the senior exporting officials in the Argentine government. For twenty grand, we could ship him anywhere those sons of Allah want."

"I thought they were ready to chuck the entire deal if the extract wasn't delivered within the next few weeks."

Stone flicked an ash on the rug and rubbed it in with his shoe. "They don't really have a choice. They'll take what they can get. If not, we get rid of him in Argentina and split five mil instead of ten."

"What if the doc refuses to re-create it?" Harrison picked at his wired teeth.

"When it comes to unfriendly persuasion, those Muslims have had two thousand years of practice. After enough of his Christian blood has been spilled, he'll do it. If not . . . it's not our problem."

"What about McGuire?"

"We'll have to take care of that," Stone said. "Before we leave the island."

"They'll hunt us." Harrison gulped the last of the milk. "They'll probably think we sold out to the other side."

"We've hunted enough people to know how to stay hidden."

Harrison crushed the milk carton. "Courser will be the first one they'll go after once we've snuck across the border."

"We'll have to take care of him, too."

Harrison sat back, rubbing his stomach. The milk hadn't helped.

"I want to be the one to do it," he said solemnly.

Stone swirled the ice around in his glass. "Courser?"

"No." He scratched his sore jaw. "McGuire, I owe her."

2:25 p.m.

JAMES LOCKTON OPENED the two six-foot-tall metal lockers by the wall shelves where he had hidden the extract. Taking out a red wet suit, he held it up in front of Alex.

"It was Susan's," he said. "Too small." He retrieved John's blue wet suit. "This one should fit. Try it on." He lifted two scuba tanks out of the second locker.

She squeezed into the wet suit's top. "A little tight in the chest, but it'll do."

"Good." He removed the rest of the diving gear and put it on the worktable. "John always refilled his tanks after using them." He checked the regulators. "Should be good for an hour, as long as you don't go too deep. Nick used to borrow Terry's old suit until I bought him one for his birthday." He checked Terry's wet suit. It was still in good condition. "Nick loves to dive. If he had his way, he'd live underwater." The sudden smile that memory evoked, faded like a shallow footprint in a dust storm. He laid the wet suit on the workbench next to the other equipment. "There's airtight plastic bags on the shelves in the locker where the wet suits were. You can put your clothes in them."

Alex watched him drift away again.

She knew what was on his mind.

He was wondering if he would ever see either of them again.

"I can't do it, James," she confessed. "I can't leave the island without you."

"You have no choice." He arranged the gear into two sets, like an orderly laying out his officers' battle uniforms.

"Yes, I do. I'm staying with you."

Lockton glanced at her sternly. "I'm making the trade."

"I don't trust him."

"It doesn't really matter, does it? Nick's all that counts now."

"But..."

"He won't kill me. He needs me to re-create the extract," Lockton explained. "I'll be all right."

"I know you, James. You won't make the extract again."

She was right.

He would never re-create the virus.

Even if it meant his life.

Last night, he had sworn an oath to John Walters and his family.

"As soon as we make the trade, Stone will come after you. He needs Nick to ensure I'll re-create it. And he needs you... dead."

Although she knew it was the truth, she despised hearing it. "James, he'll kill you. Sooner or later, he'll..." She closed her eyes and a tear slithered down the curve of her nose.

"I love you, Alex. And I love Nick. I have to get you both off this island. Once Stone has me, neither of you will be safe." He lifted her face up as if it were a priceless jewel. "Promise me you'll do it. Please?"

His finger gently outlined her cheekbone until she opened her eyes.

"Promise me?"

She looked over his shoulder at the two flat, lifeless wet suits draped over the edge of the table. "I promise."

"Good." He kissed her quickly and hopped onto the wing of the hydroplane. "Now let me show you how to drive this crate."

4:11 p.m.

LOCKTON HAD INSISTED on making the trade in Sarah's horse pasture. Having ridden there often, he knew the area well.

Stone was told that he would not see Lockton or Alex until Nick had come through the gate and was standing in the open pasture. The trade was to take place at five-thirty, as twilight slipped into night. He was also told to call Control two hours before the trade and report sighting Lockton and McGuire on the west side, south of Corbin Beach. That would reroute most of the patrols in the eastern sector, making it relatively safe to conduct the trade.

Lockton drilled Alex as they hiked up the hill to the pasture. "Don't wait for high tide. Go as soon as it's dark," he reminded her. "Now which switch lowers the boat ramp onto the tracks?"

"The top switch. Bottom two control the winch." Alex scanned the woods to the east as she followed him.

"And the ramp cable?" Lockton queried.

"Can't unlatch it until the boat's floating in the water."

"Good."

Alex had to jog intermittently to keep up with Lockton's pace. Going over the plan kept his mind busy. He needed that. Thinking about his son's captivity turned his stomach into a pit of acid.

"Distance to the mainland?"

"Approximately five miles."

"Compass bearing?"

"Eighty degrees."

He continued to quiz her on the operating procedures of the hydroplane and its relative speed in relation to different weather conditions until they reached the edge of the woods north of the pasture.

"We're still an hour early," he said.

There was no sign of Stone or any patrols.

Having borrowed the $8 \times 20 \times 25$ mm zooming monocular John Walters used to record the international ships that traveled Puget Sound, Alex crouched behind the peeling alder and surveyed the area near Sarah's trailer.

Lockton knelt beside her. "Stay here."

She grabbed his arm as he started to rise. "Where are you going?"

He smiled. "To get a little traveler's insurance."

5:27 p.m.

ALEX AND LOCKTON WATCHED the dust trail rise in Sarah's driveway.

Stone parked the Subaru in between the trailer and the barn. Harrison walked over to the fence and slowly surveyed the empty pasture.

"Can you see him?" Lockton asked.

Alex focused the monocular on the car and zoomed in. "He's getting out now. Stone's behind him."

Lockton leaned up against her behind the tree. Alex wished there was more time. So much had been left unsaid. She swiveled around and crushed him against her, as if trying to squeeze the next ten years into ten seconds.

"I'm coming back for you," she whispered into his ear.

"You can't." He stared across the field. "You promised. If Stone gets his hands on either of you, I'm lost."

Nick crawled through the fence. The clouds were high and flat in the sky. Nothing moved. The forest was silent, the air, vacuum-still.

A flock of crows cawed and flew across the pasture to the barn. "They're ready," Lockton said.

Starting at her feet, Alex tightened and relaxed all the major muscle groups in her body, then began to breathe through her nose, slowly and evenly. When she was ready, she removed the .38 from her belt and cocked it.

They marched out of the woods. Alex stood guard while Lockton slipped through the fence. Neither Harrison nor Stone had taken out their weapons. Alex leaned her forearms against the top edge of the fence to steady her aim.

Nick had been ordered to walk, not run, to the middle of the pasture. Stone had told him that if he ran, they would shoot his father. Harrison had shown him his Ruger .357 to make sure he understood. It took all of Nick's willpower not to dash across the field as soon as he saw his father.

They met on a slight knoll, fifteen yards east of the solitary shade tree in the center of the pasture. Lockton crouched down and Nick threw his arms around his neck.

"You all right?" he asked, hugging his son gratefully.

Lockton tried to stand, but Nick wouldn't let go. "Daddy, don't go. We can run into the woods. Over there where it's close."

Lockton had to pry Nick's arms off his neck.

"Go to Alex, Nick," he ordered sternly.

"I won't," Nick cried, grasping at his father. "Daddy, please..."

"Do as you're told, Nick!" Lockton shooed Nick toward the north fence. "Go to Alex."

"No!" Nick punched his father's hands away. "I won't go."

"We made a deal, Doc," Stone called out impatiently. "Wouldn't be wise to break it. Not at this distance."

Harrison withdrew his Ruger.

Lockton grabbed his son's wrists.

"Nick, you have to go," he snapped.

"I won't!"

Lockton slapped him. The startled look on his son's face broke his heart. It was the first time he had ever struck his son. Nick's arms fell limply to his side and his lower lip began trembling like a worm on a hook.

Lockton turned his son by the shoulders and pushed him.

"Do as you're told!" he commanded, loathing himself for what he had just done. "Now!"

Nick shuffled resignedly toward Alex. Looking back constantly to make sure Nick didn't stop, Lockton crossed the other half of the field. Nick ducked through the fence just as Lockton reached Stone. Harrison began to frisk him roughly.

"He's clean," he said, backing away.

Stone shoved the barrel of his P220 SIG-Sauer .45 against Lockton's temple.

"Get them," he barked at Harrison.

Knowing Stone wouldn't shoot his only living link to the extract, Lockton tackled Harrison. Stone hit Lockton at the base of his skull with the butt of his pistol and he flopped over onto the grass, unconscious. Harrison got up and started running across the pasture.

When he saw Stone strike his father, Nick bit Alex's hand and tried to scurry back through the fence. Hoisting him over her shoulder, she bolted up the path.

Harrison was gaining fast.

By the time she reached the bend in the trail, he had already leaped the fence. She heaved Nick onto the Western saddle on Joey's back and mounted behind him.

"Daddy." Nick wept, holding the saddle horn. "He hit Daddy!"

Harrison sprinted around the bend in time to see them gallop over the small ridge forty yards up the trail.

5:56 p.m.

ONE OF THE THREE FIRE TEAMS, not redirected to the northwest side, was taking a ten-minute break in a narrow clearing on a hill above a deer trail. The smoking lamp was lit.

"Ah, Corporal?" One of his men pointed down the hill.

The corporal jumped to his feet. "That's her!" He scrambled over the rock for his M-16.

Alex glanced up through the trees at the clearing.

"Halt!" the corporal shouted. Alex kept Joey at a trot. "Halt or I'll shoot!"

Alex spurred her boot heels into Joey's ribs. The horse bolted up the trail as a spray of bullets ripped through the branches above them.

The patrol clambered down the hill in pursuit.

Alex pulled in the reins when they reached the fork in the trail, dismounted and helped Nick down. The path to the southeast wound two miles around back to Joey's pasture. The horse snorted and tossed his head. It was dark now, and there was still no wind.

"Time to go home, Joey." She petted his forehead, down to his black, flared nostrils. One big brown eye watched her curiously. "I owe you a wheelbarrow full of carrots." Joey whinnied and Alex stepped aside. "Go on. Go home, Joey." She swatted his muscled haunches. "Go home."

The gelding cantered up the trail that led back to his pasture as Alex smoothed away their shoe prints in the mud.

Nick looked drained and withdrawn. She crouched down beside him. "We've got less than two miles to go. Climb on. You're going piggyback."

Chapter 35

LOCKTON AWOKE as Stone and Harrison were laying him on the pool table. His skull was pounding and his neck muscles felt like petrified wood. He could barely turn his head.

"Put the cuffs on him." Stone turned on the stained-glass lamp above the pool table.

Harrison yanked Lockton to his feet, hooked his arms behind his back and manacled him. The cuffs cut deep into his wrist bones.

"If my hands drop off, I won't be much use to you," Lockton injected.

Stone glared at Harrison. "Loosen them."

Harrison slammed Lockton against the lab door and let the cuffs out a few notches. The way Harrison was acting, Lockton was pretty sure his plan had succeeded. Harrison elbowed him in the kidney and backed away. Lockton turned, trying not to show the pain. He was enjoying Harrison's frustration.

When the big man sneered, he grinned. "Aren't you a little old for braces?"

Harrison clenched his fist.

"Don't push your luck, Doc," Stone warned.

The basement phone rang and Stone took it. As he listened his eyes kept darting back and forth. "Where did the patrol spot her? I see. So they were heading east. Yes, it's a terrible thing. I hope you find them before they hurt anyone else. Or the boy."

Stone slammed the phone down.

"What happened?" Harrison asked.

"Not here."

Lockton laughed. "She made a horse's ass out of you, huh, Harrison?"

Stone dove between them before Harrison could get his hands on Lockton.

6:37 p.m.

STONE SPREAD OUT the map of Vashon on the dining-room table. Harrison was still seething. Twice in less than twenty-four hours, McGuire and the doc had gotten the better of him.

It was only a matter of time, he kept reminding himself, before he would even the score.

"They found the horse standing by the pasture fence," Stone pointed on the map. "The patrol origi-nally spotted McGuire here. They said the trail forked here. The other path led in this direction."

Harrison tapped the coastline between Dolphin Point and Cowley's Landing.

"Maybe." Stone stood back, arms folded in cogi-tation. "If they continued on the trail." He leaned over the map. "But why there?"

"They had to have access to a house in order to make the calls," Harrison speculated.

"Not just a house. An empty house. And all the houses on that beachfront—" he clapped his fist into his open palm "—have been evacuated."

"Isn't that where that Walters kid was from?"

Stone slapped the map. "Why the hell didn't I think of that before?"

7:45 p.m.

"PATROL," Nick whispered, closing the crack in the blanket nailed over the window in the boathouse door.

Alex covered the flashlight with her jacket and checked her watch. Right on schedule. The patrols were still passing at half-hour intervals.

In fifteen minutes, it would be time to go.

"Let's get into these wet suits," she suggested. They both stripped. As Alex squeezed into her suit, she reassessed all their options.

If they attempted to make contact with Control, Stone would kill Lockton. There was no doubt about that. If they remained on the island, it was only a matter of time before they'd be found. If they weren't shot on sight, they'd be locked in Security for testing. If Alex tried to warn the authorities then...again, Stone would kill Lockton. If she didn't, Stone would eventually kill her and take Nick back. He had already gotten in and out of the Nike base once with no problem.

Strictly a no-win situation.

James was right.

They had no choice.

They had to run the blockade.

8:06 p.m.

THE TWO SOLDIERS GUARDING the evacuated beach-front paced behind the wooden horses barricading the road. They had been told a Richard Stone would be driving out and were to let him through. It had something to do with getting more water samples from houses where the epidemic had begun.

When they saw the headlights turn off the main highway, one sentry casually moistened his fingertips, pinched off the end of the joint they had been smoking and put it back in his pocket.

Stone pulled up to the barricade. The blonde checked the official sticker on the windshield before approaching the driver.

"You Richard Stone?" he inquired.

"That's right." Stone showed him his driver's license.

"The beach patrols have been alerted. But I'd still be cautious. With those two crazies out there, everyone's pretty jumpy."

8:10 p.m.

ALEX SAW THE PARKED CAR as she climbed over the small rock jetty north of the cement ramp that led into the boathouse. Lying behind two mossy boulders, she watched a figure circle the Walters house, keeping close to the wall, and enter through the kitchen porch.

Whoever it was, didn't want to be detected. Alex waited. When she saw the flashlight in the master bedroom upstairs, she dashed to the boathouse and tapped on the door.

"Alex?" Nick started to turn the doorknob, but she held it closed.

"Blow out the candle, first. Someone's here."

Alex slipped inside, gathered up anything that looked out of place, and stuffed it in one of the lockers.

"Get in the cockpit." She took the blankets off the cement and spread them over the hydroplane. After climbing in with Nick, she pulled one over them.

"Who is it?" Nick asked, curled against her.

"Don't know. Now, hush."

Fifteen minutes later, the boathouse door opened.

The blanket on the door!

Alex suddenly realized she had forgotten to take it down.

The closet door opened and closed. Then the first locker door squealed.

"You!" a voice cried. It came from the beach. "In the boathouse. Come out with your hands on your head."

"Damn," Stone muttered. He slammed the locker closed, holstered his .45 and walked outside. He was instantly blinded by their flashlights. Raising his hands, he slowly advanced toward the beach.

"Stone," he announced. "Richard Stone. You were told I..."

"Okay," an almost feminine voice sang out. "It's him. Lower your weapons."

Stone shaded his eyes. "You mind?"

"Sorry, sir." The lights darted away from his face.

"Your patrol pass here often?"

"Every half hour, one of our teams passes here."

"Seen or heard anything unusual in this area?"

"No, sir."

They had definitely been in the boathouse. The blanket over the window had convinced Stone of that. He grudgingly began to admire the doc's resourcefulness. If he had been on the run, Stone theorized, he wouldn't push his luck, either.

Never stay in the same place twice.

Too risky.

Stone watched the patrol march up the beach. They had called from the Walterses', all right. Probably spent the night in the boathouse.

Just a day late, he mused. And a dollar short.

He walked back to the car to check his map again. The doc knew the island, but McGuire didn't.

He decided to drive farther up the beach road.

They just had to be around there somewhere.

Chapter 36

ALEX COUNTED TO SIX HUNDRED before crawling out from under the blanket. In another five minutes the patrols would be at their farthest distance from the boathouse. She began to feel around in the dark for the candle.

"Looking for this?" Nick asked. She lit it and glanced at the time.

Three more minutes.

Tossing the blankets off the hydroplane, she hopped back up to the worktable and pressed the wall switch. The metal rollers on the sliding aluminum door clanked up their tracks.

Why not just blow a bugle to announce our departure, she winced.

A quarter mile down the road, Stone heard the faint clanking of metal against metal. He put the car in neutral and leaned his head out the window.

It stopped.

He turned off the car and got out. All he could hear was the faint engine rumble of a blockade ship and the gentle lapping of water on the beach below.

Then he heard another rusty metal sound, like the squeal of a braking tractor.

"Shit!" He jumped back into the car.

When Alex reached the bow of the hydroplane, she was chest deep in frigid water. It felt icy until her body heat warmed the layer of moisture between her skin and the wet suit. After unlatching the ramp cable from the bow, she pushed the boat around.

Using the cable latch-ring on the bow, she hoisted herself into the hydroplane. Crawling back into the cockpit, she slipped onto the seat Nick had created with flotation cushions. He straddled one of the scuba tanks behind her.

When Stone saw the open boathouse door, he darted down the cement ramp to the beach. As soon as he heard the rumble of an engine, he caught the stern of the hydroplane in his flashlight beam. Holding the light steady in his left hand, he aimed his pistol and fired.

Two beach patrols began to run toward the muzzle flashes.

Like a startled deer escaping a car's headlights, the hydroplane leaped out of Stone's light. Nick could hear the bullets pinging in the water as the sudden acceleration sent him tumbling back against the other tank. Although Stone knew they had sped out of range, he continued to fire until his clip was empty.

The running lights on the eighty-two-foot Coast Guard cutter, *Stevenson*, were bearing down from the northeast. Two smaller vessels, the forty-one-foot Coast Guard cutter, *Halsey*, and a thirty-eight-foot police boat were approaching fast from the south east.

There was still no wind and the water was smooth. It was now a matter of speed.

ALEX MCGUIRE kept her compass bearing at eighty degrees. Her fifty-five knot speed and course were keeping her at about the same distance from the two smaller vessels approaching from the south. The larger ship, off her port bow, was farther east and moving at an angle to cut off her escape route.

A bright tunnel of light swept over the *Suzy Q*'s bow, halted and returned.

"I think they've spotted us," Nick said, shading his eyes from the glare.

"Time to show them what the *Suzy Q* can do." Alex pushed the throttle forward. The boat shot out of the light and flew across the surface of the water. A plume of water followed it like the tail of a jumbo jet.

They were up to seventy-five knots when the *Halsey*'s port-wing searchlight flickered across their stern.

Suddenly 20 mm cannon shells began to pound the water like the fists of a vengeful god.

Alex pushed it to eighty knots. The pursuing vessels' searchlights began to zigzag through the darkness.

They had lost their target again.

Nick popped up behind Alex and looked back at the island. A pair of lights, like the glowing eyes of an owl, were bearing down on them.

"Something's coming!" Nick cried over the screaming of the engine. "Fast!"

Chapter 37

THE HYDROPLANE'S relative position, course and speed were relayed to the Cobra attack helicopter, now en route across the Sound.

The Coast Guard cutters, *Stevenson* and *Halsey*, directed their searchlights into an arrow-beacon toward the target. The pilot held the gunship at three hundred feet as it sped toward the arrow's point.

"There it is," he said, pointing.

"We have visual contact with target," the gunner informed Operations.

"Engage the target until destroyed or neutralized," the colonel ordered.

The pilot glanced anxiously at his gunner.

This was not a war game.

The target wasn't a dummy.

There were real people in that boat . . .

A woman and a child.

The pilot dived to a hundred feet and bore down on their target. The gunner's face tightened as he prepared to fire the 40 mm cannon.

NICK KEPT WATCHING the bright lights come across the sky from Vashon. They didn't seem real to him.

Nothing did. Not since his father had slapped him. He had done everything Alex had told him, but it was as if he were watching their escape from a darkened seat high in the balcony of a theater.

As soon as the *Stevenson* ceased firing, Alex backed off on the throttle. Above sixty knots, she had felt as if she had no control of the boat. Nick tapped her shoulder and she tilted her head back, never taking her eyes from the steadily approaching lights of the beachfront homes immediately south of Fauntleroy Dock.

"It's almost on us," Nick yelled.

Alex looked back at the sky. The helicopter was closing in. There was no way to outrun it.

"Put on your gear," she told Nick. "Quick!"

She helped him strap on his tank, then hitched on her own. The lights from the helicopter illuminated the boat, as they fitted on their masks. Alex cut the engine.

"Sir, let's make one pass and strafe the bow," the pilot suggested.

The gunner nodded in agreement. He didn't want the blood of a woman and child on his hands, either.

Firing three rounds a second, the 40 mm cannon opened up with a deafening whir, like the high-pitched buzzing of a mosquito the size of a cow. Waterspouts burst in a line, fifty feet east of the hydroplane's bow. The helicopter shot past them and tilted in a turn.

"Let's go," Alex said, supporting Nick's tank as they climbed out of the cockpit and slid down the short, fiberglass wing into the water. "Hold onto my shoulders and kick."

With Nick riding piggyback, they began to swim away from the boat, just under the surface of the water.

They were less than a half mile from the mainland.

The helicopter returned and opened fire. After a three-second burst, it stopped.

Alex's head popped up out of the water. Nick bobbed up behind her. The helicopter was hovering directly above the hydroplane, now floating dead in the water.

"Let's head for the park," Alex said.

They dived fifteen feet down and began swimming, hand in hand, toward shore.

8:51 p.m.

"Sir, the target has been neutralized," the gunner radioed Operations.

Green was leaning back in the chair beside the monitor at the control center. He had been in phone contact with the colonel ever since the escape began. "Tell them a boat will be there in less than five minutes, Colonel. They'll pick up McGuire and the boy."

The colonel relayed the message.

"Ah, sir? We have a problem," the gunner said.

"What is it?"

"They're not here, sir."

Green rocked forward on the chair. "What?"

"Repeat that," the colonel ordered.

"They're not here, sir. They're not in the boat."

"Well, where are they?"

"I don't know, sir."

Green looked out the bay window at the mainland. Suddenly he stood up and held the phone with both hands. "Colonel, tell them to look for bubbles."

"What?"

"Bubbles," he repeated. "In the water."

8:53 p.m.

AFTER THE SECOND BURST of weapon fire, Lockton was frantic. When he heard Stone's voice in the basement den, he pressed his ear against the laboratory door.

"What was it?" Harrison asked.

"That Cobra stopped the boat," Stone said. He had been keeping in close contact with Control ever since he had arrived back at Lockton's.

"Are they dead?" Harrison asked.

Sweat rolled around Lockton's ear, causing his cheek to stick to the wood.

"They don't know," Stone grumbled.

"What do you mean?"

"I mean, they can't find them. They're gone."

Lockton stumbled, rubber-legged, back to the counter by the sink.

They made it! Jesus Christ, Almighty, they made it!

He opened a drawer under the counter, took out an eyedropper and put it on the glass plate next to the beaker he had taken off the shelf. From the top drawer of the desk, he removed a hand mirror and leaned it against a stack of books beside the glass plate so he could see behind his back.

He pinched some of the beaker's liquid into the dropper. Twisting his hands over the glass plate, he dabbed three drops on the short steel chain. Hissing smoke rose off the metal as the sulfuric acid disintegrated the chain link.

With one quick tug, his hands were free. He carefully put a drop of acid in each cuff's lock hole. In a few moments, he was able to unlink the cuffs from his wrists.

Don't think on their level, he reminded himself, you're not a spy, you're not trained in hand-to-hand combat or weapons construction. Use the resources available—the ones you're most familiar with.

He rubbed the swollen lump at the base of his skull as he checked through the shelves below the counter.

Suddenly the date April 22, 1915 popped into his head.

The second battle of Ypres.

The beginning of modern chemical warfare.

Six thousand cylinders of chlorine gas were wafted over Allied lines by the wind.

Lockton opened the cabinet across the room from the sink and took out the five-pound bag containing the powdered chlorine compound, calcium hypochlorite.

If they wanted a C.B. weapon, he would give them one.

Chapter 38

ALEX SURFACED in ten feet of water. They were only twenty yards from the seawall protecting Seward Park's manicured lawns and stately trees. Outside the perimeter of light under the lampposts along the walkways, the park was dark and empty. A raccoon skittered down the path along the seawall to the spilled remains of a toppled trash can.

Two police vessels were combing either side of Fauntleroy Dock. One circled southward, pulling the hydroplane. The other slowly chugged toward the park. Its searchlight scanned the black, still water. Alex ducked as it swept toward the seawall.

They discarded their tanks and Nick held on to Alex's shoulders as she swam in to shore. There was only six feet of open beach between the edge of the water and the seawall. Nick hugged the bottom, his head above water, while Alex checked the park for any sign of movement.

The oncoming police vessel's searchlight rippled over the water behind them in a slow westerly arc. It was less than a hundred yards away.

"How are you doing?" she asked, crawling back into the water.

Nick lifted his mask onto his forehead. "You did most of the work. I just hung on."

"You did great." She rubbed his back.

After they took off their masks and fins, Alex looped them onto Nick's weight belt and let it sink to the bottom. She kept her own weight belt on because it held the plastic bags containing their clothes and her pistol.

"Keep low," she instructed.

They skirted across the beach and crouched against the stones. Alex rolled over the wall and scanned the area again. Nick waited until she waved, then scampered over the seawall and joined her by the fallen trash can. A searchlight passed across the grass as they ran toward the woods.

Twenty yards north of the trash can, four police officers in SWAT uniforms marched around the point just as Alex and Nick were running across the open picnic area.

"Hold it," one SWAT team member warned. "Something moved. Over there. Into those trees."

Sergeant Cooper moved up beside him. "What was it?"

"Not sure. Two figures. Just saw them for an instant."

"Spread out in the trees," Cooper ordered. "Twenty feet apart. Maintain visual contact."

As the SWAT team advanced through the woods, Alex and Nick changed into their clothes.

"We forgot shoes," Nick pointed out, tucking in his shirt.

"No one will notice." Alex stuffed their wet suits under the rhododendron bush. Nick was breathing heavily. He pulled his knees up against his chest to stop from shivering. Alex brushed his hair back. "You're not doing so well, are you?"

"I'm okay."

She squeezed his knees. "Nick?"

"I feel kinda . . . cramped," he finally admitted.

She pulled him onto her lap and vigorously massaged his limbs. "You stay here. I'm going to the pay phone. In ten minutes, you'll be in a nice warm car on your way to Pam's. You remember Pam, don't you? She went fishing with us that day you caught your first salmon."

"That skinny lady with the funny laugh?"

"That's the one."

"I liked her." Nick was too worried about his father to really care where she was taking him.

"Be back in five minutes." Keeping within the border of the woods, she jogged around the stone gazebo and up past the picnic tables to the parking lot closest to the Fauntleroy ferry terminal. The pay phone was in the southeast corner under a streetlight.

She did not like being illuminated, but it was the nearest phone booth. Besides, now she was just another West Seattle resident. Barefoot perhaps, but who would notice?

Her first call was not to Pam with the funny laugh. It was to Steven Stolks, a CIA computer specialist who lived in Bellevue, a ritzy, upwardly mobile suburban city across Lake Washington from Seattle. Her father had introduced him to her when she received her orders to go to Vashon, Washington. If there was ever a problem, he had assured her she could trust Stolks. She knew Stone was confident she wouldn't dare notify the Company as long as he had Lockton.

That, she hoped, would be their trump card.

If they could find a way to intercept Stone before he suspected a trap, they stood a chance of saving James. It was risky, but there was no other way.

She explained the situation as quickly as possible over the phone. "I'll call you back as soon as I get to Pam's house," she concluded.

As she reached up to plunk in another quarter, she saw Nick walking toward the picnic benches. She missed the coin slot and the quarter clanked on the cement.

Two black-clothed SWAT team members, one pointing an Israeli Uzi at Nick's head, were escorting him toward the parking lot.

Alex reached under her untucked shirt for the .38 holstered in the waist of her jeans.

"Don't," a voice warned.

She removed her hand from the pistol and looked over her shoulder.

A double-barreled, sawed-off shotgun was pressed against the glass.

10:08 p.m.

LOCKTON RETRIEVED the large, economy-size pack of Contac cold capsules from the top drawer of his desk and emptied their contents into the sink. After putting on a pair of surgical gloves, he packed the gelatin capsules with the powdered chlorine compound and recapped them.

Unbuttoning his shirt, he dropped the capsules into one of the gloves and folded it as tightly as he could without crushing the capsules. He taped the glove into his armpit and rebuttoned his shirt. Opening the circuit box by the door, he flipped the two top switches.

The laboratory ventilation system whirred to a stop.

Taking the five-gallon plastic bucket out from under the sink, he poured in almost a pound of calcium hypochlorite. He pushed the bucket against the wall next to the door and sprinkled a few drops of water into the compound.

The conversation in the den immediately drew his attention.

"They caught them in the park by the ferry dock," Stone said. "She was in a phone booth."

"Think she'll talk?" Harrison asked.

"Not as long as we have the doc."

Lockton didn't need to hear any more. Nick and Alex had made it to the mainland. They would probably be put in the Harbor View security ward and tested for rabies. Once the results were verified, they would be freed.

Lockton entered the S.E.M. room, closed the door and waited.

In twenty minutes, white noxious fumes were billowing from the plastic bucket. The lab quickly filled with the poisonous gas. Keeping the wet towel wrapped tightly over his face, Lockton ran to the lab door.

"Help!" he hollered, banging on the door. "Get me out! Poison! It spilled! Hurry!"

"What do you think?" Harrison asked, glaring at the door.

"With the doc, who knows!" Stone took out his BIG .45 and stepped back. Lockton continued to scream and pound on the door. "Better open it."

Harrison swung open the door and Lockton stumbled out, masked by the wet towel. The white cloud poured into the den. Harrison's eyes felt as if they had just been lashed by the stinging tentacles of a man-of-war. The gas quickly attacked their throats and lungs. Like a linebacker, Lockton threw his body into Harrison's rib cage. Harrison crashed back over the pool table, gagging for air.

Stone stepped in and kicked Lockton in the chest, straightening him up like the well-oiled blade of a gravity knife. Drawing back, Stone pointed his .45 at Lockton's eyes.

"Nice try, Doc," he coughed. Harrison lifted himself off the pool table and slammed the lab door closed. "Open the damn window!"

"It's stuck," Harrison said, trying to smack the frame up with his palms.

"Break it!" Stone turned Lockton around and held him by the back of his collar. "Upstairs, Doc."

He ripped the towel out of Lockton's hands and used it himself. Harrison threw an end table through the window breaking the frame and ripping out the screen, then ran after them.

Upstairs, the fresh air afforded only minor relief. Having been the one to open the door, Harrison had received the worst of it, but all three men's throats and eyes felt as if they were on fire.

Stone shoved Lockton down on the living room floor.

Harrison walked up and kicked him in the stomach.

"You bastard." He kicked him again.

"That's enough." Stone pulled Harrison back. "Go splash cold water on your face."

Barely able to see, Harrison fumbled his way into the kitchen.

"Need water," Lockton wheezed. "Running water. Lots of it. Quick. Could blind us."

Stone yanked Lockton back to his feet. With his weapon jammed against his neck, he pushed him into the kitchen.

"Harrison. We have to shower." Stone poured more water on the towel and patted his eyes. "We'll go in shifts. Take the doc upstairs and throw him in the kid's shower. I'll use the master bathroom."

"Bastard," Harrison kept mumbling. "Fucking bastard."

10:32 p.m.

THERE WAS a small, shallow cave on the ridge above the burned-out Winnebago. Nick and Thor used to play pirates there. It was only six feet deep and had a tendency to flood during the winter rains. A fallen fir tree blocked most of the entrance with its tangled web of upturned roots.

Thor had gone to the cave to nurse his wounds after his battle with Patterson. It had his master's scent and that had given him comfort.

In a few hours, the sickness had struck.

Like maggots on a rotting carcass, his brain was now completely infested with the virus.

Thor scratched his way up through the tree roots. Saliva foamed from his mouth.

The sickness had become unbearable.

He staggered across Cove Road, crossed Lockton's driveway and circled around the house, sniffing at the once familiar scents.

Although he cut his paws on the broken glass outside the basement window, his diseased mind never registered the pain.

10:34 p.m.

HARRISON STOOD in the bathroom doorway and watched Lockton strip. Once naked, Harrison ordered him to slowly turn in a circle.

"All right, in the shower."

Lockton closed the tinted glass door, turned on the water and let it spray over his face. As he adjusted the temperature, he heard the sink running and the sound of splashing water.

Lockton quickly unscrewed the shower head.

The sink stopped running.

He watched Harrison's blurred figure through the glass. After he had ambled back out into the hall, Lockton turned off the shower.

"Hurry up, will ya," Harrison yelled into the master bedroom where Stone was showering. "I'm dying from this shit."

Keeping his back to the door, Lockton untaped the rubber glove, poured the capsules into the shower head and screwed it back on. Taping the glove into a small ball, he hid it behind the shampoo bottle on the shelf above the soap dish.

"Time's up, Doc," Harrison stated, returning to the doorway.

Lockton got out and grabbed a towel. Harrison began to strip in the hall, never taking his eyes from his prisoner. By the time Harrison was naked, Stone was dressed and heading down the hall.

Lockton wrapped the towel around his waist and started for his bedroom. "All right if I put on clean clothes?"

Stone followed him into the room. Lockton put on his old gray sweatsuit. When he heard the shower door close, he quickly slipped on his jogging shoes.

Harrison turned the water on and raised his face to the spray. Moaning in relief, he held his eyelids open to wash them out.

In thirty seconds, the gelatin capsules liquified.

Like tiny shards of hot glass, the chlorinated water shot directly into Harrison's eyes.

He was blinded immediately.

Howling in shocked agony, he fell, face first, through the shower door. His front teeth cracked against the tile floor and his stomach retched violently.

Held back by his wired teeth, vomit filled his throat. When he tried to inhale, it flooded his lungs.

He began to drown.

As soon as he heard the crash, Stone shoved Lockton down the hall. Before opening the bathroom door, he ordered Lockton to lie facedown on the floor. With his pistol trained at his head, Stone swung open the door.

The sight of Harrison's bloody, writhing body stunned him. As he bent to help, Lockton kicked the door with both feet. Stone went sprawling over Harrison's body, cracking his forehead against the edge of the sink.

Vaulting over the stairway banister, Lockton ran down the stairs.

It took Stone a few moments to regain his senses. The fall had almost knocked him out.

Bouncing against the hall wall, he struggled toward the stairs. Blood trickled down his face.

"Doc!" he screamed, wobbling like a newborn colt. "You're dead meat, Doc!"

James Lockton ran into his study and yanked at his top desk drawer.

It was locked.

The key was on the key ring in his pants pocket upstairs.

He jammed the ivory letter opener between the drawer and the desktop and pried it open. Grabbing the .38, he dashed back out into the hall.

Stone missed the last two steps and plummeted into the front door. He shook his head to clear his blurred vision.

Lockton stepped around the corner.

"Drop it," he commanded, aiming the .38 at Stone's chest.

Stone's sudden sharp laughter startled Lockton. Because of his raw throat and lungs, it turned into a coughing fit.

"That the .38 McGuire gave you?" Steadying himself against the wall, he started up the foyer.

"Stay back!" Lockton warned.

When Stone raised his .45, Lockton pulled the trigger.

Click.

He pulled again.

The hammer struck another empty chamber.

"Works better when it's loaded." Stone was finally able to stand without support. His vision was rapidly improving.

As Lockton slowly stepped back into the living room, he passed a half-full bottle of Johnny Walker Black on the table below his old friend's photographs.

Sweeping it up by the neck, he threw it in the same motion.

Stone fired.

It felt as if someone had hit his shoulder with a sledgehammer. Lockton flew back across the rug as the bottle smashed against the front door, missing Stone's head by inches.

Stone hobbled up the hall, never taking the .45's sight off Lockton's heart. Lockton dragged himself back with his one good arm.

Stone's face was cement gray.

There was no life left in it.

He halted by the photographs. "Looks like we both lose, Doc."

Suddenly there was a loud growl.

When Stone spun around, Thor leaped.

As they fell, the pistol flipped across the floor.

Stone tried to protect his neck as the dog tore at the side of his face.

Lockton pulled himself toward the gun. His wounded arm was completely useless. He was beginning to feel nauseous and faint.

Stars were blinking around the room like confetti.

"Thor!" he yelled, picking up the .45.

The dog glanced up from Stone's body, hackles raised. A threatening growl erupted from deep in his chest.

The dog stepped over Stone's body toward Lockton.

"Thor, no!" Lockton raised his knees toward his chest and rested the barrel between them. The pistol felt like a hundred-pound weight. "Thor, stay!"

The dog snapped its teeth and crouched to attack.

Lockton shot him through the head.

Using the coffee table for support, Lockton managed to get to his feet. He took a cloth napkin from the dining table and tied it around his arm as a tourniquet.

When Stone rolled over, he saw Lockton standing over him with his .45.

"Do it," Stone pleaded.

Lockton's trigger finger twitched.

"Shoot, you bastard!"

Lockton lowered the gun and walked to the phone.

Epilogue

May 21, 1986

JAMES LOCKTON WAS SITTING on the back porch reading the Seattle *Times*. It was a warm, sunny late-spring afternoon. In the distance, the state ferry, *Klahoya*, was docking at Southworth.

Lockton adjusted the sling on his arm. In another week, the cast would come off.

Out on the beach, Nick was wrestling a stick away from his five-month-old golden retriever, Torch. Lockton put down the paper and watched them play.

The day after the quarantine was lifted, Richard Stone had died of rabies in the security ward at Harbor View Hospital.

The biological weapons project had died with him.

He was its last victim.

When Lockton had threatened to go public with his story, the CIA had warned him that if he did, he would be arrested for the murder of Thomas Harrison and Alex would be prosecuted for breaking the laws of quarantine.

Lockton had been forced to make one last deal.

All charges would be dropped in exchange for secrecy.

Because of the cover-up, the mutant virus would forever remain a medical enigma.

The CIA had also concocted an explanation of events surrounding Harrison's and Stone's deaths. The official police report stated that a few drops of water had accidentally spilled into a bucket of chlorine, creating a cloud of noxious fumes. Harrison had volunteered to go down to the basement to open the window. While showering, he had gotten sick from the effect of the gas, crashed through the glass door and drowned in his own vomit.

Before they could go to his rescue, the rabid dog had attacked. Stone had shot at it, missed and hit Lockton. Although wounded, Lockton had been able to retrieve the pistol and kill the dog.

It was a bizarre set of events, but no more so than any number of other events that had taken place on the island during the quarantine.

On April 23, 1986, a month after the quarantine was lifted, James Lockton and Alex McGuire were married. Mrs. L. had even agreed to be one of the bride's attendants.

The sliding-glass door opened and Alex walked up beside Lockton's chair.

"That was a long trip, just for milk and eggs," he said.

"I had a doctor's appointment," she confessed.

Lockton sat up anxiously. "Why? What's wrong?"

"You remember that night we spent in the boathouse?"

"Yeah?"

Alex smiled. "It had to have been that night. You were in the hospital for the next two weeks."

He tossed the paper on the table. "Alex, what are you..."

"James." She slid into his lap, beaming. "We're going to have a baby."